An emotional freight t...

Addictive – THE POOL

As **bold** and **gritty** as it is **fabulously
glossy** and readable, it's a **provocative,
important read** – OBSERVER

Compulsively readable – GUARDIAN

Gossip Girl goes to **rehab**...
Clean **hits the spot** – i NEWSPAPER

Sharp, gripping and **tender** – ATTITUDE

Compelling – FINANCIAL TIMES

Hard-hitting and **unapologetic** – SUN

Praise for **MEAT MARKET**

Guaranteed to be your **summer read** – GLAMOUR

Combines **blockbuster appeal** with piercing commentary
on **modelling, body image** and **consent** – OBSERVER

A powerful **counterweight** to light-hearted
literature that still portrays **modelling as
the stuff of dreams** – GUARDIAN

Heartbreaking, painful, and **worth every second** ...

ALSO BY JUNO DAWSON

FICTION

Margot and Me

All of the Above

Under My Skin

Say Her Name

Cruel Summer

Hollow Pike

Clean

Meat Market

NON-FICTION

The Gender Games

Mind Your Head

This Book Is Gay

Being a Boy

What Is Gender? How Does It Define Us?

What's the T?

WONDERLAND

JUNO DAWSON

Quercus

QUERCUS CHILDREN'S BOOKS
First published in Great Britain in 2020 by Hodder & Stoughton

1 3 5 7 9 10 8 6 4 2
Text copyright © Juno Dawson, 2020
The moral rights of the author have been asserted.

A CIP catalogue record for this book
is available from the British Library.
ISBN 978 1 786 54105 5

Printed and bound in Great Britain by ClaysLtd, Elcograf S.p.A

The paper and board used in this book
are made from wood from responsible sources.

Quercus Children's Books
An imprint of
Hachette Children's Group
Part of Hodder & Stoughton
Carmelite House
50 Victoria Embankment
London, EC4Y 0DZ

An Hachette UK Company
www.hachette.co.uk

www.hachettechildrens.co.uk

AUTHOR NOTE

Wonderland is a work of fiction but deals with many real-life issues including mental health, self-harm, sexual assault and drug use.

Support on these topics can be found via the organisations listed at the back of this book.

Love Juno x

To Other Max

Alice! A childish story take,
And with a gentle hand,
Lay it where Childhood's dreams are twined
In Memory's mystic band,
Like pilgrim's wither'd wreath of flowers
Pluck'd in a far-off land.

Lewis Carroll – All in the Golden Afternoon

Sometimes
I
dream
that
I'm
falling.

I fall and fall
light as a lullaby
my fingernails clawing at thin air.
Blue sky
above and below
down and down
down
and down.

And it's funny because
in real life
when I saw the woman fall
it was all over in a second
and her head cracked like an egg
on the kerb.

I

ALICE'S INESCAPABLE FATE

Wake up, Alice.

The nasal voice finds its way to me in the honeycomb of my daydream.

I don't remember nodding off, but I was somewhere far lovelier.

I open my eyes and see the silhouette of Flossy Blenheim looming over me, her frizzy mane of hair like a halo. Behind her, marigold afternoon sun bakes the top of my head as I snooze on the desk, my folded arms for a pillow.

'Can I help you?' I say, annoyed at having been so rudely awoken.

'Ms Grafton wants to see you in her office. Again. Good luck.'

Uh-oh. I've no *Get Out of Jail Free* cards left. Oh, worse things happen at sea, and I've had a fair innings. I think, this time, I might really be expelled. And what a terrible shame when the poetry corner of the Upper School library is *such* a premium spot for a nap.

'Time is ticking,' Flossy says sniffily.

Isn't it always? 'Then I shan't delay her further.' I gather my books into my army surplus satchel and give Flossy, fascist handmaiden, a curt nod.

The cloisters of St Agnes are rather lovely without anyone else around. At this time of the day, most girls are in fifth period, bellies full of whatever beige shortcrust stodge they served in the dining hall at lunch. A ghost of garlic and cabbage lingers, and I can't help but wonder if garlic and cabbage pie was on the menu. There are no lows to which British cuisine will not stoop.

If this is death row, I'll milk it, idling through the handsome redbrick arches and ornamental gardens. I shall say this for my soon-to-be alma mater, it's certainly very pretty. Sunshine splatters down on the courtyard, illuminating the veiled marble statue of the school's namesake: the patron saint of chastity and virgins. Ironic, really, that St Agnes is presently Ground Zero for a particularly virulent strain of chlamydia. Good thing Aggy is also the patron saint of gardening.

From inside the classrooms, I hear teachers barking instructions; a screeching violin recital and a very hammy rehearsal of *Antigone*. I take a moment, enjoying the sun on my face. You can almost feel the freckles emerging some days.

I reach the Coulter Building and sigh deeply as I push the heavy doors. Time to take the plunge, I suppose. Can't avoid my fate a second longer and there's only so many bullets one can dodge. Coulter smells freshly polished, my Docs echoing down the endless wood-panelled halls.

The Principal's office is near the front of the school, where she has a personal secretary. I hover for a moment at Jean's desk. Jean and I go way back.

'Ahem.' I politely clear my throat.

Jean, a human cobweb, looks up at me with watery grey eyes. I wonder sometimes if she's actually a long-departed spirit who happens to haunt this desk. 'Take a seat, Alice.'

I do so on the familiar old sofa: Frankenstein's monster, all bolts and green leather. I take out my grandpa's brass fob watch and ping it open. This watch sailed all over the world when he served in the navy. He always told me he'd won it arm-wrestling a one-eyed Triad member in Hong Kong, although I remain doubtful of that. Regardless, now it's mine and I love it. With heavy eyelids, I watch the second hand go round and around, and I find it soothingly hypnotic as I await the verdict. I shouldn't, given I rather suspect time is something I'm rapidly running out of.

If I squint, the watch looks like a face.

I suppose that's why they call it a clock face, imbecile.

'Miss Dodgson?'

I snap out of the trance. The novelty of being a Miss never gathers dust.

'Ms Grafton is ready for you now.'

I click the pocket watch shut and stow it back inside my blazer. I feel it tick-tick-ticking against my chest, playing my ribs like a xylophone.

The sofa wheezes as I push myself up. I catch sight of myself in the gilded mirror and smooth my kilt, straighten my tie – not that a tie can save my neck. I tug at the hem of my kilt so I don't get admonished and/or slut-shamed.

My Doc Marten soles, much the same as my soul, are worn thin and parp with every step to the office door. I give a polite knock.

'Come in.'

I enter Grafton's office, which I oft think is deliberately

intended to intimidate the younger ladies of St Agnes. With its oak walls and glowering portraits of former heads it has all the appeal of stepping into an iron maiden. It's little wonder Grafton's demeanour is always so dour. Perhaps I shall buy her the jauntiest spray-paint-pink orchid in M&S by way of a parting gift.

'Take a seat, Alice.'

I slip into my usual spot.

Today Grafton is wearing a salmon Harris tweed that rather clashes with her strawberry-blonde hair. She's something of a squirrel, or perhaps a chipmunk. Certainly the sort of rodent to stockpile nuts in her cheeks.

'You know what I'm going to say,' she begins, making semi-circular arcs in her swivelling chair.

'Then you hardly need say it,' I reply as sweetly as I can.

Five years we've been playing this game of chess. I mean, she must, on some level, enjoy it, or she'd have cut me free as a Second Former. 'Alice ...'

'Sorry.' I purse my lips and mime locking them shut. For good measure, I toss the imaginary key over my shoulder in the direction of the bin.

She opens a leather file approximately the size of a telephone directory. My criminal record. 'Mrs Beech tells me you haven't attended a single chapel this half term.'

'Well, Ms Grafton, I'm keeping my spiritual options open and—'

She cuts me off cold. '*And* you leave me with no choice but to issue a formal warning about your hair *again*.'

I play with a faded turquoise lock. It's long now, although I keep my fringe grazing my eyes, ever-convinced it goes some way to hiding my fivehead. 'What?' I ask innocently.

'It's *blue*.'

If my hair isn't blue, how will anyone know I'm transgender?

'Natural colours only,' she says for the millionth time.

I smile slightly. 'Ms Grafton, I think I left *natural* behind years ago, don't you?'

She stiffens in her chair. 'I can't make exceptions for you, Alice.'

Although she has, many times. I don't think Ms Grafton is a fully committed transphobe, but she wasn't exactly rolling out a red carpet for the first ever trans girl to attend St Agnes back when I started. She was certainly more supportive than some of the governors: fossils, dinosaurs and *Sunday Times* readers the lot of them. Sometimes I wonder if what she actually resents is the fact she's not allowed to advertise my mishap gender to make the school look more woke. She remains the only person here who knows all my skeletons by name. And there are so many to count. She turns the page in the ossuary.

'Your grades are at rock bottom.'

'Yes. And I think that's rather unfair.'

'You do?'

'Had I turned in the assignments, I expect I'd have done quite well on them. It seems unjust to grade non-existent essays so poorly.'

I think I see her shield a hint of a smile by pretending to wipe her lip. 'Alice. You're one of the brightest girls at St Agnes ...'

I can't and shan't argue with that. It's truly a curse more than a blessing. Oh, how I wish I could goldfish through my school career: turn up, sit, gossip, eat, sit, go home, forget.

'When you transferred here, you came with a flawless academic record ... even with everything you were going through. Your grades were exemplary for your first few terms and then ... well, I don't know. If only you could apply your brilliant mind to what you're actually supposed to be doing, you could go so far ...'

'Where?'

'I beg your pardon?'

'Where, precisely, could I go?' I ask.

'Wherever you want! With a top-flight education from St Agnes, the world would be your oyster. Alice, you're the very definition of potential. You already proved you could be anything you wanted to be.'

What's that supposed to mean? I successfully fought off my gender, so getting through Oxford should be a cakewalk? If only.

When I say nothing, she continues. 'Obviously you've been ... unwell ... but it has been a year, and your mother tells me the therapy is going well and ...'

'Yes,' I say quickly. 'I am feeling much better, thank you.'

She makes what I can only describe as lazy jazz-hands. 'Then why haven't your grades improved?'

I refrain from telling her that 'my grades' weren't my primary motivation in recovery. It's honestly a miracle I'm still breathing. Can't we celebrate that instead? They ought to make certificates: *Congratulations, Alice! You survived another week!* Gold stars all round.

I say nothing. My grades haven't improved because I don't care for them to. I don't. I just don't care. It's a con, you know. School, exams, grades. All ways of keeping us battery hens. And it's a class thing. You don't need grades when you have strings, and so education is a carrot dangling over a treadmill to stop the proletariat from revolting. *If you get all your exams you can go to Oxford where Little Lord Xanax is already sitting in your seat. He might let you sit on his lap if you're lucky.*

Grafton sighs and slaps my folder shut, jolting me out of my thoughts. 'Alice! Are you listening to a word I'm saying! This is enormously frustrating. I shall have to speak to your mother. Is there a good time to contact her?'

'I'm afraid that will be difficult. She's on tour again.'

'Ah yes, I've been meaning to read her new one.'

'The husband did it,' I say at once. 'I mean, I haven't actually read it, but he almost certainly did.' My father's absconsion eleven years ago, leaving my mother penniless with two infant daughters, seems to have cut deep creative scars. I haven't read *all* of my mother's books, she really does churn them out, but the husband is *always* at least *partly* responsible for the corpse that's uncovered within the first five pages.

Another sly smile. 'And when will she be back?'

'Well, she has to work her way up North America and Canada. She's presently in Texas.'

Grafton is sighing so much I can't help but think she's slightly asthmatic. 'Very well.'

'Am I dismissed?'

'Not so fast. I wanted to talk about what happened in the Blume common room.'

Sometimes your face flinches before you can seize control of the muscles. Grafton, no doubt, picks up on this tic.

'Alice, we've had our issues but violent outbursts aren't usually your style.' A good-cop tilt of the head. 'What's going on?'

'Nothing.'

'It must be something. Lucy Prendergast told me you had to be held back from Genie Nugent.'

I look her in the eye. 'Genie Nugent is a simpering idiot and a liar to boot.'

'Name-calling, Alice?'

It *is* beneath me, but deeply satisfying nonetheless. I shake my head slightly.

'What lie did she tell?'

I don't want to say it aloud in case it makes it true. 'That Bunny Liddell killed herself.'

And now it's Grafton's turn to flinch. 'Balderdash,' she says after a moment.

'That's what I said. Only with different vocabulary and also my fist.'

'Tea?' She goes to pour herself a cup from a floral pot with a chipped gold spout.

'No, thank you.' I would kill for a tea, but I won't give her the satisfaction.

Grafton plops one pink sugar cube into her cup and stirs it in. 'Alice, if I've learned one thing during my tenure at St Agnes it's to ignore idle gossip.'

Me too. I don't for a single second believe Lexi Volkov is raising ponies on a ranch in Colorado either.

Grafton continues. 'Bunny has … taken time away before …

12

and she's always come back. Safe and sound.'

Take your time, Alice, you need to learn some patience.

Take your time.

Impossible, I think. Time is not ours to take or hold, pour or contain; it isn't solid, liquid or gas. Sometimes – some time – I wonder about who set time. Who decided sixty seconds make a minute, sixty minutes an hour, twenty-four hours a day? The Earth, the sun and the moon very much do their own thing, but I think it's interesting that man (and I'm almost certain it was a man, no woman would have the deluded self-confidence to claim mastery of the universe) tried to regiment the terrifying globe of fire above our heads. Curiouser still that we all go along with it so obediently.

But I digress.

Bunny.

'We were supposed to meet,' I say quietly, looking up at Grafton. I haven't told anyone that, not even Dinah.

Ms Grafton takes off her glasses. 'I wasn't aware you were close with Bunny. She's not in your circle of friends.'

That would be difficult. I have only one friend and two people do not a circle make. We're more of a line.

I shrug. I'm not going to soil the memory of *that* night with wet clay words for my head teacher. *Previously on 'Alice's Adventures'...* A replay bursts across my mind's eye in vivid technicolour: the waltzers; her honey-blonde curls strewn across her face; the violet glitter on her eyelids; the fillings in her back teeth as she laughed; the skinhead who spun us faster as we screamed. They're red hot pokers to torture my poor heart are those memories. I suppose I must like the tummy flip.

13

'Alice?'

'We didn't know each other that well. We don't.' The truth.

'She'll be fine,' Grafton says dismissively. 'The police and her parents aren't overly concerned at this stage. It's only been a week.'

In any other world, an eighteen-year-old vanishing without trace for a week would be cause for great alarm, but this is London high society. Last summer, so it's said, Bunny Liddell flew to her parents' beach house in Ibiza for the whole of August without telling anyone until she turned up on a podium at Pacha. The winter before that she was found, after a frantic search, in her aunt's Chamonix ski lodge toasting marshmallows with Lady Louise Windsor.

Bunny goes.

And comes back.

But I may well have been the last person to see her. Or the second-to-last person to see her alive.

Oh, it aches.

I so clearly remember waking up in the king-size hotel bed, and being the only person in it.

II

AN INTRIGUING CLUE

I don't know why I go from Grafton's office to the dorms, but I do. I've always been a day pupil so the boarding house holds a certain exotic appeal. Dreams of Malory Towers, midnight feasts, parental abandonment and all that. I'm quite sure that those of us who get to go home at the end of each day are considered less hardy than those who bond over bleary-eyed, top-knot canteen breakfasts.

Oh, I'd have loathed it. Not only does the mere *thought* of communal showers make my stomach spasm but I've been known to visualise killing up to six people each morning before breakfast.

Pupils at St Agnes are homed in Houses. Homely. The east wing is for Wenlock and Highden, the west wing for Cullimore and Blume. As artsy types, both Bunny and I are in Blume. Sixth Formers have more private rooms and Bunny shares with just one other girl in room D14. I know because I looked it up after last week.

The door is locked.

I rather suspected it might be. I knock, then rest my forehead on the cool wood.

What was I thinking? That the door would be wide open and I'd find a secret clue, meant only for me, that somehow everyone else – including the police and Ms Grafton – had missed?

Well, why not, it happens in a lot of my mother's novels.

If this were a novel, I'd use a hairpin to pick the lock.

But this is not a novel.

At the very most it would be a sentence within one.

I press my cheek to her door. I want to smell her again: shea butter and menthol cigarettes. 'Bunny? Are you in there?' I knock again.

The thing with 'intrusive thoughts' is how goddamn intrusive they are. I picture her naked, blue and grey, washed up on the banks of the Thames. Blubber flesh, swollen and bloated, lips purple and split. Her glazed eyes stare at nothing. Fish counter girl on ice flakes.

I shake my head.

It's not real, and my imagination isn't always my pal. I steady myself against her door frame and take a deep breath. I'm fine.

Resigned, I slump downstairs to Blume common room. Most girls are in sixth period by now and only a couple of Uppers – both CrazyRichAsians who have accessorised their uniforms with Balenciaga – are playing on their phones in front of the fire.

I wonder where Dinah is.

Sixth period. She has Classics.

Which is where I should be according to my timetable, but Latin is all Greek to me and I can think of far better uses for my tongue.

I'm about to leave when I see the pigeonholes.

My little slot is overflowing with flyers, invites from various societies, newsletters and important notices which clearly weren't that important since I've squarely ignored them without consequence.

Again, I'm sure I'm not the first to check Bunny's pigeonhole for vital clues, but I can't seem to resist.

I think back to last week.

'Alice, I think I'm in trouble.'

It has to be worth trying. It's always worth a try.

The pigeonholes are sorted alphabetically by surname, and I find hers. Bunny has been at St Agnes since her parents went through a very public divorce a few years back. Her father, a publishing magnate, lives in New York. Her mother, Miss America back in the day, replaced Vicodin with crystals, and splits her time between New Age cults and rehab from what I can gather.

It's empty. Anything left in here, I imagine, has been taken by Grafton.

Still, I reach inside anyway.

I feel the wood at the back of the cabinet and I'm about to give up when my fingertips trace something stuck in the side.

I try to scrape it out with my nails, but it's stubborn.

It's probably some charity campaign from years ago: Antonella Hemmings's food drive for refugees or some such. It feels glossy, though, waxed.

I work it loose and pull it free.

Oh. After all that, it's just a lousy playing card someone has scribbled on in black marker.

The Queen of Hearts.

III

DINAH

Wonderland? What's that supposed to be?

'Alice?'

I thrust the playing card into my blazer pocket. It's Dinah, clattering into the common room with her cello case.

'What are you doing in here?' she asks. The instrument is almost bigger than she is.

'Nothing,' I say, probably too quickly. 'Why aren't you in Classics?'

'I had my music exam, remember?'

'Oh yes.' Completely forgot.

'Hardly any of the lesson left, and I assumed you probably wouldn't go back to class. So, how did it go with Grafton? Are you expelled?'

'Not yet.' I flop down onto one of the tan leather sofas, so worn it's like sinking into a block of tofu. I'm yearning to google Wonderland, but it'll have to wait. Dinah doesn't know about my night with Bunny and I'm in no hurry for her to find out.

It's complicated. No one would ever think to connect Bunny and me. I rather think she banked on that. By keeping it all a secret I could be keeping her in trouble, or I could be keeping her from whoever it was she was so afraid of.

A conundrum. A quandary.

Dinah blinks, waiting on my response.

'You know what she's like,' I say. 'She wants to speak to my mother when she gets back, but I rather think that by the time she does, she'll have forgotten what she wanted to say.'

Dinah sits beside me. 'Please don't get kicked out,' she says. 'What would I do without you? I'd have to join the Korean Clique.' She lowers her voice so the girls on the other side of the common room won't hear.

'Dinah, you're from Chicago, you've never even been to Korea.'

'Well, who else would I be friends with?'

'You'd cope.'

'They hate me because I dress like a mole. That's what Min Ya says. Or at least that's what Ji Li said she said.'

'Min Ya is a walking billboard. Ignore her,' I say loudly enough for her to catch. I curl my septum piercing out from inside my nostrils now I'm clear of the office. 'Grafton won't expel me because she knows I'll get the grades in the end. Probably. If I take the exams.'

Dinah peeks at me over the top of her glasses. 'Is something wrong?'

'No. Why do you ask?'

'You seem distracted. Yes, even more so than normal.'

I sink further into the sofa, legs wide, shoulders hunched. I shrug and tell a little lie. I think lying is acceptable if it protects another from harm, less so if it only serves to protect yourself. 'You know me, Dinah, whimsical, flighty, fickle. I don't have an obsession to obsess about at the moment and it's deeply unsettling.'

Dinah gets the cutest dimples when she smiles. 'Not even Henry?'

'Absolutely not,' I say emphatically. 'He belongs to two weeks ago. And now he's banished to the Island of Lost Men indefinitely.' That's what you get for sending unsolicited amateur pornography after standing someone up. Unforgiveable.

Dinah laughs gaily. It's all very well for her, she has Kevin back in Illinois. I'd rather like a boyfriend who required no further investment than wishing him a good morning, a good night and telling him how much I missed him occasionally. 'Do you want to go into town?' she asks. 'Get a milkshake or something? Or cupcakes?'

I spring up off the sofa. 'Dinah. Let's get started on diabetes.'

Fat Cow is the best gelato place in Kensington, but it's only a four-minute walk from St Barnabas and St Agnes so it does get exceptionally crowded at four p.m. every weekday. Luckily, Dinah and I get a head start by cutting class. We even get a mermaid-green vinyl booth to ourselves, which almost never happens. We're not nearly popular enough.

I order a *Strawberry Boudoir*, Dinah a *Chocolate Mudslide*. I pluck the cherry off the top of the whipped cream pyramid and pop it from its stalk with my teeth.

'Watch this,' I say, disposing of the stone. 'I can tie a knot in the stalk with my tongue.'

'No you can't!'

'I bet you ten pounds!'

'Deal!'

21

I get to work on the stalk, wrapping my tongue around it. I imagine it looks *very* sexy. I do not care for 'sexy', it's so unimaginative, so posed. That said, I'm coming to realise that collector's item girls like me don't really have to try. The fact I exist is enough. The fact I'm young is a bonus. I'm a blow-up doll.

My stomach cramps again.

It was different with Bunny.

'What are you doing this weekend?' Dinah asks, catching some chocolate sauce with her finger as it trickles down the sundae glass.

Trying to establish what this playing card means. 'I don't know, not a lot,' I say, poking the cherry stalk around my mouth. It tastes of stick. I'm beginning to wish I hadn't bothered. 'Lori's home for some reason.' There isn't a room my sister can't suck the joy out of, so it promises to be a dreary weekend.

'There's a garden party at the American Embassy tomorrow afternoon. You could come with me and my aunt?'

I shake my head. Not my scene at all. It's a positive correlation: the more formal something is, the more likely I am to disgrace myself somehow. The day my mother got her OBE at Buckingham Palace must never be spoken of. It was not, I know now, the right time or place to air my views on colonialism.

'Oh, come on, Alice. You never do anything.'

'I jolly well do. I do *nothing*. Actively.' With a great flourish, I whip the cherry stem out of my mouth, successfully tied in a knot. 'There! You owe me ten pounds! Pay up!'

At that moment, some of the rugby team from St Barney's spill through the door, all fists, chins and shoulders, like some masculine tumour. Royce Hart leads the pack, drunk on testosterone, while Maxim Hattersley brings up the rear, hobbling in on crutches. I heard he was either drunk-driving or some Arab prince from Eton had his leg broken for diddling his girlfriend. Both are plausible.

He catches my eye as he limps past. I scowl and stare into my milkshake.

'Oh my god, he's so hot,' Dinah says, blushing.

'Maxim? He's a Neanderthal.'

'A really hot, ginger Neanderthal. Red hot!'

'Dinah, you have Kevin!'

'He's a thousand miles away! I'm allowed to look! Come on, Alice … you must fancy *someone*. You *always* have a crush.'

I could tell her about what happened in that hotel room, I don't think she'd judge, but the memories I have are like Polaroids. If I hand them around willy-nilly, they'll get all smudged with fingerprints.

'The weekend starts right here!' Royce hollers from the next booth. 'Mate! Mate, the next three days are wall-to-wall pussay!'

His teammates cheer loudly. I roll my eyes at Dinah. They're pigs. Why any girl would bestow the gift of her body upon those oafs is quite the enigma. They aren't deserving. I hoover up the last of my milkshake with a hearty slurp as a text message comes through. It's from home, from Felix: *hello love. do not forget felicity after school.*

'Oh, crap.'

'What?' Dinah asks.

'I need to go. I'm late.'

'Late for what?'

I smile. 'Bedlam.'

23

IV

QUITE MAD

Of course, I think it's wonderfully fitting that I attend weekly therapy sessions on the site of an old asylum. The Chorley Institution for Imbeciles (a little harsh, surely, even by Victorian standards) was mostly demolished in the eighties, but some blocks were converted into housing. It's from here that Dr Felicity Baker practises.

I ring the bell and she buzzes me into the building. As ever, I wave at Kel, the daytime security guard. He hardly glances up from his iPad, but waves back.

'Good afternoon, Miss Dodgson. How's the weather out there?'

'Glorious, Mr Mwangi! You off at six?'

'On the dot!'

He probably thinks I'm a lunatic. I pass his desk and walk down the long tiled hallway towards the elevator. Although the halls are filled with towering palms and lined with contemporary art, they can't quite mask the fact this was once a hospital. How many sick, sad, mad people were wheeled, dragged, down this arched corridor? Some days I think it's very sad, others quite cool, some plain morbid. Is London so overcrowded that we've taken to jollying up places where countless people died, frothing at the mouth, electrodes strapped to their heads?

The lengths people will go to for period features, honestly.

Once in the lift, I dig the rogue playing card out of my blazer pocket. 23/5? Is that a date? I check my phone and today is the 22nd May. Although the lift is going up, my heart sinks. Tomorrow? What happens tomorrow? If this was a threat of some sort, what will tomorrow bring for Bunny? It isn't an explicit warning, but there's something a bit sinister about its vagueness.

Oh, Bunny. Why?

It didn't have to be this way.

She just fucking left me there in that hotel room, one more soiled towel for the chambermaid to tidy. She fell asleep in my arms, and when I woke up …

She came to her senses. Why would she want to be with you, you're—

I shake the thought off immediately.

The lift reaches the fifth floor with a ping and the doors slide open. I step out and see Felicity already waiting for me in the doorway to her apartment. I'll give her this, she's always very stylish. Today she's in grey slacks, a cream blouse and banana-yellow slingbacks. If I make it to adulthood, maybe I'll dress like her. I can't look like an angry child's crayon sketch of a human girl for ever. I'd hazard she's in her mid-thirties, with just the most lush, thick chestnut hair.

'Hi, Alice, come on in.'

She guides me through her flat and I do what anyone would do with their therapist: try to glean clues as to who she really is. She gives precious little away in our sessions and my online stalking has proven fruitless. I once saw a piece of stray mail addressed to a Mr G Doukas, and she has a wedding ring, so I'm *guessing* that's her husband. Beyond that her apartment is as impersonal as an influencer's Instagram.

We head for her study, which I find to be worryingly like the one in *Get Out*. The day she produces a china cup, she won't see me for dust. It's a bright airy room, lined with bookshelves and her many qualifications framed on the wall. Two armchairs sit either side of a coffee table, and she takes her seat, crossing her legs elegantly. It's a cliché to say she moves like a dancer, but she really *does*. I know she is one because there's a picture on her desk of her as a girl with a woman, I assume her mother, and she's wearing a tutu. It's the only real clue that Felicity is a human and not a therapeutic cyborg.

I'd be a fucking *excellent* detective.

Which I may well have to be if I'm going to find Bunny.

'So, Alice,' Felicity starts. I am not to call her Dr Baker. She says it's too formal, but I think they don't want me to think of myself as someone who needs doctors in her life. 'How are you this week?'

'Tip-top.' Our sessions always start this way.

She smiles slightly. I've been coming to her for a little over a year now. Some weeks I blast into whatever I'm feeling, barely pausing for air, and others … I find I have nothing I want to say. She must sense this week is the latter.

'Good. It's good there's nothing urgent on your mind.'

I could tell her about Bunny, she *has* to keep it confidential, but I wonder if telling her about the night in the hotel will open a can of worms she'll want to spend weeks fishing with. I really don't want that.

'Any more adventures on the dating apps?'

She means hook-up apps. When I was in the treatment centre last year, there was this older trans girl, and she informed me there was a thriving market for #girlslikeus if you know where to look. Since then, I've had quite an active, app-based sex life, and Felicity thinks my experiences with married men from outlying commuter towns hint at low self-esteem. I think everyone else gets to have sex, I don't see why I shouldn't send a few risqué bathroom pics. I haven't been brave enough to go meet any of these gentlemen-with-pretend-names in their hotel rooms as yet – for trans girls, curiosity kills more than just the cats – but I want to. I do. I'm starving.

'No,' I tell her. 'The Daddy Issues were becoming problematic.'

She smiles again. It was only too easy for her to link my dalliances with much older men to my absent father, and I would hate to be predictable.

'I had an email from your mother,' she goes on.

'Oh. OK.'

'She tells me you want to stop taking your medication.'

It's not a question, but she waits for a response. 'I don't think I need them any more.'

She frowns a little. 'What makes you think that?'

'To be honest,' I say, warming up, 'I forget to take my tablets half the time anyway, so I can't need them badly, can I? And it's been, what, a year since things got really scary?'

It's been long enough now that I can't really remember exactly how it felt. I know it was bad, but I couldn't put it into words.

'Have you considered that the medication might be why it's

27

been better? I mean, this is a conversation for you and your doctor really, Alice.'

'But you are my doctor! And you've helped loads. When I start having intrusive thoughts, I know what to do with them now.'

'I'm glad the strategies are working, I am, but the medication you're taking is strong stuff, Alice. We don't know what side effects there might be if you come off your pills.'

I nod. I know. I feel like I'm stronger now. Felicity has taught me techniques whereby, if the walls in my head start closing in, squeezing the air from my lungs, I don't freak out or struggle any more. Instead, I ACT. I *Accept* the situation, *Choose* a positive solution and *Take* action.

It's truly a bummer that my brain doesn't work like most people's do, but I've had to make peace with that. I'd assumed that once I finally got my hands on those hormones, everything in my life would be magically perfect. While I'm delighted with my perky little boobs, I was profoundly disappointed that my urge to cut myself didn't vanish with the first milligram of oestrogen to pass my lips.

Sometimes I *think* I want to die. I *don't*, it's a convincing lie, but that's what my brain is telling me. Felicity refers to it as 'low mood'. Yeah, I'll fucking say. Once, being alive was so physically painful, an actual bone-ache, I wanted it to end. Admitting that to myself feels hugely empowering, I am no longer ashamed. The shame made everything that much worse.

I could gladly go without hearing the words 'born in the wrong body' ever again, but I do think I was born with a *faulty* one. It seems likely that my brain will never work the way it should, but I feel like I'm starting to *know my own brain*. If

I can tell the difference between what's real and what isn't, I don't really want to spend the rest of my life taking medicines. Between the hormone pills and the anti-depressant pills and the anti-psychotics, I'm a human maraca.

'You've made exceptional progress,' Felicity says. 'But will you promise me you won't do anything rash until you've seen your family doctor?'

'I promise,' I tell her. 'I feel like I'm fully in control. I'm not going back to how I was. Never.'

'Alice,' Felicity says calmly. 'Do you think you need to be in control?'

'Yes, I do.' I clench my teeth together. I mean it.

V

CURIOUSER

I unlock the gate to The Mews, which tells me there's probably no one home. I go through our little garden, past the lemon tree. I enter through the kitchen where the Kit-Cat clock tells me it's twenty past six, its tail ticking back and forth.

'Hello? Lori? Felix?'

I look down the spiral staircase into Felix's studio. My stepfather makes neon light installations for trendy cocktail bars and West London women who think they're edgy. They favour fridge magnet philosophy: *IF YOU CAN'T HANDLE ME AT MY WORST, YOU DON'T DESERVE ME AT MY BEST,* or some other dreary Monroe or Hepburn quasi-empowerment nonsense. *YOU GO, GIRL.*

'Felix?'

Good. I have some Nancy Drewing to do, and don't want to be disturbed. I find my laptop where I left it this morning: on the kitchen table. The cleaner has left the mail next to it and I spy a tower of books in Jiffy bags for Mummy. Every crime writer in the world wants a quote from Lulu Carroll on their cover.

Our house was featured in the property and homes section of the *Evening Standard* a couple of years ago – and it does sometimes feel like I live in a magazine rather than a home.

The kitchen – the work of some Danish architect – is light and bright, a lean-to on the main house, with a glass wall and ceiling. The hobs and fridge gleam cold and steely, while the island homes an enormous goldfish bowl filled with white orchids and their tentacle roots.

I slide onto the bench and open my computer. There's not a lot to go on and this card could have been jammed in Bunny's pigeonhole for weeks, if not months. That being said, tomorrow *is* the 23rd May. Coincidence?

I suppose last year had a 23rd May, as did the one before that. Where to begin?

Searching for *Wonderland* brings up a theme park in Berlin. One of Bunny's many sojourns perhaps. Next, I google *Wonderland 23/5*.

This throws up a different link.

::::: **WONDERLAND** :::::

What else to do? I click it.

The Queen of Hearts cordially invites you to

WONDERLAND IV

23-25 May

Who: You alone
When: 4 p.m. 23rd May
Where: Further details will be supplied after registration

Dress Code:
1. Great British Masquerade
2. Disco

RSVP HERE

I click through.

N A M E: _____

N O: _____

Hmm. Well, I can't very well put my own name, can I, given how I wasn't invited? I'm scarcely invited to any St Agnes gatherings on account of how irritating and strange everyone thinks I am, and that's nothing to do with My Big Trans Secret. Three years ago, Jake Quinlan was the first trans student at St Agnes, and he transferred over to St Barney's with minimal fuss. I never intended to 'live stealth' but things were *so* gnashingly awful at my last school, and I have no desire to wade through that circle of hell again. It gets a bad rap, but the closet has kept me safe thus far.

Everyone thinks I'm a girl. Good. I am.

The website seems to be active though and it would be something of a coincidence that this Wonderland, whatever it is, falls over the May bank holiday weekend. A perfect opportunity for a party.

I see little alternative.

N A M E: Bunny Liddell _____

N O: _____

I find her number on my phone and type that in as well before changing my mind. What if the 'Queen of Hearts' wishes to send more information? I enter my own number and hit send.

I stare at my phone, expecting an instantaneous response.

33

Nothing.

Oh, except for a picture message from my mother – after all these years of touring, she still can't get over how enormous American breakfast portions are. That said, her photo depicts more pancake than any human body could accommodate.

'What are you doing?' I didn't even hear Lorina enter.

I slam my laptop shut. 'Nothing.'

'Are you looking at porn in the kitchen?'

'Of course. I don't look at porn anywhere else.'

She scowls. 'Alice, you're so queer. And not even in the dimly interesting sense of the word.'

I raise an eyebrow curtly. If only she knew.

Lori looks a lot like me doing fancy dress as a regular human. She's got my 'natural' mousey brown hair, and dresses like she's trying to harpoon a future Tory politician. Court shoes and chinos. I expect she fits right in at her tedious clubs and societies at Oxford.

'What are you doing home?' I ask. 'It's term time.'

'Reading week before finals. I promised Mummy I'd keep an eye on you.'

It was with some reluctance Mother left for her tour after everything that happened last year while she was promoting her last book.

'I don't need looking after, I'm not a child.'

'That's perhaps the most childish thing you've ever said. Trust me, there are plenty of things I'd rather be doing in Oxford.'

'I shudder to think. How's the acapella group?'

Lori takes some mango juice out of the fridge. 'I'm choosing to ignore that because you're making fun of me.'

34

'You're right, I am. But I still don't need a babysitter. I'm *fine* now.'

She pours herself some juice and puts it back in the fridge without offering me any, which makes me think she's most *definitely* a Tory. 'Mother is worried about you.'

'She has no need to be.'

Lori sits at the breakfast bar and scrolls through her phone. 'Doesn't she? Yes, you seem a lot better but you're making a complete fucking hash of school.'

'Well, we can't all be *Deputy* Head Girl, Lori.'

'Snide.' She lowers her phone, sufficiently irked. 'You have one funny little friend; you don't date; you hardly even go out; you just haunt the house like some sort of poltergeist.'

'All true and all by choice.'

'I don't get it. Like, you got what you wanted, you're a girl now. Go live your life.'

'*Got what I wanted*. Sure, yeah, that's what it was.' How wonderful, I flowered at fourteen. I suppose I'm done.

She tuts. 'You really do live in your own little world, don't you?'

It's funny, isn't it, but since day one, my sister and I haven't got on. There's a picture of Mother in hospital holding newborn me and the side-eye from Lorina has some powerfully dark energy. We share some genes and little else.

'And what's wrong with that?' I reply. 'Have you *seen* the world outside? It's a festering pustule. If I could, I'd upload myself to the internet, where everything would be exactly what it isn't out there.'

'Simpleton.' Lori rolls her eyes, unimpressed. 'You talk a

good game, I'll give you that. You're not stupid. Your problem is that you're lazy. Lazy or scared, I can't decide.'

Consider my button pushed. 'Scared? I'm not scared.'

'Yes, you are. If I'd been through what you went through last year, I'd be scared too.'

'I'm *not* scared!'

'Alice, it's fine! I don't blame you, but you've cultivated a very small world of which it's very easy to be queen. You do *nothing*, so there's nothing to fail at.'

She looks pleased as treacle with her pop psychology. 'I've just come from therapy, thanks, Lori. I don't need a double session.'

'Sooner or later, you'll have to leave the nest. That's real life: you fly or you fall. I rather suspect you'll do the latter.' She picks up her phone and swishes out of the kitchen before I have a chance to compose a devastating comeback. So frustrating, I strongly feel there was a fucking brutal read brewing at the back of my mind.

Scared? Fuck you. I'm not scared. I'm just *bored*.

Although I confess I do sometimes wonder if I spend too much time alone, whether the black mould in my head might come back. Better, I think, to keep myself busy. And what more altruistic way to pass the time than trying to piece together whatever happened to Bunny?

My phone vibrates on the kitchen table. I turn it over and see I have one new message from Wonderland.

My stomach kicks like a mule.

I open the message, a solid wooden cube wedged in my throat.

DEAREST BUNNY
WELCOME TO WONDERLAND IV
PURCHASE ACCESS AT THE LINK BELOW

I click on the accompanying link.

Oh.

I see.

It seems a ticket to Wonderland costs precisely one thousand pounds.

VI

OLIVIER TWIST

And that's only the most basic package. A luxury 'glamping' ticket. Someone should be punished for inventing that contradiction in terms. A cool grand, it seems, will get me two nights' accommodation in a 'deluxe secure tepee with elevated bed and electrical outlets'. Bloody awful.

A teenage girl's bedroom is her library and I kick my way through the leaf litter taking up most of the floor. I've enjoyed the first chapters of hundreds of books. I close the door behind myself, and can hear Lori playing maudlin music down the hall in her own room. I think I'm safe. With hefty garnet drapes blocking out the last of the sun, my bedroom retains a dark, womblike warmth. Just the way I like it.

I turn on the fairy lights coiled around the frame and sit on my bed, scrolling through my phonebook. If anyone I know knows Wonderland it'll be Olivier.

He answers on the third ring. 'Bonjour, mademoiselle. Ze usual?'

'I don't want weed, Olly.' I'm still *mostly* off pot since I lost, then found, my shit. Felicity once explained how the medical jury is still very much out on the link between psychosis and marijuana, so while they're deliberating, I'm keeping my smoking to a minimum.

He pauses. 'Then what eez it you want? I am very, *very* busy, darling.'

Knowing Olivier Marchand, I dread to think. Last year he was expelled from St Barnabas for fellating one of the prefects in the music room, only to successfully overturn the sentence by arguing it was an artistic expression of his sexuality. And that's why he was filming it.

'I'm after information,' I tell him.

'Good. For a minute, I thought eet was a social call.'

'Ew, hardly. Where are you?'

I hear him sigh impatiently. 'I'm in Harrods. What eez it, Alice, mon petite cunt? I has a hair appointment.'

'OK. What's Wonderland Four?'

Another pause, this one heavily pregnant. 'Eet is nozzing and certainly nozzing for you.'

'What's that supposed to mean?'

'Alice, eez not for people like you.'

I give my phone the stink-eye. '*People like me?* What's *that* supposed to mean?'

'Eet's a socicty thing.'

'I'll ask you thrice … what do you mean by *that*?'

'Oh, come on, Alice, you would hate it. You don't even like fun. Eet's a party. No ordinary party. A party to end all parties for ze richest kids in London. Everyone eez dying to get an invite.'

Dying literally or figuratively? After Bunny had been gone for a day or so, I went down a Google spiral of missing kids. If they don't turn up after the first few days, they're nearly always dead.

'I'm rich,' I whine. I'm faintly disgusted by how that sounds on my lips, as true as it undeniably is.

'Your mother eez. But there's rich and there's *rich*. You know what I mean.'

I muss my hair. 'I really don't.'

'How do you say … Old Money.'

'Olivier, what on earth are you talking about?'

He sighs impatiently. 'Money is not in your *blood*, Alice. Your mother had to work for eet, born poor. If you were truly rich, she wouldn't have had to work a day in her life. Your name ees worth nothing. Important people from important families: *zat* is who Wonderland is for. You know what? I shouldn't be saying any of thees. Eez meant to be a secret, although literally everyone knows, so …'

The whole thing sounds *very* Bunny Liddell. 'Where is it?' I ask.

'I don't know.'

'Are you going?'

'I could not possibly say.'

So that's a yes.

'Olly …'

'I don't know, Alice! Fuck! Step off my dick! Every year ze location changes. Every year eez different. Zay only tell you on ze day.'

'And presumably only if you pay …'

'Exactly. I find eet very 'ard to believe you were invited.'

'I don't care for your tone.'

'I don't care for your face.'

I break cover and laugh. 'You little bitch.'

'Bisoux.' He hangs up on me.

I lie back on my bed and rub my temples, trying to massage some sense into my muddled head. It's all nonsense: Bunny; secret parties; the Queen of Hearts. For some reason, as silly and trivial as it all sounds, the notion of the party profoundly scares me. Lori's words tower over me: the world that exists inside my head is boundless, but the one I physically live in is, like she said, very small. My whole universe exists between home and school and therapy, with the odd milkshake thrown in for good measure.

The likelihood of Bunny turning up on that narrow stretch seems highly improbable so I might need to stray beyond the picket fences of my Comfort Zone.

It's nauseating though, the notion of a party filled with people I loathe, somewhere I don't know.

There's a reason they call it a Comfort Zone … it's comfortable. What sort of a fool actively seeks discomfort?

I hop off my bed. With a cigarette lighter, I light the end of a joss stick and let the cypress incense fog the room. I know Bunny *was* invited to Wonderland. What was it Olly said? A party for all of London's trust fund children? Bunny, heir to the Liddell Magazines fortune, certainly belongs.

Only one thing for it then. I need a thousand pounds.

VII

MUSINGS ON TIME

Felix arrives home at about seven, his unruly hair slicked back and his portfolio tucked under his arm, suggesting he's been out a-schmoozing clients. I hear him clattering around in his workshop, and follow him down the spiral stairs to the basement. It smells of solder, smelt and his almost chocolatey cigars.

My mother definitely has a type: penniless artists. My father, I am told, once fancied himself a performance poet. I often wonder if I've been immortalised in an ode to his guilt at leaving us the way he did.

I've only seen my biological dad once in ten years. Not a good day. My *logical* dad, Felix, is as wonderful a stepfather as one could hope for. Mother married him when I was eight, he's all I've ever really known and I love him.

I was not an easy child.

I was born a grenade.

If he wants to be a girl, where's the harm? I once overheard Felix tell my mother as she sucked in breaths through her tears. She used to shut herself in the utility room and turn the tumble dryer on to smother the noise. You don't forget shit like that when you're trans. *Who else does it even affect, Lou? Just let him ... be her ...*

What an absolute fucking mensch, honestly.

I don't like to think about the day I met my 'real' father. Ironically, it doesn't feel quite real.

'Hello, poppet, how was your day?' Felix asks as I hover on the threshold of his studio.

'Fair,' I tell him, declining to mention the run-in with Grafton.

'What would you like for dinner? They had some divine swordfish at the market today.'

'I'm not eating fish any more, Felix.'

'Oh, sorry, poppet, I forgot.'

I don't blame him, I do slide in and out of vegetarianism. I have a historical weakness concerning roast dinners. This time, however, I'm determined to see it through. I think it's perfectly simple: If you love animals, don't fucking eat them. 'That's OK. I'll make us something. Pasta maybe? Or that cheesy gnocchi thing?'

He puts down the mail and scrutinises me over tortoiseshell glasses. 'OK, what do you want this time?'

'I take offence at that. I often cook.'

He regards me with great scepticism.

'Very well. May I have the emergency credit card, please?'

He frowns. 'Is there an emergency?'

'Not as such, I just don't have enough in my allowance to pay for the ski trip.'

'*You* want to go on the school trip?' The edges of his mouth curve.

'What?'

'Alice, you *hate* organised fun. And wouldn't there be dorms and showers and stuff?'

He knows me too well, and the prospect of five days of changing in toilet cubicles is acutely terrifying. I wouldn't go on a school trip in a million years.

'True,' I lie, 'but I'll figure something out. Dinah's going and I fear missing out more than I hate fun. And anyway, both you and Mummy keep saying I should try new things, and what's newer to me than a weekend in Val-d'Isère?'

'Very well.' He shakes his head and digs his wallet out of his jacket pocket. 'Here you go.' He hands me the platinum card.

Safely back amongst my books, I sit cross-legged on my bed and click on the Wonderland link.

Not for the first time, I ponder if I should call the police.

Sure, Miss Dodgson, we'll hop to it just as soon as we've tackled knife crime and acid attacks.

But, Officer, I really think an errant heiress might be going to a secret party.

I enter the credit card details.

I remind myself that this is a lot of money.

It's a ritual Mother has instilled in Lori and me. Mother got her big break when I was about seven, so I only *vaguely* remember the black patches on the ceiling of the council flat in Penge. I don't recall how she used to hide jars of baby food in the bottom of the pushchair to shoplift them. I don't *really* remember the coin-operated electricity meter or the food banks, or being a human pass-the-parcel around the neighbours while Mummy worked shifts at the all-night garage, writing her debut novel on her phone to keep herself awake.

But I do *know* all of those things because she tells us the stories regularly. Mother sees the thoroughbred girls I go to school with and doesn't recognise herself in any of them. We got lucky. There are a million parallel worlds, running closely alongside this one, where we didn't. You couldn't slide a Rizla between them. Mother is talented and hard-working, make no doubt, but she is also at pains to tell us about the importance of timing.

A week or so either side, she'd have never seen a post online from a literary agent asking for submissions; a month or two later with the manuscript, and her first editor would have been on maternity leave; a Hollywood producer just so happened to pick up a copy of her book, quite by serendipity, at Heathrow airport WHSmith.

And, of course, that's overlooking the gruesome event that inspired the whole book in the first place. The woman we saw die.

I remember *that* part oh-too clearly. I sometimes hear that horrid, wet thud as she hit the pavement. Imagine a ripe tomato hitting the kitchen tiles. It was a busy afternoon, and Shoreditch High Street was bustling, but everyone stopped still, dumbstruck. Silence so greasy you could feel it on your skin. Brains need a second or two to make sense of what the eyes are seeing sometimes. Then all the people started screaming, but I couldn't look away. I didn't blink until Mummy grabbed me and held my face against her thigh to shield me. It was all so fast.

Anyway. Call it fate, chance or destiny, we're all very much smaller than the cogs of time. They turn with or without us. They spun before I was born and will continue to do so when I'm dust. I like to think about that sometimes, it makes me feel pleasingly irrelevant. Nothing I do matters.

Of course, nowadays, we get hams and hampers from Selfridges and Mother carries a rainbow array of Gucci Marmont purses, but never for one second are we allowed to take our fortuitous timing for granted. I swear if I listen hard enough, I can hear the cogs grinding.

I hit 'submit'.

Processing payment.

Payment successful.

And then I get another text from Wonderland.

THE MOCK TURTLE TEAROOMS
SOUTHWARK
4 P.M.

VIII

A TIMELY FLASHBACK

'I'm late.' She'd collided with me at the fairground on Clapham Common.

What's not to love about a visiting funfair? The pounding house music; scream if you wanna go faster; the air sugar-sticky with toffee apples and candyfloss. Oh, and hormones, so many hormones; shaken up in us, the rides like centrifuges.

I had been waiting for Henry outside the ghost train, thirty minutes after the designated meeting time. The entrance was the gaping open mouth of a bright red, horned devil. A 'haunted' electronic wail emanated from the bowels of the ride and that was when she crashed into my shoulder.

'Ow!'

'Sorry,' she breathed, not stopping to look up at me.

'Bunny?'

She whipped her afro back. As someone who's been fetishised, I don't want to fetishise her hair, but it is fucking iconic: a bouncing cloud of honey-coloured curls. Her eyes were wide and wild. A rabbit in the proverbial … well … yes.

'Oh, it's you.' She looked me over. 'Alice, right?'

'Yes.' Sometimes people are running *towards* something, and sometimes they're running *away* and you can always tell the difference. 'Are you OK?'

'I'm late.' She burst into tears. 'She hates it when I'm late. I'm gonna be in so much trouble.'

I never know what to do when people cry. I seldom cry, I've never understood what it achieves. 'Hey, it's all right.'

'It's not! It's really not. And now, on top of everything, I'm late.' She spoke with that singular mid-Atlantic drawl that sounds like a Brit doing a bad American accent or vice versa. Bunny has been bouncing back and forth between boarding schools since she was six.

I took my little teddy backpack off and handed her a Handy Andie. She blew her nose.

'Just breathe.'

Her breath came in shallow pants. 'I think I'm having a panic attack.'

'Here.' I untucked Grandpa's fob watch from inside my jacket. 'Whenever I feel anxious, I just watch the second hand go round and round until I feel normal again. I find it soothing.' I placed it in the palm of her hand. 'You open it like this …'

She watched it a while. 'It's lovely.'

'It was my grandfather's when he was in the navy.'

'Is that the time?'

I nodded.

Bunny closed her eyes. 'She's going to kill me.'

She said it in such a grave manner, I wasn't wholly sure it was a figure of speech. 'Who?'

Bunny was silent, fixated on the pocket watch. 'Are you here alone?' she asked eventually, snapping out of her trance.

I felt my face flush. 'I … I was supposed to be meeting a boy from St Barnabas … Henry Beaumont. Do you know him?'

'No.'

'I'm starting to suspect I've been stood up. Can you believe it? Ghosted at the ghost train. Poetic, I suppose.' I swallowed a chunk of disappointment. I'd met Henry via the app – of course – and had entertained brief *Love, Simon* fantasies about having a PG 13 high school romance. Well, I guess that bubble burst. There was a comfort in knowing he couldn't really out me as trans without outing himself as someone who posts faceless pics on queer dating apps.

Bunny snapped the pocket watch shut and handed it back.

'Are you OK now?' I asked.

'No. Probably not.'

'Hang on to it for a little longer if you want.' I don't know why I said that when I'm notoriously bad at sharing. Half the toys in our attic have 'CHARLES' territorially scrawled on them in Sharpie.

Bunny looked at me like she was seeing me for the first time. Her face changed; her pained expression softened. 'Your eyes are really, really blue. They match your hair.'

'Thanks,' I said.

'I never noticed before. Fuck it. I suppose I'm so late, it makes no difference if I'm even later. Care to ride the ghost train, Alice?'

'What? You and me? Together?'

She was uneasy, twitchy, scanning the fair. It didn't occur to me then that her invite might be more of an attempt to hide herself. 'Well, I can't go on by myself. It sounds silly, and I know the ghosts and ghouls are fake, but I still get scared. The fear is real.'

I smiled at her. 'Fear is abstract.'

'So is time, but you have this.' She held up the fob watch.

I laughed. All these years, passing each other in the hallways two or three times a day, and I'm not sure Bunny and I had even said more than two words to one another. I didn't think she'd be like this. She's so, so princess-pretty, I imagined her beautiful head was a basket full of kittens and pink mohair.

'OK then. I'll look after you.' I offered her my hand.

'You promise?'

'I promise.'

She slipped the watch into her jacket pocket and we ran, hand in hand, towards the devil's grinning mouth.

IX

ADDRESS FOR ALICE

Back in the closet. This time my mother's walk-in.

When I was four years old, I wrapped a lacy tablecloth around my waist and told my mother I was a girl, and would like to be addressed as such from that point onwards. At first, she thought it was hilarious. Tears streamed down her cheeks as I ham-fistedly smeared cerise lipstick around my little cherub mouth.

The joke went stale faster than an organic loaf, and the tears soon changed their genre.

Don't be silly, Charles. It isn't funny any more. Just stop it. Act right in your head, for crying out loud.

When she left us with babysitters during her nights at that petrol station, I'd go into her room and raid her wardrobe. I'd stand in front of her mirror trying on her jewellery and clothes and make-up. That afternoon, the one when the woman fell off the balcony, I'd been daydreaming, staring at the mannequins in the window of the hipster boutiques, and planning how I'd look when God finally acquiesced and turned me into a girl.

And here I am back in Mother's wardrobe again, only this time it's a far more luxurious one. The 'Great British Masquerade' dress code is giving me a headache so early on a Saturday morning. Perhaps I shall go as a telephone box or a blue passport. Oh, how I miss the days of watching Cartoon Network in my pyjamas until lunchtime.

Dinah optimistically describes my style as 'kawaii steampunk' but that rather suggests I have any guiding sartorial sense. I buy things I like. I loathe shopping, but enjoy discovering. Clothes, I think, should come to their owner and not the other way around: my grandfather's fob watch; Felix's old marching band jacket with the shiny brass buttons; the Doc Martens I saw in a charity shop window; Mother's frilly eighties blouses; a top hat I found in a skip in the street.

All good, but something's missing.

I shouldn't really be in Mum's room, not least because it's where she and Felix probably still have maintenance sex when she's not touring. She does, though, have the most wonderful walk-in closet. When she was having the house renovated, she had two requirements of the architect: a walk-in wardrobe and a free-standing bathtub. With those two things, she claimed, she would know she'd 'made it'.

Because Mother is on tour, Felix has left the duvet in a flump on the bed, and his dirty clothes litter the floor. I have to step around his skid-marked boxer shorts, wondering why men are incapable of proper wiping. Felix plays five-a-side on a Saturday morning and Lori is out too, at a spin class, working very hard at going nowhere, meaning I have the run of the house. It's a bright May morning, honeysuckle plump with summer promise. Warm, not yet hot. London will be giddy today when it leaves its coat at home.

Unashamedly basic, Mother collects shoes and handbags she rarely uses; I think a great many men have collected much sillier trinkets and never been called 'basic'. I ignore her triumphant display of bags, mounted like stag heads, and rifle through her dresses. If I remember rightly ... yes!

Mother won the Specsavers Prize for Crime Fiction a few years ago and I distinctly remember her being very excited by a new Vivienne Westwood dress. I pull it off the rack now, thrilled she hasn't given it to charity as she often does. Oh, it's perfect! Even lovelier than I remembered: duck-egg blue with pink and lilac tartan stripes, scoop neck and a cloud-like skirt. What could be more Great and British than something called 'Anglomania'?

I pull off my robe and slip the dress over my head. Mother is curvier than I am, obviously, but it just about works. I got my flat ass on hormone blockers when I was thirteen so at least my body never went *too* far in the wrong direction. I zip up the side and grab a chunky leather belt to cinch it all in at the waist. I have some elbow-length gloves in my room that'll cover the shiny silver scars on my left forearm.

I wasn't planning on keeping on the stripy socks, but I rather like them with the dress. I admire myself in the mirror. The skirt is voluminous, so I won't even need to tuck too tight which is a blessed relief. It's a laugh that trans people are often accused of being perverts when it's everyone else who is obsessed with our crotches.

Very Alice, I approve.

Well, that solves the outfit. As for the masquerade part ... surely Mum and Felix have some fucked-up *Fifty Shades* stuff hidden away somewhere. I have a rummage through her boxes and find only one very modest vibrator and a crusty tube of KY

Jelly. I can't decide if I'm thrilled or disappointed.

Instead, I locate a black lace scarf on a hook on the back of the door. I go back to my room and arrange it haphazardly around the brim of my rescued top hat in a large bow. It's not perfect, but the makeshift veil more or less conceals my face, if not the blue hair. That I'll have to secure in a knot and wish for luck.

My stomach flopgurgles. I am not Bunny Liddell. There is no way I could be confused for Bunny Liddell. I'm the whitest white girl, so pale, I'm almost see-through. Bunny is mixed race. There's bound to be some sort of gatekeeper, or bouncer, or similar iPad-wielding fascist, and they probably know Bunny. Everyone knows Bunny.

One step at a time, Alice. I tell myself that all I have to do in the first instance is get to the Mock Turtle at the given hour. Problems become less problematic if tackled one at a time.

I've decided not to pack an overnight bag. Yes, I've paid for the full weekend, but I fully intend to drop by for the afternoon, make sure Bunny is either a) in attendance and safe or b) elsewhere and enigmatic, then make a swift exit. The thought of spending all weekend away from the safety of my bed-womb is bloodcurdling to say the least.

Downstairs, I leave a message on the fridge under a dodo magnet from the Natural History Museum: GONE TO TUTOR, ALICE XXX.

Only slightly more believable than telling Felix I'm with a friend.

X

THE MOCK TURTLE

The Mock Turtle is a quaint, toffee-box tea room. About five minutes' walk from Tower Bridge towards Bermondsey, it's tucked down a side street, away from the frappuccino fingers of tourists. Why, unless you were looking, you'd hardly know it was there. The front door, painted in deepest crimson, is sandwiched between two convex leaded windows. Through the smoky glass, I can just about make out the elderly customers enjoying afternoon tea in dim lamplight.

So far, precisely nothing is screaming 'London's most exclusive secret party'. It looks like heaven's waiting room. I was hoping I might get some sense of how to trick my way in if I were to observe other guests arriving, but I've been lurking outside for fifteen minutes and nothing. No hope of getting lost in a crowd.

With a sigh, I cross the road and slip inside the tea room. As I push through the door, a bell tinkling merrily overhead, I'm greeted by a wave of warmth and the aroma of fruit teacakes slathered with butter. A couple of old ladies sip through pursed lips, glancing at me quite pointedly over their china. I suppose I *do* look *somewhat* outlandish. I remove the top hat and tuck it under my arm, weaving my way through the three-tier jungle to the only available table.

The walls – an even deeper sanguine red than the door – are chock-a-block with framed oil paintings, mostly of cats dressed like humans. I think my favourite is one dressed like a cavalier in a ruff. Decorative teapots of all shapes and sizes fill a shelf that runs all the way around the café and I'm very glad I'm not responsible for dusting them. A gramophone scratchily plays swing classics, and it somehow makes me even more claustrophobic.

I could not feel more awkward if I tried. I'm a hangnail, a snaggletooth.

I smooth down my dress and sit, forcing my knee to stop bouncing. Instead I cast my eye over the array of cake stands on the counter. Quite a spread: slabs of death-by-chocolate cake and Victoria sponge bigger than bricks, with buttercream cement; daintily iced cupcakes and pastel macarons; doughnuts oozing jam and custard; raspberry ripple meringues that look uncannily like breasts with ripe nipples. I lick my lips.

An elderly woman in a hair net and apron appears at the side of my table. Her name badge says Mary Ann. 'Hello, treacle, what can we do for you?'

I haven't thought this far ahead. 'I … I'm not sure.' I lean closer to her. 'Do you know how to get to Wonderland?'

She regards me over her half-moon spectacles. 'You what now, love?'

'Wonderland? The party?'

'I ain't got the foggiest what you're on about, love. You all right, darlin'?'

Well, I suppose that's that then. 'Yes. Thank you, I'm fine.'

Her cheap lipstick has left waxy flakes on her thin lips. 'What about a nice cocoa? That'll sort you out.'

'Yes.' I sigh. 'That'd be lovely, thanks.'

Mary Ann shuffles off, jotting my order on her notepad. I rest my head in my hands.

Once more, I remember waking up in the big empty bed at the V Hotel. I reached out with my arm, expecting to feel Bunny's warm skin, only to find a cool pillow. And resting on the pillow, my pocket watch.

A shadow falls over the table and I look up. It's Mary Ann carrying a small tray which she places in front of me.

'Here you are, petal, this is on the house.'

It's a tiny glass bottle filled with a ruby-red liquid, a cork stopper in the top. 'What is it?'

Mary Ann winks theatrically. 'Only one way to find out, darlin'. Just one thing …'

'What?'

'I need your phone, sweetheart.'

A thought so horrifying, I almost vomit on the spot. 'My phone?'

'No phones where you're going, I'm afraid.'

The penny drops. Secret parties wouldn't stay secret for long with camera phones. I did it! I found Wonderland! Reluctantly, I hand it over and she gives me a plastic chip with a number on it.

'Thanks, poppet. You'll get it back at the end.'

'The end of what?'

She winks again and walks off with my phone. It feels a lot like she's removed a vital organ. I'd rather she'd taken a kidney to be frank, I have two of those and I can't watch memes on either.

I turn over the label which dangles from the neck of the bottle.

I read the message to myself. 'Drink me.'

Curious. I look around the tea room. No one else seems to have the aperitif. It's the colour of Campari or cranberry juice. I tease out the cork and give it a sniff. It smells like neither, it's marzipan-sweet, with a trace of cinnamon.

What else can I do? I take a sip. It's delicious. I gulp the rest back and a second later the vodka kicks. At least I *think* it's vodka. Schnapps maybe? Whatever it is, it's strong. I judder from the inside out.

Moment over, I realise there's something in the bottle ... a small black key. I swill the last dregs and shake it into the palm of my hand. Why, it's so dinky it looks more like the key to a jewellery box than a door.

What do I do with this? Logic dictates there is a lock to fit the key, and presumably I'm supposed to find it. If Wonderland is a treasure, it seems there is to be a treasure hunt first.

As my finger traces the bottom of the bottle, I realise there is something embossed into the glass. I turn it upside-down and the writing is backwards, so I hold the top of the bottle close to one eye like a telescope. Sure enough, the letters spell out GO DOWNSTAIRS.

I'm almost impressed.

'OK,' I mutter to myself. 'I'm game.'

I clear my throat and gather my things, tucking my chair under the table. I see there's a narrow staircase leading down to a cellar. A signpost points to the WC. Checking no one is looking, I duck down the stairs. The ceiling is so low, I have to stoop to avoid hitting my head.

As I descend, I realise my vision is swimming ever-so. Gosh, how strong was that shot? I feel a toastiness in the pit of my stomach. It's been a while since I drank.

Never one to do things in moderation, I used to drink to blast myself out of my head. I have only attended one St Agnes house party at Reena Aziz's place and I ended up locked in the bathroom cutting myself. Or so I'm reliably informed. That whole year is something of a fog.

I run my hand along the flocked wallpaper to steady myself. The same calliope music is piped down here and it feels like I'm entering a funhouse.

I think of Bunny and why I'm doing this.

For one night, I was her girl.

I shake my head, trying to rid it of the wooziness. It only makes it worse: the basement corridor and the black and white floor tiles seem to curl and twist under my feet, like a boa trying to swallow me whole. My goodness, it's disorienting, like some topsy-turvy Escher print. Sometimes I miss my blackout drunk nights. It was nice, temporarily, to switch off life. Oblivion is silence for noisy little minds.

I find myself in a long, dimly lit basement hallway – a vast gilded mirror at one end and a fire exit at the other. The party must be outside. Managing to plant one foot in front of the other, I pass the toilets and make it to the fire escape: a sturdy chestnut door at the end of the corridor. I grab the handle and yank it open with gusto, only to find more of the same oppressive wallpaper. What? A fake door. I look over my shoulder. There's only the mirror at the other end of the hall.

A door to a brick wall. A flashing green EXIT light points down to the floor. I tut.

'Well, that's helpful.'

Only then I realise, it's not directing me to the floor, it's pointing at a tiny little wooden door, no bigger than a mouse hole.

'You have got to be ...'

I kneel down to examine the hatch. It's like any old door, only much smaller. It reminds me of Lori's doll's house which I was never allowed to play with because I was – according to everyone else – a boy.

'Let's see, shall we?' I take the key out of my coat pocket and try it for size. Sure enough, it fits. I twist the lock and, taking care not to break the miniature handle, I push open the door.

'Oh wow ... that's too cute.'

Peering through the door, I can see into a garden party – from shoe level. Outside, dozens of pairs of well-heeled feet mill around and I hear a jovial hubbub of conversation. I think I've found the party.

Which would be great if I were the size of a gerbil. At a push I could slide a hand through the doorway, but I can't imagine how odd that would look to the people on the other side. I try a different tack.

'Hello?' I press my mouth to the doorframe. 'Hello there? Can you hear me?'

I'm crouched on the floor, shouting through a hole. This is all very undignified.

I peek through the hole once more, hoping I'll recognise someone, anyone, who can give me some sort of a clue of how to get in. The garden beyond the wall seems to be sloping downhill, presumably to the river. The incline means I can obliquely see some of the guests at a distance. The fancy dress costumes aren't making this any easier: further down the garden, I can make out a colourful assortment of peacock feather headpieces and beaked Venetian masks, but I can't tell who anyone is.

And then the crowd parts and, in the centre of them all is a white rabbit. I think that would be rather clever, Bunny hiding in plain sight as a rabbit. The girl is skinny enough to be her; I suspect Bunny has a somewhat fractious relationship with food. She's wearing white tube socks and platform trainers with a shift dress and the rabbit head. Her legs are about the right colour, too. All that matters is that it *could* be Bunny Liddell. The mask itself, much too big for her body, is shabby, and unintentionally scary, like one of those memes about terrifying Easter Bunnies.

'Bunny?' I mutter to myself.

But then I think again of our night in the V Hotel.

'Alice,' she says, 'I think I'm in trouble.'

'What kind of trouble?'

'The serious sort. The sort I can't get out of.' She turns away from the window, but still can't look me in the eye.

'Bunny Liddell – your escapades are legendary ...'

'Not this time. This isn't the same.'

If Bunny was running away, and I think she was, why would she come here and advertise the fact?

Even if she wouldn't, or couldn't, come here, I feel like I'm finally getting a glimpse into her strange, secret world. That night in the hotel, she was a bunny tangled in barbed wire. She was caught up in something, I'm sure of it. The look in her eyes belonged to a girl who'd swum well out of her depth.

And it's something to do with … these people. Some of them, undoubtedly, are the same people who ignore me at school. I'm blissfully invisible, and I can use that now.

There has to be a way in.

I clamber to my feet, my head-juice sloshing, and look around. In front of me is the tiny door, behind me – at the far end of the corridor – is the grand mirror. From this angle, I see that the mirror must be some sort of distorting glass, the sort you'd find in a funhouse: everything at this end of the corridor looks a million miles away, the chequered tiles stretching on and on.

But doesn't that mean …?

Feeling my way down the hall, I move closer to the mirror. My reflection grows larger and larger with every step. When I'm within touching distance, I resemble an ogre or some such, my legs like tree trunks, and this time – for once – it isn't body dysmorphia.

And, when I step to one side, the reflection of the itty bitty door at the far end of the corridor almost looks to be a normal size. It nearly fills the mirror, so large I could fit through it. A wide smile creeps across my face.

'Got you …'

I frisk the frame until I feel a lock with my right index finger. 'Bingo!' I slip the key in and it complies with a polite click. It's not a mirror at all … it's a *door*.

A gentle breeze, laced with freshly mown grass and sticky sweet Pimm's greets me.

I'm in.

XI

ALL ARE BORED

I replace the top hat, lower the veil over my face and step outside. The mirror conceals a perfectly mundane doorway onto a paved courtyard. I expect, on a normal day, the café has a back patio on which customers can enjoy a view of the Thames. Today, as soon as I step amongst the tables and parasols, a waitress, dressed head-to-toe in red, hands me some sort of greenish aperitif in a hi-ball glass.

'What is it?' I ask.

'It's called a garden party.' Her stiff smile tells me she's counting down the hours until she's free.

I take a sip through the now ubiquitous paper straw. Oh, I know they'll save the polar bears and turtles, but I do so loathe the moment when the straw turns to cold mush against my lip. The drink itself tastes of cucumber and, very potently, tequila. 'Crikey,' I mutter. Truly we are a nation that embraces alcoholism. You're considered a problem if you aren't a problem drinker.

'You're welcome,' says the waitress and weaves away with her tray.

The party is already well underway. I'd guess there were maybe three hundred guests loitering on the three tiers of the garden all the way down to the riverside. A bikini-clad DJ – I vaguely recognise her from somewhere – waves her arms around behind a laptop, pretending to mix, but is almost certainly just playing songs off Spotify.

The masquerade costumes make it virtually impossible to tell who anyone is. I must know some of these people from school and I wonder if I should have made more of an attempt to hide my turquoise hair – it's a blue ball at the nape of my neck, just hidden by the brim of the hat.

I take another sip of the drink – goodness me, it's strong – and scan the garden. I see the white rabbit – Bunny? – holding her glass aloft, winding her waist to the music. It's hard to tell who she's with.

As a side note, I wonder how she's managing to drink through that rabbit head. Possibly not the most pressing concern, but still food for thought.

And there's another odd phrase: food for thought. What food would thoughts prefer if they had a preference? Almost certainly cake, I should imagine.

Shit, am I drunk already? I used to be able to drink sailors under the table at my best/worst.

As I'm staring, I get the impression Rabbit Head is staring back. It's hard to tell, but she stops dancing, and the googly eyes are pointing directly at me.

I start towards her.

'You're not supposed to be here,' a voice says close to my ear.

Startled, I whirl around and find myself face to face with a black cat.

White rabbits and black cats, whatever next?

The girl in the cat hoodie is very pretty indeed. Underneath the hood – the edges of which are peaked like feline ears – a pair of green-blue eyes smeared in metallic purple almost burn out of the shadows. Pretty poor effort at masquerade, I think, I can more or less see her whole face. She grins broadly and I see a row of perfect white teeth, a highly adorable gap between the front two.

'It's cool,' she purrs. 'I'm not meant to be here either. And I'm no grass.'

I stall. I should have been readier for this sort of thing. 'I … I don't know what you mean.'

'Alice Dodgson. Did I see your name on the guest list? No. Does your name belong on the guest list? Also no. You don't belong here.' She smiles again. She seems friendly enough and doesn't exactly look like the bouncer. There *is* security, but they wear the same red shirts and ties as the wait staff.

'I'm sorry, do I know you?'

'No.'

'How do you know who I am?'

Another smile. 'There's not a lot to know.'

'Wow.' I can't pretend that didn't sting a little. 'Is that a read?'

'I know my drag queen vernacular, and you can read that read however you wish.' She speaks sleepily, languid, almost like she's stoned. Perhaps she is, I'm starting to wish I was. My heart feels like it's beating too fast, my palms are clammy.

A boat sounds its horn. I look over my shoulder and see that some of the party people have started boarding a cruiser down at the jetty. Rabbit Head follows the crowd towards the river.

'What's going on?' I ask the cat girl.

'All aboard for Wonderland …'

'This isn't it?'

'Oh, this is just the un-party.'

I roll my eyes. 'I don't have time for riddles.'

The girl looks genuinely disappointed. 'Well, that *is* a shame.' The hood rides back just far enough to reveal she has a buzz-shaved head. I maybe shouldn't assume she's a she. They could very well be a they, or even a he. I, of all people, should know better.

'The boat goes to the party?' I see the rabbit board the yacht via a gangplank. Oh, fuck me, I really don't want to get on the boat, but I don't see how I can avoid it. She's getting away.

'Looks that way.'

'Can I get a straight answer, please?'

'From me? Unlikely.' She smiles even more broadly.

'Is it coming back?' The notion of a boat ride into oblivion isn't especially appealing.

'I'm not being vague, I don't know,' the cat says. 'No one knows. That's the point of Wonderland. It's a trip into the unknown.'

Yeah, I've been there before. It's overrated. Very low Trip Advisor rating from me. I don't see what choice I have, though. I nod towards the beefcake with the earpiece. 'Are you going to rat me out?'

'I'm a cat, not a rat. Why would I do that? Although I don't know why you'd *want* to be at this carnival of cunts. Guess you have a reason,' she sighs.

'Do I need one?'

She shrugs. 'No one *needs* a reason to be.'

'I couldn't agree more usually. But I *need* to be on that boat.'

'Go ahead. I'm not stopping you.'

'Aren't you coming?' She's the only person who's even acknowledged me here, and I figure it'd be easier to blend in if I had a companion.

Another sigh. 'Maybe, maybe not. I'll let you know.' She waves at me with gloved hands. I know why I am, but why *she's* wearing purple leather gloves on a perfectly warm spring afternoon is anyone's guess.

'Well … wait …'

'Things to do …' the cat says, backing away against the tide of people pushing past us to get to the ferry.

'Do you at least have a name?'

'Not traditionally, no.' She smiles and vanishes into the crowd.

'Oh, for crying out loud.' I turn my attention to the boat. I tap a guy in a plague mask on the shoulder. 'Excuse me, where is the boat going?'

'Wonderland,' he replies, his voice muffled.

'More specifically?'

Through the holes in the mask, I see his pupils are already dilated like saucers. 'We don't know. That's the whole point. Just go with it …' He hurries away.

The foghorn mournfully bellows again and I force my feet to move. *Let go.* Lori's words haunt me again. I don't really *do* letting go. I am holding on exceedingly tight, every minute of every day, digging my fingernails into the flesh of life and leaving smile marks. I like it that way. If I don't, it's Humpty Dumpty time again.

There's nothing in Alice's world that Alice doesn't control.

I conjure Felicity's therapeutic tones telling me to gently acknowledge (and then ignore) the most catastrophic potential outcomes. The most catastrophic potential outcome is always *Alice, you might die*. You welcome that thought in, sit it down with a cup of tea and a chocolate digestive, and give it a firm talking-to. If I board this boat, I *probably* won't die. That's a very unlikely outcome. I haven't brought an overnight bag, so I can go to the party for a couple of hours, talk to the white rabbit and find out if she's Bunny, then come home. I paid for 'glamping' so I deduce the boat must going towards *somewhere* on dry land in order for us to camp, rather than the open sea.

Thinking it through, it's not so scary, and not so 'unknown' after all.

I just want to see Bunny.

I want to know she's OK.

I want to know if she feels ...

Well.

Let's not get carried away.

I reach the lowest level of the gardens via mossy stone steps and walk onto the wooden planks of the jetty. I feel seasick before even boarding.

Dutch courage.

My brain doesn't even have time to wonder which brave Dutch alcoholic originated that phrase as I down the contents of the glass and board the ferry.

It's time to let myself fall.

XII

CATERPILLR

There is a second DJ, on deck on the decks, and the bassline seems to rattle the hull. Tropical Euro house. Ghastly. The cruiser has three levels. We boarded on the middle deck and were then shepherded towards the top for some sort of welcoming committee.

An only-too familiar redhead in a kitsch blue sailor outfit holds up a loudspeaker. 'Boys and girls and those clever enough to transcend the binary, welcome aboard the *SS Wonderland*!' There is a deafening cheer. 'I am your captain, Rose, and allow me to introduce your pursers, Lily and Violet.'

Two more Elvgren sailor girls appear – one in green and one in yellow. All three are from my year at St Agnes. Rose, Lily and Violet – collectively known as the Flower Girls.

They are all very pretty but very awful.

Rose is the shrill redhead, Lily is a petite Singaporean and Violet is a voluptuous blonde. They make for a loathsome bouquet. Rose is a busybody – constantly trying to save the whales, or end period poverty, or ban airbrushing, but each short-lived campaign is always rather more about her than it is about any genuine cause. She has to be seen to be being seen and her activism lasts as long as the spotlight does.

Lily is a carnivorous little gossip. When Mr Gough gave her

a D grade on a History essay, she put it about he was touching choir boys from St Barnabas – particularly cruel as he is one of very few out gay members of staff. It *had* to be investigated even though there wasn't a shred of evidence and Lily watched it all unfold with barely concealed glee.

Violet – the sweetest-smelling of the three, if you were forced to choose – is simply too stupid to defy the others and that, in my book, is just as bad a sin. We do not stan a passive bystander. I judge people by the company they keep.

'The pursers are here for your safety, but mostly your enjoyment, so do please help yourself to party favours!' cries Rose.

Another hearty cheer almost perforates my eardrums. Rose activates a rave horn and the fleet of waiters lift cloches to reveal trays of pills. Good grief … are they …?

I've seen them once before. I swipe a pill off a silver tray as a waiter passes and hold the little heart-shaped white tablet closer to my eye. On one side are tiny letters: *EAT ME*.

'Don't be greedy, party people!' Rose says with a wink. 'You don't wanna peak too soon!'

All around me, people place the pills on their tongues or knock them back with drinks. I feel woozy enough after the cocktails but stow the tablet in my jacket pocket.

'I'm coming up … I can feel it.'
'What's it like?'
'I love you …'
'No, you don't! That's the pill talking.'
'I'm warm, I'm warm inside. Like caramel …'

'The first time is the best. If I could capture how that felt again ... let me share the high ...' Bunny strokes my face and kisses me again. And that's why they call it ecstasy. I get it now.

Well, you never know, do you? That night Bunny told me that MDMA is basically the same stuff they put in anti-depressants, and I knock back those like they are Tic Tacs. Both puppeteer the serotonin and dopamine in your brain.

But no. The last thing I need right now is to feel *less* in control, and it'd be just my rotten luck to end up six feet under like Antonella Hemmings did. Instead I swipe a glass of champagne from a different waitress. I need to calm my nerves more than anything else and they are flaring up. I don't know why they call them 'butterflies', which suggests something rather airier than the present stampede of hooves in my stomach. I try to focus on the beautiful murmuration of starlings currently swooping over the Thames.

'Anchors away!' Rose screams and we start to move.

I grip the side of the boat, watching as the Mock Turtle grows more and more distant. I shouldn't get too drunk. I should pay attention to where we're going. Are we going east towards Essex or west towards ... whatever's past West London? Surrey?

I look across the deck and I can't see Rabbit Head or the enigmatic cat girl anywhere. I'm on my own. Luckily, no one seems to pay me much mind. There's an array of wigs: candyfloss-pink afros (for shame); platinum Louise Brooks bobs; inevitable Native American headdresses (for yet more shame). My hair is fairly tame by comparison. I could be anyone.

The boat chugs along, and after turning around, seems to be heading west.

A new thought occurs to me as I see another tray of pills whizz past. I haven't packed my medication. Every morning I take a 10mg tablet of aripiprazole and another of escitalopram on top of my oestrogen, which I take before bed. I forgot to take both this morning. But then, like I said to Felicity, I've been forgetting a lot, and I've been *fine*. I cling to that. I haven't noticed a change.

Although just the memory of how bad it was is scary.

Fearing it might come back is almost as destructive as the depression itself.

The boat rocks gently as it glugs over the Thames, and I grip the side tighter. I'm suddenly acutely aware of there being nothing stable beneath my feet.

I bat away bats of panic as they fly at my face. I will not break now.

For the first time in a really long time, I can't get away. Every molecule of my being is telling me to retreat; to return to my ivory tower in Notting Hill, but I can't. I *physically* can't unless I throw myself overboard.

And that, my friends, is terrifying.

I look around. I see a lot of gums and teeth, everyone wide-mouthed; laughing, howling like hyenas. I don't understand how they are all enjoying this. None of these revellers know where this vessel is heading, and only I seem to care. How can they dance through all these clanging alarm bells?

My legs go to jelly.

I might need a momentary sit-down to go through Felicity's de-escalation techniques.

First things first: where am I? The pleasure cruiser is rather like a waterborne hotel. Leaving behind the twee English garden party theme, the vibe on the boat appears to be Riviera Chic – there are palm trees dotted around the top deck. This level seems to be a dancefloor so I opt to head inside and go down a level.

The next deck is a bar area. The noisy St Barney's rugger buggers bray like the donkeys from *Pinocchio*, chugging down yards of ale. Maxim Hattersley is presently having beer poured down his throat via a funnel. He's wearing a baby-blue velvet tuxedo and a matching top hat falls off to be caught by none other than *Pierrot* Olivier Marchand, his white hair freshly bleached. I promptly swerve downstairs again before he sees me.

Near miss.

The lower level is a welcome oasis of tranquillity. I can only dimly feel the bass from the party above. I suppose it's normally a restaurant and the space is divided up into plush, powder-pink velour dining booths. A gold palm leaf shade hangs over each table.

Felicity says anxiety is little more than an excess of adrenaline flooding the body. Your primitive brain, still pre-programmed from our cave-dwelling days, tells you you're about to be gobbled up by a Tyrannosaurus Rex or some such and so your body prepares to run like hell or attack it with a sharp stick. The fact that the modern-day equivalent of a dinosaur is having to speak to someone on the phone is neither here nor there.

I think I can relax now. It's less intense down here. It feels like all that adrenaline – getting to Southwark; getting into the garden; boarding the boat – is ebbing out through my feet and seeping into the floor. It's *fine*. I will be home later tonight and can take my medication then.

Looking out of the window, I see the Globe theatre and I slump into an empty booth.

There's a polite *ahem*. 'Who are you?'

OK, I *thought* it was an empty booth.

A chubby younger boy sits opposite, his feet not even touching the floor. He's smoking a joint out of a gap in the porthole.

'Oh my gosh! I'm so sorry, I didn't realise anyone was sat …'

He deliberately blows a plume of grassy smoke into my face. 'Who are you?' he says again.

I waft it away. 'Well, that's rude.'

'It's rude not to introduce oneself.'

'You haven't introduced yourself,' I reply indignantly.

He sucks on the joint. He's so baby-faced, it's almost absurd. 'I'm Willie Zong.'

Oh. I've heard of him. I was expecting someone bigger. You'd imagine the son of a man who owns China's second largest phone company to be … well, big. 'I know who you are,' I say, although it sounds very strange now I've said it.

'Let me guess. You were expecting … something else?'

You'd think, with all his money, he'd get his teeth fixed. Wow, that was bitchy. One cannot help the occasional nasty thought rearing up from the sewer, but one can admonish oneself each time, and try to counter them with more positive thoughts.

'I'm Alice,' I deflect.

'I know.'

'You know? Then why ask?'

'I didn't ask for your name, I asked *who are you?*'

Oh hurrah, more riddles. I never tire of them.

'Yes. And I said: I'm Alice.'

He relights the joint and takes another deep toke. 'You want some?'

Why not? It's all a balancing act of uppers and downers and I could definitely cope with being fuzzier around the edges right now. He passes it over the table and I take a hit.

'I know your name,' he says. 'It's my business to know people's names. But what's in a name? Names are nothing.'

I remember what Olivier said about the value of my name. 'I don't know if that's true.'

He ponders this. 'You're right, certain names –' he takes a sort of bow – 'have a certain cache. But they are ephemeral. All of them. A few words here or there … a rumour … an allegation … and even the most prestigious name can turn toxic. Names change. I should know. Little Zong Wei-Li flew a few thousand miles and became Willie Zong. So much easier for the Caucasian palate to swallow. A little change to play the game.' He has a slight lisp and I wonder if he's maybe gay.

'My mother changed her name.'

'Indeed. Would Louise Carol Dodgson sell as many books as Lulu Carroll? Hard to say.'

I frown as I feel the familiar fuzz-buzz wash through my head. 'How do you know so much about me?' And exactly how much does he know?

'I know a lot about everyone. Except you. You're a bit of a blank canvas as it happens, Alice.'

Good. I've worked hard to keep it that way. I didn't go

75

through ten years of feeling like a freak to become a freak-show attraction at St Agnes. *Roll up! Roll up and witness the terrifying transsexual you read all about in the tabloids!* It feels like I'm melting, becoming one with the cushion underneath me. 'And what's that supposed to mean?' I want to tweeze it out of him without admitting a thing.

'I just think it's fortuitous that we happen to meet. As a St Agnes girl I know your academic history: such early promise ...'

'Thank you.'

'...such low yield.'

I wrinkle my nose, but can hardly argue.

'I know what websites you access from the computer labs – K-Pop and kittens mostly – and your stunning lack of extra-curricular participation. I know your family history: rags to ... slightly more impressive rags.'

'Hey now!'

'And I know you have an unexplained school absence from about a year ago. You had almost three months off. Intriguing.'

'It really isn't. Burst appendix,' I lie, and I don't know why I lie. My mental illness should be no harder to admit to than the physical one I invented, and yet ...

Willie is seemingly fobbed off. 'But *who* is Alice? There *must* more to you than blue ...' He points to his greasy, Kim Jong-Un haircut.

I'm a little blindsided. An autumnal fog rolls through my head and I'd love nothing more than to fall asleep, but Willie has irked me now. 'I wasn't aware I posed such a conundrum.'

'You can't possibly be as dull as you seem.'

I mean, it's a concern, isn't it? I remember lying in the hard bed in the unit, digging through the detritus in my head and wondering if there was anything to me except tablets. Am I destined to be defined by a maximum of one word, *trans*, or two: *trans* and *mad*?

Willie prattles on. 'I suppose there's the Alice you think you are, and the Alice others perceive. Perhaps the real Alice exists somewhere between the two.'

'You sound stoned.'

'I am. Very. But I'm also right. It fascinates me.'

Christ alive, stoned people are tedious, but I'll bite. 'Why?'

'I find everyone else's motivations quite easy to understand. Love, money, revenge, et cetera. What brings *you* here today? These people aren't your friends and this *definitely* isn't your scene.'

'Is it yours?'

'It's my business to be here. And don't answer questions with a question.'

In that case I shall ask him what his business is in a moment. 'I'm looking for someone.'

'Yourself? Or someone else?'

Te-di-ous. 'Someone else, obviously.'

'Ah. Bunny Liddell.'

That sobers me. 'How did you know?'

'You're not the only person … looking for her.'

'Who else is?'

He starts to roll a fresh joint. 'People I … wouldn't want to cross. I'm stoned, not stupid.'

'What *is* your business? Aren't you in Lower Three?' That makes him fourteen at most.

'Correct.' He pinches the ends of the spliff with precision. 'I'm in the secrets business. I'm an entrepreneur. My father taught me from a very young age how to identify a gap in the market, and monetise need.'

Somehow, through all the clouds, a light bulb flickers on. 'No. Surely not? Caterpillr?'

He says nothing but smiles and lights his joint.

'Fuck. Off.'

Caterpillr is an app. Pretty much everyone at school has it. Except me, but of course, I do so enjoy being the odd one out, don't I? Anyway, I can play on Dinah's phone and still appear superior. When socialite.com stopped being fun – imagine logging on to a website any more – people started to subscribe to Caterpillr instead. Say you're at school, or out and about, and you spy someone doing something they oughtn't be doing. You take a sneaky picture and send it to Caterpillr. The app then uploads and transmits it, anonymously naming and shaming.

It's a curious thing. When it first launched, people were *terrified* of being papped. Any notion of sharing a sociable line of coke or ketamine in the loo in your members' club du jour evaporated almost overnight. But over time, as is the way with these things, to appear on Caterpillr became edgy, a badge of honour. In London society circles, you're *no one* if no one wants to follow your exploits. Like day follows night, people soon started staging phony moments, only for the wily Caterpillr to start slapping a big red "FAKED" sign over the posts. Genius.

'That's you? Why?'

He says nothing, neither confirming nor denying.

'Oh, I get it! Advertising ...'

Between every third post an advert pops up.

He merely shrugs. God, he must be raking it in.

My eyes feel so heavy. 'That app lives and dies on anonymity. Why are you telling me all this?'

'I've told you nothing.'

'Oh, Willie, come on ...'

He smiles. 'Who would you tell? Who would listen? *Who are you?*'

I'm too tired to argue any more. 'I don't rightly know.'

'What do you want?'

'I don't know that either.' I rub my anvil head, which feels too heavy for my neck to support it. 'How strong was that weed, Willie?'

'Finest Hawaiian Gold. Just go with it.'

'*Go with it?*' I ask.

'Just fall into it. Don't fight it. Relax.'

Everyone wants me to loosen up, let go, relax. But I can't, not for a second. My mind wanders, fogging up. 'I once saw a woman fall ...'

For the first time, he looks surprised. 'Really? Who?'

'It didn't look very relaxing.' A tear finds its way out and splats onto the table. 'She died. It was awful.'

I remember. A thud, a silent second, and then the screams.

'Alice, are you OK?'

It feels like the whole ship is capsizing. 'I just need ... I just need to rest my eyes a moment.'

'Take all the time you need. When you know, let me know.'

I lie myself down on the seat and tuck my feet up. 'Let you know what?'

He vanishes in a cloud of blue smoke as my eyes close. 'Who is Alice?'

The last thing I hear is a phone camera clicking.

Damn.

XIII

IS THIS A DREAM? IT FEELS LIKE I'M FLOATING, NO, SINKING. I'VE CRIED SO MUCH, I'VE FLOODED THE WHOLE BOAT. SALT WATER STINGS MY EYES AND I TRY TO SWIM. TABLES AND CHAIRS AND CUPS AND SAUCERS FLOAT ALL ABOUT ME AND MY DRESS BILLOWS AROUND MY LEGS. HOW IS IT I'M ABLE TO BREATHE UNDERWATER? UNFORTUNATELY, DWELLING ON THIS SEEMS TO HAVE REMINDED MY BODY THAT I CAN'T PERFORM THAT FEAT. OH, CRIPES. I SWIM TO THE NEAREST WINDOW AND TRY TO PUNCH THROUGH THE GLASS. IT'S NO GOOD. ON THE OTHER SIDE OF THE PORTHOLE IS BUNNY. SURPRISED, I LET MY BREATH GO IN GREAT BUBBLES. SHE LOOKS INSIDE, BUT SEEMS NOT TO SEE ME. SHE FADES AWAY INTO THE BLACK OF THE RIVER, SOMETHING PULLING HER DOWN. BUNNY. I TRY TO CALL TO HER. BUNNY …

XIV

THE QUEEN OF HEARTS

I wake with a start, ready to fight. I gulp in a lungful of air, most grateful I'm not drowning. Instead, and quite by surprise, I vomit across the table. It's bright red, very liquid, dribbling over the edges like a puke waterfall. Potent pot. Well, this isn't very ladylike at all. I wipe my mouth with the back of my hand.

Luckily, there's no one around to see my digestive pyrotechnics.

In fact, I'm the only person on the whole deck.

And the music has stopped.

And we're not moving.

I twist myself around and look out of the window. The glass and concrete of the city have been supplanted by lush green fields and broccoli trees as far as the eye can see. And birds; the birds I can hear singing sound much too twinkly to be inner city pigeons, who coo like they have a sixty-a-day habit. How long did I sleep for? Willie is long gone.

I remember him taking a picture of me. Or at least I think he did. It figures that *he'd* somehow manage to smuggle a phone in. If he's posted that picture to Caterpillr, I'm in bother.

The sick burns the back of my throat and I look around for water. There's none at the table but I remember there were bathrooms on this deck. I find my hat on the floor, retreat to one of the little cabins and lock myself in. I look perfectly vile, my face olive green, lips pasty pale. I cup some water in my palm and spoon it into my mouth. It helps. Then, I use what little make-up I brought and try to draw some life back onto my face with blusher. I succeed only in making myself look like I'm auditioning for the Fourth Form production of *Cabaret*. Trans girls have to be especially wary of make-up in case people mistake you for a *Drag Race* contestant.

It feels like the ship is tilting, but this time, I'm fairly certain it's all in my mind. Sobering up, reality drops on my head like a cartoon piano: I'm miles from home, without a phone, without my medication, all alone.

For crying out fucking loud, what was I thinking?

Tears sting my eyes. By myself, in this toilet stall, I can allow myself one tear. I'm not going to drown.

Maybe I should have just left Bunny to the hounds.

'Have you ever been to a hunt, Alice?'

'Of course not.'

'They're a tradition …'

'So was slavery.'

'Touché. And you're right. I was dragged to them as a child and they were heinous. There must be something about the scent of blood, the promise of a kill, because as soon as the dogs got hold of the poor fox … well. Everyone seemed to lose their shit.'

'What happened?'

Bunny threw the tail end of her hotdog into the Thames. 'The dogs tore it to pieces and everyone clapped and whooped and cheered. Everyone became … well, I remembered.'

'Remembered what?'
'That we're animals too.'

Oh well. I suppose I'm here now.

If it's really, really bad I do still have the emergency credit card. I wonder what a taxi back to London is? I tell myself it could be much worse. Mummy wouldn't be thrilled, but I've spent money on more ridiculous things and so has she. I once again check my privilege. If need be, I can pay my way back home.

And it is really, really bad.

I slip outside onto the deck and thank goodness for fresh country air. I rinse my lungs and breathe out a toxic London smog. My bogeys shall be yellow once more. I seem to be the last person left on the boat. No one thought to wake me.

As I disembark the yacht via the gangplank, I see a funfair ahead. How can I not think back to meeting Bunny outside the ghost train? My heart cramps. Love, thus far, feels very much like knitting needles jabbing my chest and I wonder why people are so keen on it.

I fall into step behind a couple of other stragglers leaving the boat and pull the veil over my face again.

This is all terribly impressive. We seem to be at a private dock. The jetty leads to vast, rolling gardens, where the fair has been erected. Beyond that is thick forest leading up to an imposing mansion house overlooking the water. I have absolutely no idea where we are, but I sense it's early evening; pretty lanterns are strung along the dock and lights twinkle on the rides. Ubiquitous trance blares from the funfair, rattling my skull.

The air smells of fried onions and churros and I think vomiting has left a vacancy in my stomach. I shall make eating my first priority. I vividly picture a soya hotdog, piled high with veggie chilli, and my mouth waters.

I pass a merry-go-round, keeping my head down. I see Lily and some other St Agnes girls posing on a menagerie of exotic carousel creatures: an owl, a dodo, a mouse, a monkey, an eagle. The contraption looks to me to be an antique, pre-Disney – the poor beasts' expressions range from mildly haunted to downright menacing. The girls scream as they go round and round in circles, hanging off the brass poles like strippers.

Again, what I'd give to be even able to *pretend* to be that carefree. I'm sure that pretend is what some of them do. For a time, I followed Lily, Rose and Violet on Instagram and I fail to believe anyone is a) so consistently contented or b) quite so invested in eggs on toast. Is our collective self-esteem so wafer-thin that we rely on compliments from strangers for sustenance?

I'm sure if I put my mind to it I could conjure some hoary metaphor about the Flower Girls going around in circles in quest of some impossible perfection, but it seems almost too obvious. I have my shit, and they must have theirs, but I'm not sure I care enough to look beyond their MAC veneers.

To my right, next to the hotdog stall I see the Tweedle twins, Jonty and Jeremy, trying their luck on the strongman machine. As ever, a cloud of pretty girls in crop tops follows them rather like flies around manure. One of the twins (it's hard to say which) swings the mallet and the weight shoots all the way to the top with a clang of a bell. The girls squeal like a school of horny dolphins. To be fair, the Tweedle brothers *are* easy on the eye.

My gaze lingers on Jeremy's (or Jonty's) tanned, toned arm when a honeyed voice trickles into my ear.

'You might want to make yourself scarce.'

I keep my surprise under control this time. I turn to face the girl (probably) in the cat hoodie. 'Oh good, you again. Did I look to be in need of some frustrating gobbledegook?'

'That's not a very friendly way to accept friendly advice.' She does sound a little wounded.

'I've never been very good at the whole friend thing.' I shrug.

'Me neither.' She grins. 'Two of my five psychiatrists think I have Antisocial Personality Disorder.'

'And what do the other three say?'

'I don't know, I killed them.' Her eyes widen and, just for a second, I'm not wholly sure she's joking. 'Kidding. The other three think I have *Borderline* Personality Disorder.'

'What's the difference?'

'If you have to ask …'

She looks disappointed and goes to leave but I grab her arm. 'Wait! Can you at least tell me your name?'

'Cat.'

'Seriously?'

'Absolutely not seriously.' She looks beyond me. 'And you're on your own, I'm afraid. I'm outta here and suggest you do the same …'

Cat pulls away and dips behind the hotdog stall. I turn to see what has her so spooked.

The music stops. The rides slow to a halt.

A brief squawk of feedback and then: 'Ladies, gentlemen and all in-between, please welcome your hostess for the weekend.

86

Her royal highness, the Queen of Hearts.'

Everyone stops what they're doing and turns to face the great house. I follow their gaze.

Oh, fuckabella.

It's Paisley Hart.

And she's cradling a teacup piglet wearing a diamante collar. Why wouldn't she be?

Flanked by a handsome pair of red-clad security guards, comes Paisley fucking Hart. A clue so obvious I'm livid with myself for not figuring it out.

The last I heard, she'd transferred to Surval Montreaux in Switzerland and yet, here she is, her blood-red gown trailing behind her as she descends the grand stone stairs leading down to the lawns. Yes, yes, she's as breathtaking as ever: her chestnut hair tumbling almost to her waist in Hollywood waves, a dainty crystal crown resting on top of her head. She's very petite, her features baby-doll lovely, but she's always given off an aura of being much larger than she physically is.

How can I word this politely? Paisley Hart is a fucking cunt. St Agnes became a much nicer place when she left.

It is said a king cobra can kill an elephant with a single bite, yet I'd still rather be alone in a lift with one than with Paisley Hart. It veritably boils my piss that I waste so many brain cells thinking about how fucking perfect she looks. She is tiny, feminine, in a way I never will be *despite* a year on hormone blockers and three on oestrogen. It's an ugly jealousy and I hate myself for hating her, but she did nothing to deserve her beauty and uses it only for evil. If I had her body, yes, I'd fuck at least one of the rugby team, but then I'd use my powers for good. I'd be Miss Universe and bring about world peace in a dental floss bikini.

She pauses halfway down the stairs to receive her applause. The pet piglet wriggles in her arms. No one else seems especially surprised to see her here, which makes me think …

Right on cue, Royce Hart gallops up the stairs to meet his little sister. He has a microphone. 'What up, you bitches!' Royce cheers, already slack and wet-mouthed from beer. 'Welcome to Wonderland Four!'

There's an even wilder round of cheers. Paisley hands the pig to one of her henchmen and prises the mic out of her brother's grasp.

'Thank you! And isn't it wonderful to be here?' She smiles but it's all teeth, no feeling. 'After a little rest last year, we are back and we're bigger than ever.'

Royce punches the air, grunting like a triumphant Neanderthal. The rest of the St Barney's rugby teams chant back at him.

Paisley gives him a whiplash-inducing side-eye and he falls silent. 'Previous Wonderland parties have become legendary, but you've seen nothing yet. This year, thanks to the generosity of the Dorman family, we're at the beautiful Gryphon Hall, and we have *such* delights to show you. Let us all redefine hedonism for this dying planet. Party like the world is literally fucking melting under our feet. The Romans would blush at this bacchanal. My friends, this is a party like no other. Submit to your wildest fantasies. Test your limits. Enjoy the flesh, give in to carnal desires. Because what is life without pleasure, fun and joy? What would be the point? So let go.

Fly, children of Wonderland, fly!'

The crowd screams in anticipation and I sink back further towards the merry-go-round, somewhere I can hide.

'And now, a word of warning,' Paisley continues, holding up a finger. 'Be safe. Look after yourselves and others. Here in the queendom of Wonderland, *I* am the law, and we treat one another with love, kindness and respect. Consent is everything. No one in Wonderland does anything against their will. Is that understood?'

Another mighty roar.

'Good. Oh, and one more thing,' she adds. 'As hard as we try to keep out the riff-raff, it seems we have a couple of party-crashers …'

Oh crikey. If I were a tortoise, I'd be all the way inside my shell at this point. Does she mean me? Or Cat Girl? Or *Bunny*? No, she was invited, so it can't be her.

'It's a shame, isn't it? When a few bad apples spoil the party for everyone. Security is aware and we're working to remove the undesirable element. Do *not* take candy from strangers, party people, least of all when there's so much of *my* candy to share.'

I slip behind the merry-go-round, hiding behind a stationary dodo.

Paisley smiles. 'Enjoy the opening gala tonight. Hangover brunch is served tomorrow from eleven!'

And the music starts again. Paisley turns to her brother and whispers something in his ear. What? Who knows? But she looks simply *furious*.

XV

A MOST UNLIKELY TEA PARTY
AKA SCIENCE & MAGIC

Luckily, syrupy sycophants slither up the stairs to greet their queen, offering me a getaway window. Paisley, like any billionaire heiress, is honour-bound to exchange pleasantries, so I have some time to make my escape. Cat is nowhere to be seen. The same can be said of both the bunny who may or may not be Bunny and Willie Zong.

Not paying attention, I crash directly into Rose, still in her nautical costume from earlier.

'Excuse you,' she says. At her side, Violet gives me evils.

'Sorry,' I say automatically and duck around her. My heart rate quickens.

'Wait a minute,' Rose replies. 'Who's that under that hat?'

What? Is she Dr Seuss or something? She reaches for my veil and I swerve away. Think quick, Alice, think very quick.

'Sailor Birling,' I say with as much authority as I can muster. Sailor's as pale and lanky as me, she's rich, she graduated last year and, more importantly, her name means something. Syrup heiress.

'Oh? I thought you were in Paris?'

I tut. 'Well, obviously not.' What would Sailor say? She'd treat them like subordinates. 'Have you seen my brother?'

'He was at the pool party.'

'Thanks.' I strut away in the haughtiest fashion I can muster.

'Sailor,' Violet says. 'The pool house is that way ...' She points in the other direction.

'They should really have put up signposts.' I sigh and walk back the way I've just come.

I get lost in the crowd, avoiding the Flower Girls and Paisley, before making a looping arc through the rose garden and into the forest beyond the perimeter of the gardens. As soon as I'm under cover, I slump against a sturdy trunk and pull off the hat and veil. I'm getting hot and bothered, my skin prickly in all these layers. So much easier to hide amongst the trees.

I need a moment to gather my thoughts for they are most messily scattered. When I was a child I had some building blocks, and photographs from that time attest that I liked them sorted by size, shape and colour.

Prima Problema: Bunny. Bunny was in trouble and told me she was scared of someone. I still don't even know if she's here or not. If she's not, I'm wasting precious time.

Problema Secunda: Paisley. I could very easily believe it was Paisley that Bunny was scared of. Because I thought Paisley was finishing finishing school in the Swiss Alps, I hadn't factored her into my suspicions.

Problema Terza: Me. I'm not supposed to be here and I rather suspect Willie Zong has shared my whereabouts on Caterpillr. I have no desire to make Paisley Hart my enemy. I've so enjoyed sailing under the radar at St Agnes and should like to keep it that way.

It's only when the third acorn lands on my head that I think

91

to look up. Sure enough, my new friend Cat reclines on a branch several metres up.

'Quercus.'

'Are you dropping acorns on my head?'

'Yes.'

'Why?' I ask, exhausted.

'Oak trees in the Quercus family make acorns and they're good for attracting attention.'

'You could have just shouted down,' I shout up.

'Where's the fun in that? Are you escaping?'

I feel faintly ridiculous talking to someone partially obscured by leaves, but plough on. 'I can't. At least, I can't yet. Say, you've seen the guest list, haven't you? You said earlier.'

'I have.'

'Is Bunny Liddell here?'

Cat nods, sipping from a bottle of beer. 'She's on the guest list, but my hypothesis is that's how *you* got through the door, right? As there's only one Bunny on the list, she either used a pseudonym too or else she isn't here, in which case ...'

A raincloud goes over my heart. 'I don't need to be here.'

'Aw, don't say that. Now that you're here, you might as well enjoy yourself. Live a little.'

'Like you are? Hiding in a tree?'

'I can see everything and everyone from up here. Good position to be in.'

'Who are you? Are you a crasher too?'

'It's better you don't know.'

You know, I really didn't think it possible for there to be someone more irritating than me in the world, and yet here we are. 'If you're not willing to tell me anything about yourself, I'm putting an end to this exhausting dialogue. I feel like I'm being catfished.' I immediately regret saying that and hope she doesn't think I'm punning. Oh, there's a special red-hot poker set aside in hell for punners.

I start down the forest path and then realise I have no idea where it, or I, am going. 'Do you know where this leads?' I ask Cat, turning back impatiently.

'Well, where are you going?'

'I … I don't know.'

'Then it hardly matters which way you go, does it?'

'Oh, do go fuck yourself,' I mutter and stride away down the trail. I'm fairly sure I hear Cat laughing as I go.

It's hard not to think of the time Paisley and Lily cornered me at the pool. St Agnes has the most beautiful swimming pool: housed in a grand glasshouse, a feat of symmetrical Victorian engineering. It'd be Wes Anderson-lovely if the mere smell of chlorine didn't bring me out in a cold sweat. Between changing rooms, swimsuits and crippling body dysmorphia, it goes without saying that I never learned to swim.

PE, although torturous, never posed a problem – like, who gets naked after PE? – but it was agreed when I started St Agnes that I'd be excused from swimming sessions.

'You can't have your period *every* week,' Paisley said nastily. It was Lower Three and we were thirteen. Any girl excused from swimming that week had to do their homework at tables on the mezzanine overlooking the pool. Paisley's exquisite Liberty print notebook matched her pens and pencil case. She'd singlehandedly started a craze at school. I was very jealous. A water polo match was in full swing below, only punctuated by Miss Driver's whistle.

'What?' I said, already feeling sick.

'Are you deaf?' she shot back. 'How come you *never* do swimming? It's not fair.'

I could have said what's not fair is that I'd *never* have a period, never have kids, or even a shot at giving birth because of some biological admin error. Some lazy angel, desperate for a fag break, scribbled the wrong gender on my destiny forms.

'I'm allergic to chlorine,' I said, my voice wobbly. No one had ever challenged me before.

'Who's allergic to chlorine?' Lily snarled.

'I am.'

Paisley considered me for a second, eyes boring into my skull like corkscrews. 'Uh, whatever. You're so lucky.'

Sure thing, Paisley. I truly won in life's lottery.

This is *fine*, I tell myself as the path through the woods becomes even less certain than I am. I head vaguely uphill, assuming that at some point I'll loop back to the main house. I know from the night in the hotel that Bunny has little talent for poverty, so it seems unlikely she'll be camping with the hoi polloi. But, every time I think I'm getting nearer, the forest floor crumbles away into jagged ravines filled with vicious-looking tree bones, and I have to find an alternative route. It feels like I've been walking for ever although I suspect that's loneliness talking.

Worse still: night is falling fast; it's getting colder and I didn't grab my dream chilli dog to eat at the fair. My stomach feels hollowed out like a Halloween pumpkin.

I stop dead in the middle of a clearing, hands on my hips. This is futile. 'Have I already been this way?' I ask myself.

I wish I'd asked Cat to come with me.

The light is cool twilight indigo and I don't want to be in these woods after dark. Funny how only a subtle change in light can turn a forest from enchanting to menacing, and the branches become more like gnarled claws and teeth with each passing minute. When I turn my back, they seem to move an inch or two closer. Grandmother's Footsteps. Whether I like it or not, I'll have to head back towards the party and take my chances with Paisley.

I turn on my heels and start trying to retrace my steps.

Girlish laughter blows in on the breeze and I plant my foot awkwardly on the edge of a root. I try to cling to branches overhead, but they're too reedy and I go over on my ankle.

Down I go.

It's only a shallow trench, but I close my eyes and feel brambles catch at my arms and dress as I roll.

I slide the last couple of metres on my derrière and come to a halt. I check for damage and there's a tear on the back seam of my dress. 'Damn,' I curse. If Paisley doesn't kill me, Mother will. My hands are caked in soil and I wipe them on my now-ruined skirt. 'Well, this is going swimmingly.' At least my ankle doesn't hurt too much. I look around and I can't even see where the bloody hat has gone.

Acid-green panic juice floods my stomach and I *really* think I ought to be away from this forest before I become a Missing

Persons poster on the London Underground. God, that's a point … Felix. I should have been home from the tutor hours ago. I can't even text him with a decent lie. It's time to call off the search, before he sends out a search party. I pick myself up and dust myself off.

Only then I hear raucous laughter again, masculine this time. I thought I'd imagined it, but it's definitely *not* in my head. This time. There's music too.

Odd. I'm still a good way away from the fairground. I wonder …

It's worth investigating.

I tentatively tread through the undergrowth, invoking my inner ninja, heading down a gentle incline to the centre of a dell. In the middle of the clearing is some sort of yurt. It's grander than even a Bedouin tent; a chimney puffs out great glugs of smoke and, from the looks of it, there are smaller 'rooms' off the main chamber. It's clean too, so I'm guessing it's brand new, erected especially for Wonderland. The perimeter of the makeshift campsite is lit with cables of fairy lanterns.

Now. I know that turning up uninvited to a cabin in the woods didn't work out for Hansel and Gretel, but I've never been so glad to see human life. It's unlikely to be Paisley, so far away the main party, so I figure I'm safe. In fact, I wouldn't be at all surprised to find Willie Zong skulking on the outskirts of the action and I think he's mostly harmless.

I tramp down the rest of the hill and approach the yurt, albeit cautiously. I'll be sweet and girly and sugar-and-spice-and-all-things-nice, and ask for directions to the main house. Oh, here's a thought: what if this tent is where Bunny's been hiding out? Optimism is perfectly healthy as part of a balanced diet which also includes scepticism.

The yurt has been erected on wooden planks, set off the leaf litter, and there's even a front door to knock on.

'Hello?' I say. Light radiates from within. Someone's home.

'Who is it?' a male voice booms from inside.

I don't really see the point in lying any more. I need help and I'm a dreadful actress. I'll have to be myself and hope for the best. 'Alice.'

'Alice who?'

'Alice Dodgson.'

'Who?'

That is a very popular question around these parts.

The door opens and I find myself face to face with Olivier Marchand. He has black make-up smeared across his eyes like a raccoon.

'Olivier!'

'No sank you, we're not interested.'

He shuts the door in my face.

I hammer on the door, rattling the entire yurt. 'Olivier, you little bitch, let me in! I'm cold!'

The door opens again and he's wearing a sly smirk. 'Zery well. Come on een.'

I push past him and step into a wall of toasty warmth from the wood burner. The tent is *gorgeous*. Lanterns fill the main chamber with deeply nurturing honey-amber light, bean bags are gathered around a low bronze table. A Moroccan teapot sits on a silver tray, steam curling out of the long spout like a serpent.

'Who's this then?' asks Maxim Hattersley, who is reclining on one of the bean bags.

Maxim Hattersley is one of those seventeen year-olds who has looked about twenty-five since puberty kicked in at eleven. The precise advent of his adolescence is well-documented because he famously once gathered everyone on the Green between St Agnes and St Barnabas to exhibit that he was the first boy in his year to develop pubic hair.

These days, he's a hulk of a man – well, he looks to be a man – towering over most of the school at six-foot-four and in possession of a faceful of wiry ginger stubble. He's the same age as Olivier, but looks at least ten years older. Other than that I don't really know much about him. He was scouted to play rugby for the Harlequins, but is presently balancing one of those futuristic foot casts on a stool, so I'm guessing he's out on injury. The collar of his frilly seventies shirt has been ripped open to the chest, sleeves rolled to the elbow. He's still wearing the powder-blue top hat.

His companion at the table is a boy I don't recognise. Compared to Maxim, he's small and weedy-looking, not to mention entirely fucked, slumped face-down on the floor.

'Is he OK?' I ask.

'Dormouse? Yeah, he's just taking a time out.'

'Thees eez Alice,' Olivier says airily, joining Maxim back at the table. He's still in his jester costume: a jumpsuit of black and white diamonds with an elaborate ruff at his throat. 'She's a nuisance I know from St Agnes.'

Maxim shrugs. 'Oh, *you're* Alice. Well, in that case, you must join us for tea, neighbour. Grab a bean bag.'

'Have you got anything to eat? I'm ravenous.' I seat myself between Maxim and Olivier, opposite their comatose chum.

'We has plenty of brownies …' Olivier says and both of them dissolve into giggles. Well, that explains their glassy eyes. Still, my stomach feels so empty, I'm in no position to refuse. I help myself.

'You look like sheet,' Olivier says. 'Did you crawl 'ere?'

'I may as well have for all the good I'm doing. Are you sure he's all right?' I lean over to check the unconscious young man is breathing.

'Dormouse can't take his ale,' Maxim tells me. 'He's fine.'

'Who is Dormouse?' He does look somewhat rodent-like. I pick the corner off a piece of brownie. It's delish: rich, moist and nutty, drizzled with salted caramel sauce.

'Alisdair Dorman?' Olivier looks at me expectantly. 'Son of Viscount Dorman? You are een his garden right now.'

'He lives *here*?'

'No!' Maxim says. 'It's his parents' summer house!'

'Summer house? It's a mansion!'

'Ees a dump! Ees crumbling around their ears. They has a townhouse een Fulham.' Over the top of a silver teacup, Olivier looks at me like I'm a total pleb. 'Anyway. I sought I told you not to come 'ere, Alice, so what exactly do you sink you are doing?'

'Dude, chill,' Maxim says. 'Merrier more and all that. And also merry amore.' He raises a toast to nothing and cracks up.

Olivier's steely eyes won't leave mine alone. I squirm.

'Have either of you seen Bunny?'

'Bunny Liddell?'

Without warning, Dormouse pops up from his stupor and

bangs his head on the side of the table. 'Bunny Liddell,' he announces, 'is fucked!' He blinks at me. 'Who are you?' And then he slumps backwards, passing out flat on his back.

Olivier and Maxim share a very brief, but very much there, glance and I seize on it.

'Bunny is fucked?'

'Ee doesn't know what ee is saying,' Olivier says dismissively with a flick of the wrist.

'Have you seen her? Is she here?'

'I don't know,' Maxim says. 'But I don't know much of anything. If Bunny is fucked, I'm the fuckedest.'

'Ollie?'

'Oh, let eet go, Alice. You don't know what you're dealing wiz.'

'Paisley?'

Neither of them reply. I can go either way on hash brownies. Sometimes giggly, sometimes irrationally angry. Let's see, shall we?

'What are we drinking?'

'Mush tea,' Maxim says.

'Mycena,' Olivier adds.

'Magic mushrooms?'

'I don't know if I'd say they were *magic*,' Maxim says, 'but you know that the best minds in the world used to think that science was magic and now magic is science. It's *all* just science, but that sounds way less fun, don't you think? The last time I did mushrooms I thought I was falling, like sinking to the centre of the earth. Down through the grass and the mud and the worms and the fossils all the way to the lava … bright-red lava. The floor was lava! And all the colours had different sounds, or the sounds had colours … and you know what? It was kinda magic, even though I know it was just the effects of a chemical called psilocybin making my brain process my environment differently. Just science. Magic science.'

I think of the way the chemicals in my head can make me feel so joyous one day and then like I'm full of cement the next. 'Science is magic,' I say softly.

Maxim looks at me strangely, like he's seeing me for the first time. 'It really is. What did you say your name is?'

'Alice.'

'*Alice.*' His tongue tries it on for size.

People on drugs are *most* wearying if you yourself are not.

'Try some.' Olivier pours me a cup.

It's the colour of very weak Earl Grey. I take a sniff.

'It smells of strawberries.'

'I added zat to taste,' Olivier tells me.

Can one both imbibe and ingest at the same time? Will I die? I'd rather not. While my hallucinations were *mostly* auditory, I've had enough to last a lifetime. 'I'm fine, thanks.'

'It's good,' Maxim says. 'And you're safe here. Good trip all but guaranteed.'

'I'm not sure I want any kind of trip.'

'Why not? It's …'

'Magic?'

'Science.'

'Then why bother?' I say tersely.

Maxim leans in very close and I smell yeasty hops on his breath. 'Don't you want to take perception somewhere new and unexpected? Magical Mystery Tour.'

Been there, done that, got the prescription. 'I'm not a huge fan of the unexpected.' The pot in the brownies is kicking in. Lori's face fills my mind, apple-plump and swollen like her head's about to pop with self-righteousness, and I suddenly giggle to myself. As soon as I start to lose control, I get a grip of myself and correct my posture. What was it Miss Driver used to say in PE? *Girls! Imagine you're holding a shiny pound coin between your shoulder blades!*

'She's very uptight.' Olivier finishes his tea, his eyes now as wide as the saucers, if not wider.

'She is sitting right here, thank you. And I'm not *uptight*, I'm simply mistress of my own destiny.'

Maxim slaps his hands down on the table and Dormouse briefly stirs. 'Well, where's the fun in that?'

I smile sweetly. 'I find maintaining a vicelike grip on my affairs to be fun.'

'Fuck that!' Maxim laughs. 'Haven't you ever been in love?'

I'm a little blindsided. 'What? What does that have to do with anything?'

He squints at me. 'OK, the world is like ninety per cent science. What about the other ten per cent? Real magic. The point I'm making – in my admittedly fucked state – is that nothing *truly* magical is controllable. You can't control love, or joy, or sadness, or madness. And that's where the magic is, Alice.'

'I think you'll find they're all just chemicals too,' I say a little morosely.

He shakes his head. 'No. Love isn't science, it's magic.

Definitely magic.' He smiles wonkily and, I shall admit, for the first time I see what the other girls seem to see.

I feel funny. Funny queer, not funny ha-ha.

I don't know what to say.

Olivier clears his throat. 'Well, ze tea can't be more potent zan zhe sexual tension can eet? Bottoms up!'

I sip the sodding tea just to pull away from Maxim's stare. 'What did you do to your leg?' I ask, changing the subject abruptly.

Maxim clears his throat. 'My solicitor has advised me to keep schtum, but it involves a myriad of terrible choices.'

'Did one of them involve magic mushrooms?'

'No,' he says sadly. 'But it did involve love.'

Oh, my head feels spongier than the brownie.

Did I love Bunny?

In fingers and flesh, yes. In hearts?

We had only one night together, but what a night.

That night felt like for ever.

'How long is for ever? Sometimes, just one second.'

'Alice? Are you OK?' Olivier asks. He's lying on his back, looking up at the ceiling. Candles twinkle through lanterns.

Just for a second, I think I see something moving on the other side of the tent. A shadow sweeps through.

'Why is a raven like a writing desk?' Maxim too sinks back onto the plush rug.

Felix is a fan of a riddle. I find them very droll. 'Because it can produce a few notes, though they are very flat; and it is nevar put with the wrong end in front,' I tell him.

'Oh. That was an anti-climax.'

Beyond the tent, I now clearly see a silhouette. A slender girl with a bouncing afro. 'Bunny.'

'So fucked,' Dormouse mutters.

'Bunny! Wait!' I cry. I clamber to my feet only to trip over them.

'What? Where?' Maxim rolls over.

The shadow looks my way for a second and then darts away, very like a startled ... well. I stagger towards the door and it feels like I'm wearing clown boots.

'Wait! Come back!'

I fling open the door and it is now blackest night. I see a flash of blonde hair in the moonlight. 'Bunny!'

'Alice, you're tripping!' Maxim shouts. 'Bunny wouldn't come here ...'

'Oh, let 'er go,' Olivier says. 'She's a liability.'

It's real. I swear it. The dell smells of midnight; of wild garlic; and jasmine; and petunia; and pearly owl feathers; and spiderwebs; and I *see* a girl running deep into the woods. And it is, if I can trust my two eyes, Bunny Liddell.

XVI

SKINTEREST

Sprigs and boughs and roots and shoots all start to twist into a woodland tunnel. They curve and curl into a vortex and I run down their forest funnel. In the distance ahead of me, running in slow motion, is Bunny, gold hair bouncing. I reach out for her, but my feet feel to be stuck in toffee.

I call her name.

No sound comes out.

What were you thinking, Alice? That you'd come here and she'd love you? You'd be her saviour. A long way to come to prove to yourself you're lovable.

'Shut up!' I scream at myself.

I keep running, running from the vicious little voice in my head as much as anything else. Other Alice. We don't listen to her any more.

I can't … I can't go there again.

Claws scratch at my face and hair. She's hungry, this forest, starved. She's ancient and she hasn't eaten in millennia. She's older than man, and finds our arrogance amusing because we are but microbes breeding on her belly.

Knots blink open to reveal wet eyes, and bark lips part with stringy saliva. Little square baby teeth nibble at me.

The forest floor lurches forward and I free-fall down the

oesophagus, arms and legs cycling at thin air. I'm too shocked to scream.

I think of that woman falling in Shoreditch. Is this what it felt like? Was her stomach all up in her throat? Was it terrifying … but also … arousing? I am unbound and

Up ahead, the moss and detritus, the thorns and brambles squirm and shift like snakes into a single gawping mouth. I'm going to be swallowed, consumed. I wonder what it will feel like to be chewed, to feel my bones bend backwards and snap like chicken wings and

I'm in water.

Freezing cold water, a full body slap, snatching breath all away.

I'm back in my skin and sink fingernails into my senses.

I tell myself this is but a bad trip and, like a nightmare, I can rouse myself from it with a click of my ruby slippers.

Oh, but it's cold and

I really can't breathe

I really am in water this time

And it's chlorinated.

Oh, crumbs.

Just let yourself die. You've been fighting since the day you were born.

Fuck you.

I'll show her. I kick and push but the water is sapphire black and so, so cold. The dress weighs me down, an anchor pulling me to the seabed where my skeleton will be a shipwreck for eels and barnacles to shelter in.

It feels like my skull is shrink-wrapped around my brain and then –

Arms clamp around my ribs. I'm too heavy to fight.

Up we go.

The surface breaks and the night air, crisp as an iceberg, is the sweetest nectar I've ever drunk. A dead weight, I let my sodden body be dragged through the pool. Water clears from my eyes. I blink myself back into reality. Underwater lights come on and the pool is now far less menacing. It's holiday brochure turquoise.

Not that that makes an ounce of sense. I was in a forest and now I'm in a swimming pool. That tea has some explaining to do.

'Who is it?' a male voice yells.

'It's … that girl,' my rescuer, another guy, shouts directly in my ear. 'The weird one with blue hair.'

'I'm sorry.' I cough and splutter.

'Is she shitfaced?'

'No, I'm fine!' I lie.

'Just hold on,' my rescuer says.

I clutch the arm that circles my chest as if it were a rubber ring.

Other arms loop around me, and with great effort, haul me onto the side of the pool. Freezing cold, I stare up at the stars for a moment. Well, I think, that could have ended quite badly.

'Are you all right?'

I roll onto my side and spit out a mouthful of water. I'm seeing double.

No. No, I'm not.

I'm seeing *twins*. Jeremy and Jonty Tweedle.

And one of them is holding a GoPro camera. Oh, you have got to be kidding.

'Did you get all that?' asks the wet one.

'Dude, it was sick,' says the dry one holding the camera. 'Full *Baywatch* action.'

It seems fitting that I would have the misfortune to be rescued by YouTubers.

I cough and splutter and the wet one helps me upright and throws a plush white towel around my shoulders.

'Here, come inside,' he says. 'That was fully mad, babe! We were just chilling and then you come flying down the hill and into the pool! Bonkers! Are you OK?'

'I'll be fine,' I say, although my legs are distinctly wobbly. 'Thanks for fishing me out.'

'No biggy.' He steers me towards a trendy-looking barn conversion with the poolside wall almost entirely glass. The twin hurries me through the patio doors and onto an equally trendy Scandi sofa. It's all very Airbnb chic. I wonder if we're still on the Dormans' property or not. I have no notion of how far I ran into the woods.

The wet twin towels himself off and my eyes linger on his toned, tanned torso. Obviously I've seen it many times before on Instagram but, in the flesh, he's, well, fleshy … real. I have to stop myself from reaching out and prodding the compelling groove that runs over his hip and into his swimming shorts.

I may well be a traitor to my generation, but I don't massively *get* YouTubers, or the entire notion of 'influencers' per se. I enjoy the odd tutorial as much as the next make-up fan, but there's some perplexing content on there, plenty of which is courtesy of Jeremy and Jonty. They attend St Barney's, and their father is some big film producer, so they were somewhat (enormously) aided on their quest for online fame. And they *are* famous. The last time I checked they had some nine hundred thousand subscribers and counting. I couldn't tell you what it is they actually *do* but it seems to involve them running around, gurning a lot, and doing various 'challenges', or picking through gifts they've been sent. Whatever hypnotic spell is cast by such videos, I remain gratefully immune.

'It's Alice, right?' the wet one says.

'Yes.' I huddle into the towel and force my mouth to function. 'I'm so sorry. I don't know what happened ...'

'You fell in our pool.'

'Yes, I gathered.' I guess these chalets were once the stables. Maybe the Dormans rent them out as holiday cottages or something.

The other twin returns with two mugs of steaming tea. 'Here, drink this. It's some sort of diet tea we're supposed to be promoting. It doesn't really taste of anything to be honest, but I figured it'd thaw you out.'

'Thank you.' It smells of chicken Super Noodles. 'Is there some way of knowing which of you is which?'

'I'm Jonty,' says the one who brought me tea. 'That's Jeremy. You can tell because my hair flops to the left and his flops to the right.'

Unhelpful. 'Well, thank you.' I'm shivering hard. 'I won't keep you.'

'Don't be gay,' Jonty says.

'Jont!' Jeremy snaps. 'Problematic! Sorry about him.'

'We're not filming!' Jonty sulks. 'But you can't go out like this. You'll catch your death.'

I'm inclined to agree.

'What on earth were you doing running around out there in the dark?' asks Jeremy, throwing himself onto the sofa beside me. His teeth are inhumanly white, bookended by impossibly cute dimples.

'In the spirit of honesty, I was tripping my tits off. I thought I saw someone and followed them into the woods.'

'You don't seem too bad now,' Jonty says, sitting on my other side.

'I think the impromptu dip sobered me up.'

'Oh my days, you talk so clever!' Jeremy gapes.

'I swear I can't tell what she's saying. Like, what's impronto?' asks Jonty.

They both guffaw.

How odd. I always assumed their dumb blonde act was just that – an act. I mean, they attend one of the most prestigious schools in the world. You'd never guess. I see it at St Agnes a lot – girls who pretend to be a lot stupider than they are as soon as a boy is in the vicinity; but less so with the boys who often believe they're a lot cleverer than they actually are.

Jeremy and Jonty buck the trend. They're clueless and they celebrate it.

It's a good thing they're pretty and come as a matching set.

'How come you're not at the party?' I ask.

'Oh, we got bored,' Jonty says.

'Like, our online fam are always totally surprised by this, but we're both actually introverts,' says Jeremy.

'ISFJs,' Jonty confirms.

I may not know *who is Alice*, but I will not be defined by four letters, and want no part in the fetishisation of social awkwardness. It's hardly aspirational.

'We made the call to come chill in the hot tub before bed.'

'And anyway, we don't wanna peak too soon. The closing disco tomorrow night will be sick.'

'Disco?'

'Yeah, this year's theme is *Bougie Wonderland*. Sick, right?'

'Indeed.' I see what they've done there. Cute.

'So yeah, total rookie mistake to get fully cunted on the first night and be too hungover to party on the Saturday,' Jonty says and Jeremy nods in agreement.

'Say,' I begin, 'I don't suppose either of you gents has seen Bunny Liddell?'

'No,' Jeremy replies. 'I thought she was missing.'

'Again,' adds Jonty.

'Although Paisley asked if we'd seen her earlier too,' Jeremy adds as an afterthought.

I sit up straighter. The room still sways, like I'm on a boat. I should really eat something soon. I'm running on fumes. 'Did she now?'

'Just in passing.'

'Compelling.' That seals it. I'm now pretty much certain it was Paisley that Bunny was hiding from that night in the hotel. I'd hide too if I'd done something to tick her off. Which leads logically to the next question: precisely *what* had Bunny done to so offend the Queen of Hearts? It can't be anything so obvious as owing her money – both Bunny and Paisley have more of that than they could ably count.

'Is that who you were looking for out in the woods?' Jeremy asks.

'I thought I saw her, yes.'

'Was it her or were you tripping?'

An excellent question. 'See, this is why our teachers warned us about drugs, isn't it?' I say, still shivering in the big white hospitality towel. I remember poor Felix, no doubt fretting at home. 'Do either of you have a phone I could use?'

'No, we had to hand them in like everyone else,' says Jonty.

'Jonty tried to smuggle one in …'

'Somewhere *very* personal, too.'

'But they busted him.'

'Damn,' I say, pulling the towel tighter around myself.

'Are you still cold?' Jonty asks.

'Freezing.'

'Get in the hot tub!' he says.

'Yes!' Jeremy agrees, springing up like a puppy.

'Oh, I can't …'

'Of course you can! You're here now. Where are you staying anyway?'

'I'm supposed to be in one of the luxury tepees.' The thought fills me with dread. I saw that Fyre Festival documentary.

'Oh, how ghastly,' Jeremy says. 'Just stay with us!'

'Yeah! Like a sleepover! It'll be fun!'

I smile, but warily. I mean their whole brand is being super-cute and sexlessly PG 13, but, well, they are boys, and a smart girl never really trusts a boy. 'I should go …'

'You'll catch pneumonia! You're all wet!' says Jeremy.

'OK,' I concede. I should wait at least until I'm dry. 'But I didn't bring a swimming costume.' This is the truth, but it's also the truth that I don't own a single item of swimwear.

'Well, your underwear is already wet,' replies Jonty, '… assuming you're wearing any?'

'Jont!' Jeremy slaps his arm. 'Again … sorry about him.'

'Of course I am!'

'Perfect!' Jonty says. 'Join us when you're ready.'

'I … I can't,' I argue, running out of excuses. There is nothing in this world I hate more than my body and, although the blockers stopped it from becoming *too* manly, there's only so much tucking can hide. 'I … I'm hardly going to sit around in my knickers, am I?'

'Why not? We'll look away while you change …' Jeremy says.

Like a pair of springer spaniels, the twins gallop back to the terrace, GoPro in Jonty's hand. I wonder if they got special dispensation from Paisley to film at Wonderland, or if they're breaking her rules. I walk over to the glass doors and watch the Tweedle brothers sink into the steaming hot tub.

They look over their shoulders and, in a perfectly synchronised moment, smile back at me. Oh my. I feel *that* somewhere very personal.

Carpe diem.

Try new things.

I am stuck here. I can't imagine there are any boats back to London this late. I tell myself it's pitch black and I don't know my way to the campsite. Furthermore, camping is awful. I feel more or less sober enough to fend off Jeremy and Jonty if need be, and the girls of St Agnes – for their innumerable faults – have established a hugely reliable whisper network about which St Barney's boys are less-than-chivalrous and which are downright dangerous. The Tweedles haven't featured on either list.

They're not boyfriend material – far too concerned with appearing available to their fanbase – but they don't come with a trigger warning.

Without quite realising I'm even doing it, my hand snakes up my back and pulls down the zipper. I slip one soggy strap off one soggy shoulder followed by the other and the dress falls to the floor with a wet squish. I'm glad to be out of it; the once blue dress is now black with muck.

It's doomed. Beyond redemption. I've accepted I'll have to confess all to Mother.

In four or five years when she goes looking for it in her closet, of course.

I'm wearing mismatched underwear – a jade-green bra and millennial-pink pants with a seahorse on the front – not to be quirky, but simply because I'm a mess. Shopping for sexy lingerie feels like admitting I'm sexy. Paradoxically, I think prowling around in strappy lace would make me look even more of a sexual imposter. My body isn't quite my body yet. It's an odd, almost alien, terrain to me.

Checking the twins can't see me, I sort out my tuck where it came loose in the pool. Any trans girl knows that buying underwear a size too small goes a long way to squish everything down. Being limited to clothes that will hide my birth defect is exhausting and boring. I can't wait to be rid of the fucking thing next year. Obviously the operation – or more specifically the recovery period – is terrifying, but I figure I'll get it over and done with on a year out before college, and live the rest of my days the way I was meant to be. I just wish it weren't all such a surgical lottery. I've spoken to many a trans girl online who *assure* me my new vagina will both look and function like anyone's, but what if something goes wrong? No one wants a Frankenpussy.

I wrap my towel around my chest and pad across the decking barefoot. I feel so gross. The pool cleansed me of most of the forest, but I'm pretty sure I still resemble early woman.

'Come on in!' Jonty (or Jeremy) shouts.

'It's lush!' Jeremy (or Jonty) agrees.

There's a little ladder on the side of the hot tub. As I climb, I catch a heady whiff of eucalyptus. It's soothing, enticing, and I decide now is not the time to inform them of the likelihood of contracting folliculitis from unclean hot tubs, which can be, as I understand it, bowls of bacteria soup.

'Avert your eyes, please,' I say, my voice terse and squeaky.

The twins do so and part to make a space for me. How many girls would sacrifice a limb to be the filling in a Tweedle sandwich? I slide in between them and breathe a sigh of relief. The steaming water protects my modesty.

'Ooh, that's divine!' I say, plonking my behind on the bench. And it is. The ice in my marrow starts to defrost.

'Which of you is which?' I ask with a smile. 'I've forgotten the hair thing.'

'Does it matter?' says one.

'Once,' the other one says, 'when we were little we swapped for a while to trick our parents and neither of us can remember if we ever swapped back.'

'It was so long ago.'

'But, for now, I'm Jonty,' says the one to my left.

'Doesn't that freak you out?' I say. 'Having a genetic clone?'

115

'No,' says Jeremy. 'I don't know what it's like to be him.'

'And he doesn't know what it's like to be me.'

'In his head, everything might be totally different. How would I know?' Jeremy continues.

I grin. 'Gosh, I think you've just stumbled into the very core of identity politics.'

'Huh?' The poor boy looks very confused.

'Never mind. You were right. This is lovely.' All this time I've been scared of water and here I am, and no one cares but me.

'Right?'

'So tell us about you!' Jeremy says, sidling up a bit closer. 'You're, like, really hot but no one knows anything about you!'

'I'm not hot!' I'm lanky; too skinny; my shoulders are American-football-player size; my nose is too big; my hips are too narrow; and my boobs are little more than bee stings. Did I mention I suffer from body dysmorphia?

'Oh, she's fishing!' Jonty laughs, miming casting an invisible fishing rod.

'I'm *not* hot,' I repeat myself. 'I'm St Agnes's resident weirdo. You said so yourself.'

'Who cares what those stuck-up cunts think,' Jeremy says. 'At St Barney's we have a fairly complicated ranking system and you're Certified Fresh.'

I can't even feign surprise. I *am* surprised I rank highly, but not that us girls are ranked by fuckability. I'd expect nothing less. 'How wonderful,' I say, very sarcastically.

'Own it,' says Jonty. 'The whole trans thing. It's hot.'

And in that second, my heart genuinely stops.

XVII

ANOTHER FLASHBACK, BUT A SATISFYING ONE

'I beg your pardon?' My head is spinning. Did I just hear that correctly?

The twins look to one another and blink doltishly. 'You're the trans one, right?' Jonty says.

I wasn't aware I was in a diversity girl group.

'It's cool,' Jeremy adds. 'The trans thing. Jake Quinlan graduated last year from St Barney's and he was top bants.'

To lie and deny is my first instinct but that would feel like I'm betraying myself somehow, more than simply omitting information. I can't do it. My heart pounds almost painfully. 'I … how do you know?' It feels like there's a fist down my throat. The admission slips out as a rasp.

The twins frown again. 'Everyone knows. I didn't realise it was meant to be a big secret,' says Jonty.

'What the fuck?' I say, to myself as much as anyone else. I might vomit again. I picture it forming a scum on the water, and go to climb out.

'Hey! Don't go!' Jeremy pleads.

'It's fine!' Jonty says. 'We thought you knew we knew?'

'No! Clearly not!' Funny, isn't it? As soon as that sensation that I'm reaching boiling point in my blood kicks in, I revert to the only coping strategy I know: create a slit in your skin somewhere, let the pressure out; like piercing a sausage before it pops. I haven't cut myself in a long time, but I want to most days. It is, and I quote, a 'faulty coping strategy'.

'Sorry … but no one really cares,' Jonty says. 'You're just the trans girl from St Agnes.'

'Oh good,' I say, hardly listening. The word TRANS peals in my ears. Under the surface of day-to-day life my little duck legs have pedalled so fast to just *get by*. And it was for nothing.

'And we *still* think you're really hot,' Jeremy says. 'I mean, look at you!'

'You sucked off Henry Beaumont at the Spring Fling, right?'

'Oh, for crying out loud!' I almost leap out of the hot tub.

'Jont!' Jeremy says *again*. 'Jesus!'

'Sorry,' Jonty says sheepishly. 'But did you?'

'I fail to see how that's any of your business.'

'Fuck knows, I'm not slut-shaming you! If I was drunk enough, I'd let Beaumont finger me, he's a top bloke,' Jonty says, and both twins howl with laughter.

My heartrate slows a fraction. It's disconcerting. I thought people knowing I'm trans would be the end of the world, but it seems to still be turning. Fuck, though. FUCK.

The twins continue to wind each other up about which guys they'd consider noshing off.

'Are you guys gay?' I ask outright.

'No,' they say at the same time.

'But I *wouldn't not* in a pinch,' Jonty explains. 'I mean, hello! We go to an all-boys boarding school. Everyone knows which boys will blow you in a dark corner of the changing room during a dry spell.'

Jeremy nods too. 'Olivier …' he says sagely.

'Any hole's a goal.' They both cackle again.

'How modern,' I say quietly.

'What about you?' Jeremy asks. 'When you dumped Beaumont he told everyone you were a dyke.'

'Can trans girls be dykes?' Jonty ponders, visibly running the maths in his head.

'Of course!' I say. 'And how fucking predictable. I dumped Henry Beaumont because he's sixty-five per cent boiled gammon.' The words spray out with such venom, I suppose I must have liked him a little bit after all. I briefly thought he was going to be my happily ever after.

My world is still adjusting. So … did Henry know I was trans *before* we met on the app? Or did he tell all of St Barneys? And then I remember the party line: I shouldn't have anything to hide or be ashamed of. I *should* be out and proud, fighting the good fight. Every day is Trans Pride Day, filled with rainbows and unicorns! It's not ideal, but whoever outed me has kind of saved me a thankless task, I suppose. It's a lie of course. It stings like vinegar. I quietly relished the fact I thought I was "passing" as a cis girl. It's a guilty badge of honour and I don't want to lose it. Heavens, being trans is complex. I honestly wonder what cis people do in their heads all day long.

Jonty is still doing identity mathematics. 'So you're a straight girl?'

'I'm actually pansexual.'

'Is that like where you fancy pans?' Jeremy chuckles, only half serious. I hope.

'Sure. Why not?'

'No, you dick, it's the same as bi, right?' says Jonty.

'I don't factor gender into my dating choices,' I say loftily. I have no intention of breaking down my sexual history to the Tweedle twins, but needless to say that night with Bunny went a long way to clarifying how I've felt for the last year or so. No, that's not quite right. Rather, I faced the thing I feared and now it doesn't seem so scary.

'Is that why you're after Bunny Liddell?' Jeremy asks.

'Are you and Bunny ... well ...?'

'I don't know,' I admit. 'She vanished after ...'

'Vanished after what?' Jonty's eyes light up.

'It's none of your—'

'Business? No, but we might be able to help.'

'I don't see how.'

'Well, tell us what happened and we'll know.'

I sigh very deeply. There's not a lot to tell. I've only ever been with Henry and Bunny ... in real life anyway. The apps tell a different story.

It's not like I'm some sexual anthropologist but I do believe sex is a complicated thing that makes other complicated things even more complicated. No: I know from the married thirty-somethings of Guildford that the act of sex can be very uncomplicated if you're so motivated. I mean *desire* is complicated.

When I was in hospital, Bianca – the trans girl – taught me that my *exotic* nature is valuable currency. Some men, a lot more than I anticipated, are moths to this flame. It's not a talent I earned, but their fascination is palpable, bordering on hungered. I mean, perhaps that's true of any girl. We're regarded as prizes

120

whatever our bodies are like. And it's *powerful*: we can bestow the gift of our sexuality as and when we choose. We have it. Men want it.

I wonder if that's why we fear sexual assault so much … it's a grab for our power, not just our bodies.

Anyway, I'm no prude, but to let someone else enjoy this prize is a very great honour I feel, and so I haven't shared it freely, even when I've experienced … curiosity. Which brings me to the night with Bunny.

I shift uncomfortably. 'I'm not sure that's such a great idea. The fewer people that know, the better.'

'So something did happen with you and Bunny!' Jonty brays.

'That's not what I'm saying!'

'Well, if you don't tell us, we're going to tell everyone that's what happened anyway, so you might as well tell us the true story,' Jeremy says.

'Oh, go on. Jeremy loves a good story.'

'It's true, I do.'

'Very well.' And so I tell my tale for the first time.

Night has long since fallen by the time we leave the funfair and head towards Clapham High Street. For some reason, Bunny drags me into Tesco Express, and the ultra-white lights of the supermarket are bleach for the eyeballs.

I wouldn't ever *buy* one of those tawdry magazines, but I *am* interested to learn of *Posh's Fury at Becks* and also why *Meghan Angers Royals*. I do this by flicking through the pages on the stand.

'Just walk,' Bunny says, appearing like a ghost at my side.

'What?'

'Be cool. Just walk.'

She presses her shoulder to mine and we exit the store past the bored-looking security guard. She picks up her pace as we reach the outer edges of the common. The fairground is right the other side of the green, drowned out by London buses and the din from the Hen Do Central cocktail bars. We cut across the park, where our only company is the little troupe of street drinkers who congregate at the war memorial. They sporadically scream incoherently at each other from across the common.

Bunny slips a bottle of white wine from the sleeve of her satin bomber jacket and hands it to me. 'Bottoms up!'

'Did you just steal this?'

'They would have IDed us. Besides, I see it as community outreach.' She slides a second bottle from her other sleeve and hands it to one of the homeless people.

'Bunny …'

'What? I have one down my pants too! Red, obviously. I didn't fancy a chilled white Zinfandel pressed against my pussy.' She laughs at her own joke.

I'm not sure where she's going, but I continue to follow her along the path.

'What now?' We got bored of the funfair a while back, and Bunny was starting to look anxious again – checking over her shoulder constantly.

She unscrews the wine bottle and necks it. 'Last supper.'

'Are you ever going to tell me what's going on?'

'No.'

'Are you hiding from someone?'

Her nose crinkles. 'If I was hiding would I be on Clapham Common?'

'I can't help if you won't tell me what's wrong.'

'I'm having such a fun night, don't harsh my mellow.' She grasps both my arms. 'Alice! Shall we go missing?'

'What?'

'I do it all the time,' she says, giggling. 'It's fun! I know, to everyone else, it's irritating, like I'm the quirky literary cipher girl, but after the first couple of times I did it, I realised it's actually pretty satisfying. Haven't you ever wished you could freeze time, get your shit together and then press play again?'

Only every day.

And yet.

'I can't disappear, Bunny. My mother would freak.'

'Ah, I see. I think my mom is at a no-phone yoga retreat so she wouldn't know anything about it until at least Wednesday.'

I don't know what to say to that.

'What about tonight? Vanish with me for one night. You can even text your mother and tell her you're staying at mine.'

'Are we?' I ask. 'Staying at yours?'

'No,' Bunny says at once. 'They'll be looking for me there.'

'Who will?'

I think she's about to tell me but then changes her mind. 'It doesn't matter.'

'Bunny …?'

'In or out? Come on, Alice, do something scary. Fall down my rabbit hole.'

I take a vinegary glug of room-temperature wine. 'Very well.'

'And look at that …' An 88 bus to Camden Town pulls in alongside us. 'Perfect timing. Hop on. Get it?'

I follow her on to the bus and the door hisses shut behind me …

The V Hotel at Vauxhall glows a garish neon pink, a glass monument to poor taste on the Thames. Mirrorball panthers flank the entrance, and Bunny saunters past them and into the lobby. It's all very Las Vegas: a fountain gushes over a black marble V at the centre of reception.

'Isn't it the tackiest fucking thing you ever saw?' Bunny says, twirling past a coachload of bewildered American tourists. She queue-jumps all the way to the front desk. 'Hello, Vanya, can I get a suite, please?'

'Of course, Miss Liddell. Will your mother be staying with you?'

'Nope. Just me.' She plonks a black card on the desk.

And that's when I realise one can quite easily be a ridiculous female literary will-o'-the-wisp if one has the financial means.

She scribbles her signature on some form and he hands her a key card.

'Eighth floor! Let's go!' she cries.

We take a lift with the elderly Americans. It's very quiet, a little bell pinging out the floors until, apparently, the silence becomes too much for Bunny.

'Alice, baby, would you mind terribly if I licked coke off your clit?'

The lift arrives on the eighth floor and we tumble out, cackling with laughter as one of the women scolds us.

'Bunny!' I cry.

'Welcome to London, you cunts!' she screams as the doors close. 'If they can afford to stay here, they probably deserve it,' she says as we run, hand in hand, down endlesssssssss corridors. I wonder if Bunny has ever received a formal diagnosis for what looks suspiciously like ADHD. The carpets are so plush, my Docs are leaving footprints in the snow.

'Bunny, what are we doing?'

'We're hiding. But doing it in style. 827! Here we are!' She swipes into the room and we boulder in.

Bunny flicks on the lights. Goodness, the suite is quite breathtaking. I occasionally get to tour with Mummy and she stays in some lovely rooms, but this one is nicer – more like a studio apartment. White and clean and crisp: a living area and the bed partitioned off behind a silk veil.

Just the one king-size bed.

I suppose I can take the peacock-blue chaise, which is almost as large.

Bi-fold doors lead onto the balcony and beyond that is the sprawl of London. I unlock the door and step outside. A gust of wind blows my hair into my mouth. I am overcome by my own smallness. Jets, like insects, fly in and out of a pulsing electric hive. Everything is blue and orange and very alive, like some sort of writhing cyborg. A leviathan rising out of the Thames.

Looking down on it all, I go a little queer. If we can get lost anywhere, it's here. It's so big and we're so tiny.

It's not a pleasant sensation, one's own insignificance, but it does creep up on me every now and again.

We tell ourselves we matter.

125

We don't.

We're a gasp in all this.

'What are you thinking about?' I don't hear Bunny sidle up behind me. She's peeled off her bomber jacket and trainers.

'London. It scares me sometimes.'

'London? London's a piece of cake. You have a driver, right?'

Bunny really doesn't have a clue, I realise. And I'm not sure I have that many more. Somewhere in the distance sirens scream.

'I wonder how many people we're looking at right now. You know like how in Biology, when we get to see bacteria under the microscope? We're a virus. We keep growing and spreading and spawning. You lose count. I just wonder why we bother.'

'Why we bother what?'

'You'll think it's nonsense.'

'Try me. I like nonsense.'

I shrug. 'Why we bother doing *anything*.' She waits for an explanation. 'We're so irrelevant, don't you think? It makes me want to lie down and let time grind over me like a steamroller. Stop the world turning. Just for a second while I figure it out.'

'Figure what out?'

I shrug again. 'How … to be … OK.' The bar is that low.

'Where did you go last year?' she asks out of nowhere. 'You had a bunch of time off school. I'm normally the one who vanishes, so I don't like it when other people do. You stole my *thing*.'

I can't look in her eyes. I pull away from her and go back into the suite. 'I can't believe anyone noticed.'

She follows me back inside. 'It wasn't a big deal. I think most people assumed you'd died. Or worse, gone to a state school.' She winks.

'Cute.' Lie or truth? Maybe if I'm honest with her, she'll be honest with me. 'I was in hospital.'

'Oh no! Were you OK?'

I perch on the chaise. 'No. Not remotely.'

'What was wrong?'

My mouth opens, but only a strangled little noise comes out. I can't say it. A weirdly elegant word for something so awful. Three syllables, strung like pearls: soo-ee-side.

'It's OK, you can tell me,' Bunny says, kneeling at my feet.

'I … I had an episode. I … tried to hurt myself, so I was sectioned under the Mental Health Act.' There, I didn't need to say THE WORD.

'They locked you up?' Her eyes widen.

'Yes,' I admit. 'I tried to get out so they had to.' Because, at that point, I was convinced there were shadow men in the room with me. I thought the doctors were going to poison me. I thought the only way to stop it, to make it better, was to kill myself. Dead had to be better than what I felt, like life was a hand pressing my face to the concrete floor.

I'm nothing if not thorough, and I researched the best place in London to do it – the spot where the trains travel the fastest through a station without stopping. I'd love to say it was a grey, morose morning with sheets of drizzle and howling winds, but, as I stood on platform six, the skies were as blue as my hair.

How was I to know, with scrambled egg brains, that I hadn't put on any shoes that morning? Standing barefoot on a train platform in uncontrollable tears is a sure sign a teenage girl might not be 'in the best place' and that's how the police got to me about three minutes before the 11.37 South West service to Portsmouth was due.

Couldn't tell you how I got to the station. There are lots of patches I've never been able to fill in. Can't really remember getting to the hospital either. I remember the police woman. She looked a lot like Mummy. For a minute I thought she *was* my mum. As I fell back into her arms, I reached for her face, immediately glad I wasn't dead. I didn't want to die. I still don't.

That's the illness talking. Other Alice. She tells me I want to die.

'It was the worst thing,' I say.

'Are you feeling better now?'

'Yes. God, yes.' I sit up straighter on the chaise, trying to do an impersonation of a person with exemplary mental health. As we all know, mad people have terrible posture. 'I haven't had an episode in almost a year. I'm on medication and I have therapy every week.'

She tilts her head. 'But ...?'

'Almost as bad as what happened ... is the fear it will happen again.'

Bunny smiles kindly and takes my face in her hands. Her palms are soft and warm. 'Oh, you have so much rattling around in there. Just be. Don't think about what happened before or what might happen next. Just be here. In this room. With me.'

That's when she kisses me on the lips. I'm surprised, and pull back for a second, but then I want more so go in again.

'Is that better?'

'Sometimes it feels like I'm running out of time, but I don't

128

know what it is I'm supposed to be doing.' I'm crying and I don't know why.

'Oh, Alice. That's my line.' She takes my hand and leads me to the bed. She wipes my tears away with her thumb. 'Calm yourself, beautiful. You've got *for ever*.'

I smile up at her. 'How long is for ever?'

'Well, all we have is now.' She laughs. 'So how long is for ever? Sometimes just a second.'

And then she kisses me again and, so help me god, I taste cherry chapstick.

Regardless, it's very, very exciting. Maybe it's because she's a girl or maybe it's because it's new or maybe it's because I already love her.

And that is because kissing Bunny is lovely. All of a sudden I feel the snuggest feeling of total safety. Nothing bad is going to happen. Not here.

I kiss her back, our tongues tickling.

'Wow,' I say once she's pulled away.

'That good, huh?'

'I didn't know you liked girls.'

'I like kissing,' she replies, rolling onto the bed. 'So kiss me.'

'Wait,' I say. 'I … before this goes any further … I have to be honest with you. I … I'm … not like other girls.'

She smiles. 'Oh, honey, that's what they all say!'

I laugh, but my heart has already climbed right up into my throat and I wonder if she can hear it pounding. 'No, Bunny, you don't understand. I … I'm transgender.' The word flops out like I've coughed up a furball.

She nods slowly and I can't quite interpret her face. 'Oh, OK.'

'OK? That's all you're going to say?'

'Fuck it. Don't worry, your secret's safe with me! You're transitioning into a girl? Or out of being a girl?'

I suppose the fact she can't tell should be a compliment, although it doesn't feel like one. Either way, it's a fucker. 'I was born ... a boy. But never really was one.'

She kisses me again, fleetingly. 'Baby, it's fine. Look at you: you're a *girl*.'

In the moment, I feel so seen. I cry anew.

'But ... but my body ...'

'Your body is beautiful. Now shut the fuck up and kiss me.'

I do as she asks, and hands go exploring. Why does this feel so different? It's a different colour in my head from the boys I've fooled around with. Awkward, hurried fumbles and fingers. That was orange, yellow and red: fire colours. Right now, my head is awash with pale lilac and white-blue: water and air.

'Here,' she says. 'Take this.' From the pocket of her shorts, she slips out a little plastic baggy containing pills. She places one on my palm. It's tiny and heart-shaped with EAT ME printed on it in even tinier pink letters.

'What is it?'

'Bliss!' she says, glitter in her eyes.

'Ecstasy? I don't know if I should, I—'

She pouts. 'It's the same stuff they put in anti-depressants, you know.' She puts one on her tongue and kisses me again. I feel the pill pass into my mouth. 'Just you wait ...'

We kiss some more. We kiss and kiss until I feel a certain *whoosh* in my head and heart and throat. I grip her head and pull her into my mouth.

Her fingers slide into my pants.

And

Instead of fear

Or shame

Petals open

I buzz, buzz, buzz all over

honey electric and

'Oh my …'

'Yeah?'

'Yes.'

My back arches like something's about to blow inside me and I spread my legs wider. She unbuttons my shorts.

'That's not kissing,' I tell her.

She smiles. 'Do you want me to stop?'

'No. God, no.'

It's as good as when I do it myself. It's like we're levitating a foot off the bed. *Light as a feather, stiff as a board.* We're fucking flying.

I'm radiating waves of heat; they pour over my skin like desert winds.

The colours in my head go hot cerise pink and purple.

'Bunny!'

My whole body spasms, like I might bounce clean off the bed. I crack like thunder. She pins me down with a kiss and I ride it out. The boom ebbs away and I sink into the duvet with her still atop me.

'I'm coming up … I can feel it.'

'What's it like?'

'I love you …'

'No, you don't! That's the pill talking.'

'I'm warm, I'm warm inside. Like caramel ...'

'The first time is the best. If I could capture how that felt again ... let me share the high ...' Bunny strokes my face and kisses me again.

And that's why they call it ecstasy. I get it now.

She presses my hand against her and rubs up against it.

I want to give her what she just gave me. I'm nervous, but don't want to let on. I don't want to fuck it up. Here goes.

She's warm and wet against my skin. So, so warm.

And when she moans in my ear, I know I've found *her* spot.

She tells me what to do. A little faster, a little harder. She shivers.

It's like I'm strumming her.

I'm doing this to her and I've never felt so special.

We're pressed together so tight you couldn't get air between us and

She gasps, throwing her head back. I did that and she looks beautiful.

There's no *was that good for you*. No anxious male egos to flatter here, no winners. We lie side by side for several second-long forevers; breathing, looking at the ceiling. I don't rush to cover my nakedness, I hardly even notice. The room smells of a weird, delicious mixture of our bodies and whatever sugary perfumes we've doused ourselves in.

'Do you want room service?' she suddenly says. 'They do the most delicious club sandwiches.'

I laugh and roll onto my elbow. I'm still pulsing, my soul bigger than its skeleton. I'm glowing all over. My head is like one of those snow globes filled with glitter. 'OK! Why not? Something vegetarian.'

'Oh, I didn't know *that* about you either.' She hops off the bed and fetches the menu over. 'So are you gay, bi, pan?'

'I don't know. Honestly.'

'You're seventeen.' She fluffs out her hair with a hand absentmindedly. 'I don't think you have to have it all figured out just yet.'

'You're only a year older than me!'

'That's how I know!' She kisses me again. I'm glad it's not weird or awkward. I hold boys in quite low regard so it's never really mattered before what people think of me.

I can barely focus on the words in the menu. They seem to crawl over the page like ants. 'I'll have the grilled cheese sandwich.'

'A fine choice. So being trans, huh? That's gotta be a trip?'

I allow myself a shy smile. The glow is dimming now. I'm coming back down to earth. 'When I was nine, my mother finally caved and took me to see a specialist. I moved schools when I was twelve and started my life as Alice at St Agnes.'

'Cool. And, not that I'm collecting Pokémon or anything, but I've always wondered what it'd be like to be with a trans girl.'

'And …?'

'Are you kidding? That was fucking hot. And I can confirm – not that you're asking – that you're *definitely* a girl. That's not what it's like with boys.' I grin. I wonder if she felt the same cool blue aura I did. 'You been with girls before?'

'No.' I pull my shorts back on and cross my legs. 'I thought

I just liked boys. But lately, I don't know. Lately, when I ... you know ... I think about boy bodies and girl bodies and ... just bodies ... and it does the trick.'

'Oh, same.' Bunny mirrors my pose on the bed. 'I enjoy a balanced diet. Girls are sweet and boys are savoury. Usually.'

I laugh again.

Bunny goes on. 'In dorms, the code word is *slumber party*. Sometimes I'll invite a girl over for a slumber party and we'll wear our nicest nighties and well ... it's all good fun, isn't it?'

I don't know why, but that stings a little. I'm high on post-orgasmic brain chemistry and MDMA but, in this moment, I want to marry Bunny Liddell, not be the latest in a long line of St Agnes girls she's pleasured. 'And that's ... all it is? A slumber party?'

'I don't know. Alice, I don't know what I want from one day to the next. Sometimes ...'

'Sometimes what?'

She hides behind the menu so I can't see her face. 'Sometimes I don't see a future for me at all.'

I pull the menu away.

'What does that mean?' I wonder if we have suicidal ideation in common too.

She swings her legs off the bed and pads back over to the window. She doesn't bother to put her T-shirt back on. 'Well, it's the way I live, isn't it? Surprised I made it this far, to be honest. The stories are mostly all true, you know.'

'Prince Leonardo of Sweden?'

She nods.

'Golly.'

'What you said about time ...' She pauses. 'It sometimes feels like I'm on borrowed time. Sooner or later, it's bound to catch up with me. You can't run this fast for ever. I really fucked up.'

I'm worried now. I don't think she's talking metaphorically any more. It's not *time* she's on the run from. She has the same look in her eye that she had at the fairground: resignation. '*Who*, Bunny? Who's going to catch up with you?'

Bunny looks out of the penthouse windows over the Thames. The moonlight makes her hair liquid amber. She can't meet my gaze. 'Alice,' she says finally, 'I think I'm in trouble.'

'What kind of trouble?'

'The serious sort. The sort I can't get out of.' She turns away from the window, but still can't look me in the eye.

'Bunny Liddell – your escapades are legendary ...'

'Not this time. This isn't the same.'

'You're serious, aren't you?'

'Deadly.'

'Deadly?'

Her voice is scarcely a whisper. 'When the clock strikes thirteen, it'll be off with her head.'

What? What's that supposed to mean? 'Bunny ...? Please, you're freaking me out now ...' Maybe the pill is exaggerating fear *and* love, but I'm worried, really, truly worried.

She shakes it off. 'No! No, I'll be fine. I always am. If cats have nine lives, it seems Bunnys get ten.' She's lying. I can tell. She derails the conversation. 'So? Grilled cheese sandwich? Do you want a drink too? Oh, I'll order champagne!'

She prances to the phone on the desk and makes the call.

I'm sleepy, and drunk, and horny, and worried, and wide

awake and it's all a bit excessive. An alarm sounds underneath all the other noise. A tiny voice is screaming at me to leave this suite and go home at once. It's telling me Bunny Liddell is a sinking ship, and she'll drag me down with her.

But that's exactly why I stay.

I wake up to a cold bed. The duvet has slipped off in the night and my bare back is exposed. Stark white light floods the room. Last night, Bunny didn't want to draw the curtains because the view was so pretty.

I groan.

What time is it?

I feel like shit, my mouth like a litter tray. Why does wine make your breath smell like wet dog?

In front of my face, I see only big white bed. My grandpa's pocket watch is resting in the groove of the pillow where her head would have been. It's almost eight. Still early.

'Bunny?'

I sit up.

'Bunny?'

I climb out of bed and walk around to the en suite. The bathroom door is ajar and there's no one inside.

I retrieve my teddy bear backpack from the chaise and dig out my phone. I'm down to 8% battery and I don't even have a message from Mummy.

I stand in the centre of the beautiful room, lost for inspiration. Then I see a tablet of writing paper on the desk.

I already know what's waiting on the V Hotel notepad.

Alice,

Thank you for last night. For a second, all my worries went away and, as we know, sometimes a second is enough.

I want to thank you in person. Meet in the Blume common room tonight at 6pm?

Sorry I had to dash. I couldn't bear to wake you, you looked so beautiful as you slept.

Yours,

Bunny xoxo

I waited in the common room until midnight.

She never came.

XVIII

SKINTEREST (CONTINUED)

'Where did she go?' Jonty asks, eyes wide, when I've finished my enormously abridged version of events.

'Here?' I reply. 'There? Anywhere? Who knows?'

'That's so sad,' Jeremy says. 'How could she leave you like that?'

'I don't know.' Steam swirls around us. The water is bliss and my eyes feel woolly. It has been an extraordinarily long day and, like Bunny, it rather feels like time has caught up with me.

Jonty looks even more baffled than usual. 'You came all the way to Wonderland on the off-chance she'd be here?'

'Yes.' Admitting that is acutely embarrassing.

'Why?'

'The police wouldn't do anything. Her parents don't seem to worry that she hasn't been seen in over a week. No one else cared but me.'

'You love her!' Jonty exclaims.

'No!' Even I think that sounds like a lie. 'Well, no, not like that. It just … I don't know, it didn't seem right.'

'Sounds like some sort of love to me,' adds Jeremy. 'I can think of people I've loved in just one night. We don't measure love in minutes and seconds, do we?'

That's rather profound, I think.

What unit *would* we measure love in? Heartaches? Memories? Daydreams?

'Here,' Jonty slips an arm behind my back. 'Do you want a cheeky bean?'

I look around as he slides a hand into the pocket of his cast-off towelling robe. 'A what?'

'MDMA. This'll perk you up.' He shakes a baggy of the distinctive heart-shaped pills.

'No, thank you,' I say. 'It was one of those that got me into this mess – falling in love at the drop of a hat. It's a very, very dangerous drug.'

He pops one on his tongue, leans forward and, before I realise what he's doing, slips his tongue into my mouth.

I push him away. 'Jonty!' I didn't especially want that, but it's too late. Already down the hatch.

'Pass them here!' Jeremy commands.

Jonty takes another pill for himself and hands the bag to his brother.

'You had no right to do that,' I say.

'Oh, relax!'

'Paisley's back in town,' Jeremy says, stating the obvious.

'What does that have to do with anything?'

He shrugs. 'Paisley doesn't fuck you over. Her shit is always top-notch.'

The penny drops. 'Paisley's a *drug dealer*?'

Both brothers guffaw. 'Don't let her hear you say that! She'll have your guts for garters,' says Jonty.

'Uh, I hate that phrase!' I say, my head suddenly filled with the most gruesome image. 'Can you imagine holding your socks up with bits of intestine?'

It makes a strange sort of sense. Paisley – before she went to Switzerland – was *everywhere*. She's been in the clubs and bars of Mayfair since she was about thirteen. Who'd dare turn her away? She knows everyone and can go anywhere. Well, that revelation goes some way to explaining why someone with all the warmth of a penguin's bottom is so inexplicably popular.

'Just go with it,' Jonty tells me, leaning in closer so I can feel his breath on my lips. 'Let yourself come up. A perfect high.'

Come up, fall down. Everyone wants me in a different direction so it seems. I imagine myself clinging on to my skeleton for dear life and wonder what it is I'm so afraid of. Everyone else seems able to let go.

Minutes pass, the twins talking utter nonsense and, sure enough, I start to come up. Or, at least I assume that's what's happening, it feels like my soul is a viscous purple bubble floating in my chest, a helium balloon trying to soar right out of my body. I rest my head on the rim of the hot tub.

This is only the second time I've done ecstasy. I've been cautious, partly because of what happened to poor Antonella Hemmings a couple of years back – every school has that one poor student in living memory who got gravely unlucky – but mostly because I never dared risk the consequences of it *working*. My feelings are mine, not for sharing.

All of a sudden I feel more love than I have in my entire life and I really need to share it.

This is what love feels like!

The pool glows the most intense aquamarine blue. The steam now rises off the hot tub in candy-pink swirls. There are an impossible number of stars in the sky and they all twinkle, twinkle.

Before I know it, both Jeremy and Jonty are nuzzling my neck, their lips hunting for kisses. The love finds its way out through the pores. There is so much love to go around.

A threesome with the Tweedle Twins. Oh, Dinah *will* be jealous.

Is this a threesome? Am I seriously having a threesome?

It feels like there's a lot more than four hands tracing my skin. There are fingers on my thighs, my torso, my breasts, my face. Each twin is like one of those many-armed Hindu gods.

Let them use your body and get fucked both ends like a little piggy and

No.

You're a fucking cum slut. Worthless tranny whore.

Stop.

This isn't you.

I sink further into the water, but this doesn't feel right. I clutch my head, trying to squash the sense back in.

Why am I doing this?

My heart does feel positively swollen with love, but I'm not so stupid as to not know that's the MDMA pumping through my veins. I've only ever slept with people because I've wanted to … and this feels rather more opportunistic.

And what's so bad about that, I wonder? If it feels nice …

I kiss Jeremy and then Jonty.

But I'm not sure it does feel nice. Their kisses feel hungry somehow. Do I want this? It would be an experience. *Submit to your wildest fantasies. Test your limits. Enjoy the flesh, give in to carnal desires.*

The twins press against me, their bodies hard and wet. Firm hands grab at my breasts, pull on my nipples.

If it was right, would there be so many questions, so many wasps at the picnic?

Carnival of the animals.

Carnivores.

A hand slides up my thigh towards

I can't.

I can't let go.

'Stop,' I say between kisses.

'Relax,' one of them says.

'You're so hot,' says the other.

I push his face away. 'That's all well and good but I didn't come here for this.'

'So?'

'It's a nice surprise. Go with it.'

I know I could. Maybe I should. Think what they could achieve with two tongues.

But no.

It's very hard to quantify, but it just doesn't feel right.

'Stop!' They stop. 'Is this even *legal*?' I ask.

'We like sharing girls,' one of them says.

'We do it all the time,' says the other.

'That,' I say solemnly, 'might be oversharing.'

I pull myself up and the one to my left – they won't stay still so it could be either of them – grabs my wrist. 'Don't go.'

He's squeezing me too hard. It hurts.

There's a tipping point, I wonder if everyone's experienced it, when things go from being *OK* to *Not-OK*. I think we just reached that point. The pink champagne feeling in my chest turns sour and green. 'Let go.'

'Aw, come on …'

'I said no.' And I'm praying to god that *Saying No* is enough. It's always worked in the past but, like all girls, I live in fear of the day it doesn't.

Jonty (I think) leers up at me. 'Have you still got a dick I can suck?'

I freeze. Just for second. 'Go fuck yourself, Jonty. Let go of me, you prick.'

He lets go, thank god, and I clamber out of the hot tub, water pouring from my knickers in a very unsexy gush.

One of them mutters something to the other: 'I thought you …'

I'm wobbly on my feet. I'm still coming up. I grab the towel and wrap it around my chest. Uh-oh. I've got what I believe is referred to by scientists as 'Room Spin', the whole floor feels like it's revolving clockwise, only to then snap back anti-clockwise. This usually happens mere moments before I liberally splatter the contents of my stomach everywhere. I stagger, and steady myself against a pool lounger.

'Here,' says one of the twins, stepping out of the hot tub to steady me. 'You need to sit …'

The world is on a slope.

The other twin comes at me from the opposite direction. 'Why don't we put you to bed?'

Funny how quickly things go south, isn't it? Worse still, I'm not sure I can run this time. It's like my whole body is turning to semolina.

'Just … leave me alone … I don't feel too good …'

'Alice, it's fine … you can trust us …'

Except that I'm not sure I can.

This. This is why I don't like to lose control … fuck.

I am at their mercy.

I freeze, my whole body tenses.

A black shape swoops in from my periphery and barrels into the twin nearest to me. It's all too fast for me to process. The twin is winded, giving a loud 'oof' before crashing into the swimming pool.

What the fuck is going on?

I try to focus. It's Cat. Her eyes burn angrily from under her hood. Her teeth are bared in a snarl. A gloved hand slips into mine and she yanks on my arm, pulling me behind her.

'Hey!' the other twin says. 'What the hell!'

From her pocket she produces a flick-knife. The blade glints in the moonlight as it springs out.

'Holy shit!' He holds his hands up and jerks away from us.

'Back the fuck off, brotherfucker.' Cat holds the blade at arm's length. Her voice is low, steady. Her hand doesn't waver even slightly.

'What are you doing?' I try to pull her arm back before she has someone's eye out.

'They gave you something,' Cat says, never once taking her eyes off the Tweedle. The one in the pool is now swimming to the side.

'I know, I took a pill.' My words are slurred. I'm messy and I don't like being messy.

'No, something *else*. They put something in your tea.'

'What?' I ask. When? I'd have seen. And how does she know?

'Get inside,' Cat orders. She addresses the twin again. 'If you try to follow us, I'll cut you.'

'That's *our* chalet!'

Cat scowls right back him. 'I have checked my fucks and lo, I give none. Alice, get in.'

The whole barn is zooming in and out of focus. I can barely plant one foot in front of the other. Cat takes me by the shoulders and guides me through the sliding French windows.

'You can't do this!' one of the twins cries as Cat slides the door shut behind us and swiftly locks it. Both twins hammer on the glass, but it's impressively soundproofed.

I flop down onto the same sofa as before. 'They drugged me?'

'I heard one of them tell the other while you were changing.' Cat's many colourful faces spiral around in a vortex.

'You were watching us?'

'My eyes were open. I was in the vicinity.'

'So … watching?'

She shrugs. 'Relax. You're safe now.'

I don't know about that. The air is gelatine-thick and I'm pickled in aspic, every movement slow and laboured. It's like I'm hearing her voice via a conch shell. I'm tripping off my skull and I'm now locked in a luxury Airbnb with a strange girl with a knife. Although, I suppose, she … *saved* me, which is an odd sensation. I've never thought of myself as the damsel-in-distress sort. I don't know this girl from Eve, but I find myself – possibly against my better judgement – trusting her. The puppet strings between me and my body feel like they've been cut at present, so I think I'm going to have to.

I hate that. Hate that I need her. That's the thing with being trans, I always assumed everyone would leave me once they saw me for what I was, so I got very good at looking after myself. Well, until I couldn't.

'What did they give me?' I ask.

'I don't know. Something soluble. G maybe?'

I don't even fucking know what that is. 'Am I going to be OK?'

Her green eyes shine even in the low light. 'I'm going to watch you. So yes.'

I lie down on the couch. I cling to it like a life raft. 'You'll stay?'

'Yes.'

'Thank you.'

'Go to the bedroom,' she says. 'I'll get you water.'

I do not want to Goldilocks their bed. It only got her savaged by bears. 'I'm OK here. Where will they go?' I point at the wet, angry twins on the other side of the glass.

'I don't care.' Cat goes off in search of the kitchen.

My heart rate now feels too fast, like it's galloping. Everything feels like it's being pumped too quickly. I might pop. My breath comes in shallow pants. I'm thirsty. 'Cat …?'

She returns from the kitchen with a pint of water. 'That's not my name.' She hands me the glass. 'Sip this slowly. You're tripping.'

My hand is shaking, but I manage to lift the glass to my lips. My hands look translucent, like ghost hands. 'Then what is your name?'

'It's honestly better if you don't know.'

'Are you going to hurt me?'

'No. That I promise.'

No one can promise that. You can only promise to try. I have to lie down. It's the only way I can stop the spinning. Cat takes the water out of my ghost hands and places it on the coffee table.

'You're gonna be fine. Just gotta ride it out.'

My eyes feel so heavy. Is it safe to fall asleep? What an awful thought to fall asleep on.

As I roll in and out of consciousness, I feel Cat rest a blanket over me. My eyes open briefly and I see her curl up in the armchair opposite, keeping her vigil.

XIX

OTHER ALICE

When I wake, very bright sunshine streams through the windows and neither Cat nor the Tweedle twins are anywhere to be seen.

'If one more girl leaves me in the night,' I say to myself, rubbing mascara bogeys from my eyes, 'I shall start to take it personally.'

My tongue feels furry and I see Cat, possibly an angel undercover, has left the water on the coffee table. One can only hope this drink hasn't been spiked. I gulp it down thirstily.

It doesn't help.

I'm going to have to lie down for a while, it seems sitting up was a shade ambitious.

My head feels like it's been injected with Polyfilla. My jaw and back teeth ache keenly and I wonder just how badly I was gurning through the night. God, I dread to think how ridiculous I looked to Cat.

My hair reeks of chlorine and I'm naked aside from my underwear and a still-damp towel.

There's something about the custard yellow of the daylight which suggests I've slept through a considerable chunk of Saturday. Why haven't the Tweedles tried to gain access? Or maybe they have and I slept through it. The reality of what happened and what *could have happened* sits heavily on my chest. If Cat hadn't been there … well, I'm glad we need never find out.

I force myself to sit up again. I have no desire to be here when they do get back.

But I also need, in no particular order, a coffee, a shower and an abundance of stodgy carbohydrates. I wrap the blanket around me like a cape and blearily feel my way to the kitchen which is off the lounge. There's a whole mezzanine overhead and I cast a glance up the stairs as I pass, but I'm certain I'm alone.

The kitchen is beautiful, but it's apparent that two YouTubers have been living in it. The countertops are covered in discarded pizza boxes, bags of cookies and crushed cans of Red Bull.

I've stayed in enough Airbnbs to know the hosts usually leave coffee and, sure enough, I find a cafetiere and a bag of Waitrose coffee next to the kettle. Oh, hello, sweet saviour. Just for a second, I truly believe everything today, and for the rest of my life, will turn out all right. Such is the power of caffeine.

While it brews, I raid the fridge and cupboards and find the twins have brought a punnet of pain au chocolat. I help myself to two of the four without hesitation. They deserve a lot worse than that, the absolute shits. Now that I'm safe, the horror is starting to turn to anger. They won't get away with it. God knows how I'll prevent it … but they won't.

I know what I *should* do. What I should do is call the police at the very first opportunity. That's what one does isn't it? But I also know a bunch of police would want to go poking about in my knickers; I'd get called a liar; I'd be outed; I'd become the target of every tween Tweedle fangirl on the internet. Despite everything I'd tell Dinah to do, I know I won't call the police, and hate myself a little for it.

Feeling rather like Goldilocks again, I sit at the big farmhouse table, licking chocolate off my fingers and sipping the powerfully strong black coffee. It occurs to me I've only eaten drugs in almost twenty-four hours. It's no wonder I feel so peculiar. My stomach gurgles and I may well vomit. I really don't have time for a comedown today.

Did I hallucinate Bunny in the forest last night? I sigh. At this stage, I'm not sure it matters. Whether Bunny's here or not, *I am* and I'm a bit stuck. I wonder how often the boat returns to London and if there's an opportunity to board it today. As I finish my coffee, I decide on a plan of action: I need to leave. I'm not entirely sure where I am though, and I can't call Felix … or can I?

I abandon my breakfast things and head back into the lounge, searching for a landline. I find a socket near the TV set, but there's nothing plugged in. I trot upstairs where I find a luxurious bedroom and en suite. The bed is untouched, the boys' luggage left on an armchair. I see the corner of a MacBook poking out of a rucksack and grab it. I perch on the bed and flip it open.

'Damn.' It's password protected.

Well, it was a nice idea.

I can't be that far away from civilisation, can I, if the twins ordered pizza in? I shall just have to walk until I find a phone, or there *must* be one in Gryphon Hall itself.

The twins have colonised the en suite with dirty boxer shorts and deodorant cans. I don't understand how they've made it so gross in such a short amount of time. Still, needs must. Just in case, I lock the bathroom door. I twist the shower nozzle and a power jet quickly heats up. Steam floods the room and I step into the tub.

I let the water blast my head, watching mud from the forest swill down the plughole. The water is hot, too hot, but I like it that way. My chest turns pink and blotchy. It's cleansing. The chlorine scent quickly fades and I give my poor scalp a bloody good itch. It's all imaginary, but I like to imagine the various toxins I put in my body last night seeping out through my pores too.

I make a private vow to eat my five-a-day today.

I dry myself off and wrap my hair in a towel. The next problem is what on earth I'm going to wear. I was never planning on staying overnight and I assumed we'd be partying within Zone Six. Everything I was wearing yesterday is in a damp heap outside.

Again, vis à vis the planned gang rape, I don't feel a shred of guilt over taking Jeremy and Jonty's things. Serves them right. I return to the bedroom and rummage through their stuff. I find some brand new, white Calvin Klein briefs and pull them on. I didn't come all this way to wear boys' underwear, but I'd rather wear dry, clean boy pants than cold, dirty, girl ones. The best part of having tiny fashion boobs is that I can live without a bra for a day. One of the twins has packed a pair of powder-pink denim shorts which I rather like, and I can pull off a man's shirt too. It's a fairly neutral pale blue cotton with a white candy stripe. I'm sure a fashion magazine would call it 'boyfriend style'. I shall refer to it as stolen goods. The shirt hangs to halfway down my thighs, covering the shorts anyway. I grab a belt and cinch it all in at the waist, creating a shirt dress. All in all, it could be a lot worse.

I've worn a lot worse.

I locate the hairdryer and dry off my hair before securing it in a messy bun atop my head.

It's only now, with a sinking sensation, I realise that in my haste to leave Maxim and Olivier's yurt, I forgot my teddy backpack. Fuck. It has everything in it – my purse; the token for my phone; the emergency credit card. Shit, shit, incandescent shit. I have got to get back to their tent.

I hurry downstairs and find my boots. They're still soggy, but I'll just have to live with it. I slide a pair of stolen socks on my feet first and it's bearable. Sorry, Vivienne Westwood, you're beyond redemption. I gather up Mummy's dress and leave it in the kitchen trash.

It comes out of nowhere.

The *dread*.

It's a physical thing, like a headache or upset stomach. The overwhelming blackness of *knowing* something awful is going to happen. Somewhere, something is on fire and you can't stop it because you don't know what it is.

I have to sit down on the blue and white tiles. A dread so heavy it weights me down.

Alice …

No. I'm not hearing that. Too much to do.

Alice …

This time, her voice seems to be coming from the lounge area, so real there really could be another me in the next room.

The coffee and croissants churn in my stomach. I hardly dare breathe as I follow the sound. I crawl on my hands and knees.

The TV is switched on.

Which is odd because I didn't turn it on.

It's some Saturday morning cookery show where minor celebrities cook with a slightly less famous celebrity chef. Only this time, the chef is me. Or rather, her. She smiles out of the TV set and looks right at me from behind a stove. She's my identical twin in every way, save for a couple of important details: her eyes. They're black, gleaming like onyx. She grins, showing too many teeth. Her mouth is too wide.

You fucking worthless piece of shit.

I grab the remote and change the channel. This time it's a black-and-white war movie. Instead of a soldier, it's me, it's *her*, dressed in army fatigues. She continues to stare.

Everything you are is embarrassing. You're no fucking girl, you're a man. You're disgusting, you will always be a

I sit cross-legged in front of the TV and press my hands over my ears and screw my eyes tight shut. 'Go away!' I say aloud.

I try to focus on what Felicity would tell me to do: centre myself by focusing on my immediate physical surroundings; breathe in for seven seconds and breathe out for ten; put my fingers on my pulse and wait for my heart rate to slow.

I open my eyes, and somehow, I'm already resigned to knowing she's still there.

You are dirty. You're disgusting.

This is because I'm cold turkey off my meds.

And there I was, just for a second, thinking I didn't need the tablets any more. How thoroughly disappointing.

I remember Felicity once telling me about 'insight'. Psychologically speaking, if you *know* you're crazy, you're certifiably less crazy on the Crazy Chart. And I *know* that I am not somehow inhabiting the TV set. What I also know is that there's something wrong with my brain. They haven't quite worked out what, but sometimes it makes me see and hear things which are not there.

There is no such thing as Other Alice.

Yes, there is, you utter fucking cunt.

'Oh, just fuck off!' I scream.

I push myself off the floor and stagger back to the kitchen. It won't contain her long, but right now I need to get away from the television.

I unlock and throw open the front door and scream, more in shock than anything.

She's on the garden path.

I close my eyes again, only to realise this is no psychotic episode.

It's not Other Alice, but a security guard stomping down the path towards me. He's one of Paisley's private team, wearing the red shirt and tie. Protein shake pecs strain against the buttons. He has an earpiece and walkie-talkie.

I consider running and decide against it.

Where would I run to?

And he'd catch me in a stride.

'Alice?'

I look sheepish. 'Yes.'

'Is this your accommodation?' His thin, reptilian lips are a tight line.

'No.'

'Can you come with me, please?'

'Do I have a choice?'

'No. Miss Hart wants to see you.'

XX

CROQUET RULES

It doesn't take very long to arrive at Gryphon Hall. My skin still feels like bubble wrap. The urge to pop, to cut, is there, as it often is when I encounter Other Alice. I try to push it all down into my feet. I can't deal with that and Paisley all at once.

The buggy crunches down the gravel driveway at the front of the property where it seems much of the backstage activity is based. Trucks, staging and catering vans are all parked up, somewhat ruining the Wonderland fantasy vibes.

We drive past all of them and around the side of the house. The hall itself is beautiful, gothic even, with its spires and turrets, but as Olivier said, it's bordering on dilapidated. It's strangled by ivy and climbing nettles, some windows are boarded up and there's scaffolding on one side of the property. Once upon a time, though, this must have been fit for a ... well.

On the back terraces, it looks as if brunch is winding down, which gives me some sense of time. If brunch was served at eleven, I suppose it must be around midday now. The top terrace, overlooking the garden, fairground, and river below, has been set out with about twenty circular tables, each with a crisp white tablecloth. Waiters weave in and out, clearing away the remains of eggs benedict from the looks of things.

My security guard, Bill, brings the cart to a halt on the

periphery of the terrace. 'Follow me.'

It's a beautiful day. The sky is deep blue with only sparse cotton-wool clouds. Some guests are still finishing their brunch, knocking back mimosas and bellinis. The costumes are gone and everyone's dressed in their usual preppy Chelsea uniform of summer dresses, blouses, chinos, shirts and shorts. Tory Youthwear. There's also a lot of very large sunglasses no doubt hiding some dark circles from last night.

And, at the top table, is Paisley and her inner circle: Royce and some of his rugby friends; the Flower Girls; and present St Agnes Head Girl Jocasta Whyte. I've always thought Jocasta, also the captain of the lacrosse team and head of Cullimore House, is a bit of a ninny.

'Ah, Alice.' Paisley looks over her sunglasses. 'Join us a while. Violet: take Piglette for a walk.'

Violet starts to complain, but Paisley silences her with a glance. I fill the seat Violet vacates. The pig happily trots away, dragging the rather sullen Violet along by a pink leash.

'Hi,' I start.

'Jocasta, have you met Alice Dodgson? She's in Upper One.'

Frankly, I'm surprised Paisley even knows who I am. We haven't had a class together since second-year Latin.

Jocasta, a statuesque Zimbabwean girl with immaculate box braids, shakes my hand. 'I don't think we've been introduced. How do you do?'

'I'm well, how are you?' I ask awkwardly. This is worse than if she'd screamed at me. Paisley sips ice water through a straw.

'Super,' Jocasta says. 'Paisley was just telling me all about her plans for St Agnes next year.'

I blink. As if school weren't bad enough. 'You're coming back to St Agnes?'

'Yes,' she states. 'I've had a wonderful year at Surval Montreaux, but I think it's time to come home.'

'To come home and be Head Girl?' Jocasta downs her champagne with one hand and swipes for the bottle with the other. Cullimore girls, the sporty lot, are notorious for drinking like fish. The lacrosse team, it is said, can drink the St Barney's rugby team under the table.

'I don't know what you mean,' Paisley says coyly.

Jocasta turns to her. 'Paisley! I see right through you! This whole brunch is an attempt to butter me up so I'll put in a good word with the Cullimore girls next year.'

I briefly picture Jocasta being liberally smeared with greasy yellow butter by a giant knife. The Head Girl election is a hugely political game of chess. Wenlock – Paisley's house – is the most exclusive and has all the royals and celebrity offspring. Except me; I opted for Blume, the artsy house. Head girls usually come from Wenlock, or Cullimore if the sports teams get behind a candidate. Every once in a while a more charismatic nerd from Highden or a more mainstream Blume loser might creep up the outside, but it's only happened once while I've been at St Agnes.

If Paisley is returning in September, she will, undoubtedly, be crowned. There's no one else in her stratosphere.

'We can discuss school another time,' Paisley says. 'Unfortunately we have some business to sort out, don't we?'

'Do we?' Jocasta asks.

'Yes. I'm afraid so. You see, Alice is a party crasher, Jocasta. She wasn't invited.'

159

Jocasta looks surprised and slightly disgusted. 'Oh.'

I'm going to have to beg, aren't I? It's not going to be dignified, is it? 'I'm sorry, I—'

'It's all terribly fascinating.' Paisley cuts me off. 'I can't fathom why a self-proclaimed misfit outsider would go to such great lengths to infiltrate the most exclusive party of the year. It makes me think she must have an ulterior motive of some sort.'

I close my eyes. 'Paisley … I came because—'

'She's with me.' A boom of a voice interrupts me. I open my eyes and see Maxim Hattersley limping towards our table on one crutch.

Paisley removes her sunglasses, her jaw tightening. 'I beg your pardon?'

'You are pardoned,' he says lightly. 'Alice came with me. I invited her. As my date.'

Why does he get a plus-one? Paisley rolls her eyes. 'Oh, do fuck off, Max.'

'It's true!' He slips a protective arm around my shoulder. 'She's the last girl at St Agnes I haven't rutted.'

A small laugh escapes my lips and I cover my mouth.

'While I can believe that, I doubt you'd be her type.' Paisley looks to me expectantly, awaiting a response.

'Oh … I don't know about that,' I say. 'I mean look at him … he's … prime sirloin beef, isn't he?'

And now Maxim laughs too. 'See?' The girl on the other side of Jocasta excuses herself and he plonks himself on the spare chair. 'She's mad horny for me.'

'Well, good luck, Alice,' Jocasta says sniffily. 'He's not beef, he's a pig, and I should know.' She tips her champagne over his head and strides away.

'I probably deserve that,' he says, the fizz dripping off his nose.

'Almost certainly,' Paisley says. 'If Alice is here as your plus one, why did she break into the Tweedles' lodgings?'

An excellent question.

'My fault!' Luckily Maxim interjects again. 'We got so fucked up last night, Pais. It was messy.'

'Mushrooms … and pills … and pot, oh my!' I add clumsily, trying to play along.

'I passed out, and when I woke up, Alice had gone. She must have wandered out of the yurt and got lost. I should have kept an eye on her.'

Ordinarily I'd argue that I don't need anyone to keep an eye on me, but his lie sort of works, and is barely even a lie when you think about it.

'I did. I had a bad trip …'

Violet returns, red-faced and out of breath, Piglette trotting along amiably behind her. Violet approaches her queen and whispers something in her ear.

'Oh, really?' Paisley says. I don't hear what Violet is muttering, but it's obviously juicy. 'Interesting. Thank you.'

Paisley stands to reveal a very cute red mini-dress with a pristine white collar and buttons. I look closely and, yes, the buttons have *Gucci* written on them. Today her hair has been straightened and it's so long it sits at her waist, held off her face by a pair of barrettes. 'It's time for the croquet tournament,' she says on the exhale. 'Alice, I apologise for my rudeness. Won't you and your *date* join us for a match?'

161

Whatever Violet said, it seems to be responsible for a fairly enormous three-sixty from Paisley. I'm going to quit, therefore, while I'm ahead and still have my head.

'You know what, I'm going to collect my things from Maxim's yurt and head home, I think. You're right … I shouldn't really be here and—'

Paisley holds up a hand to silence me. 'I won't hear of it. You're here now and there are no boats until tomorrow. You may as well enjoy yourself, Alice, dear.'

I hesitate. I didn't get invited to many parties when I was little – boys didn't want me at their birthdays – but I do know one must always be polite to the host, even if she's a viper. 'I … I don't know how to play croquet.'

'It's really very simple. Come along, I'll teach you.' She smiles sweetly and it's more than a little unnerving. I think I preferred it when she was openly hostile. I can't help but think of those tiny idiot birds who pluck bits of meat from the teeth of crocodiles on the banks of the Nile. They look like they're smiling too, but I'm not in a hurry to climb in.

Paisley and the Flower Girls lead the way. I look at Maxim and we both know we have no option but to do exactly as she says. I offer him a hand up.

'Thanks for that,' I say, confident we're out of earshot.

'For what?'

'For saving my neck.'

He shrugs. 'It's true. At least partially. After you ran off I spent some time searching in the woods, but man you can run fast and I have this thing stuck to my leg.' He nods down at the plastic boot.

Olivier, in a very cute nautical striped T-shirt with jaunty red neckerchief, runs over and falls into step alongside us. 'I want you to know zat I *didn't* look for you. I don't want you to sink I care.'

I laugh. 'Gee, thanks, Ol.'

'*De rien.*' He strides ahead of us towards the croquet garden.

It's a glorious morning, wood pigeons cooing away and the manor behind us shifting and cracking in the midday sun. Last night feels a whole lifetime ago, but I remind myself not to get too complacent. I can't help but think I just received a stay of execution, not a royal pardon.

My palms are sweaty and I wipe them on my shirt tails. I think the mania at the chalet is giving way to anxiety, which is the lesser of two evils. I just wish I could call Felix and let him know I'm OK. No boats ... no way out. The walls, even though there are none, are very much closing in. I'm in the open air and I cannot breathe.

There's a polite round of applause as Paisley and the Flower Girls descend to the lawn. I guess everyone really enjoys all the free narcotics.

Among the crowd, I spot Willie Zong smoking a joint with some Blume girls I recognise. 'Do you know how to play?' I ask Maxim as we pass an ornate sundial. I run my fingers over its brass face. The shadow confirms it's half twelve or thereabouts – if I'm reading it right.

'I think you just have to get the balls through the hoops. I dunno, I'm used to bigger balls. Oh, I mean *rugby* balls obviously, I didn't mean ...'

'I got it.' I grin. His face turns sunburn-pink.

'Let's play doubles!' Paisley announces. 'I'll be red and yellow with Olivier. Alice and Max, you be black and blue. You go first.'

'Oh, we don't actually know how to play ...' I say apologetically.

'It couldn't be more simple, Alice. You and Max have one ball each and you have to steer them through the hoops, in order, with your mallet. Easy peasy.'

Lily hands me a wooden mallet and sturdy blue leather ball, not unlike a cricket ball.

'OK.' I look at Maxim who can only shrug. I guess we're playing croquet. I set my ball down at the starting post. 'I'm aiming for that hoop?' There are six in total. Paisley nods.

I go to swing the mallet like a golf club until she stops me.

'Not like that, like this.' She models how to hold the mallet correctly. I do as I'm told and tap my ball. I hit it too gently and it stops far short of the first hoop.

'See? Nothing to it.' Paisley lines up her shot and, with little effort, the red ball taps into mine. 'Ah. Now that's what we call *roquet.*'

'Huh?'

She smiles. 'Now I take another shot, known as the *croquet* shot. Watch.' She sashays to the side of her ball and, looking me dead in the eye, wallops it *into* mine, sending the blue ball spinning to the very edge of the lawn.

'Harsh.' Lily sniggers.

'And that's croquet,' Paisley says. 'It's as much about taking out your opponents as it is getting through the hoops. The only way one can progress is by removing the competition from one's path.'

The subtext literally couldn't be clearer, but I'm not sure why I'm getting such a stark warning. I pose no threat to Paisley's little empire. I wonder if … I wonder if there was something between Paisley and Bunny? That's the only thing I can think of, but how on earth would Paisley know we'd spent the night together? Things seem simpler for the boys at St Barney's where, I've ascertained, if boys don't care for one another they simply pummel each other in the face or ignore each other entirely. With girls, there's the *Dance of the Niceties* and it's a dance I'm hopeless at. But heaven forbid a girl should appear uncouth, aggressive or difficult.

'Understood.' I smile sweetly.

'There she is!' A bark cuts across the lawn.

I turn and see the Tweedle brothers stomping across the garden towards us, accompanied by another red security guard. They point directly at me. 'That girl broke into our chalet!' Jeremy yells. I think I can tell them apart in the light of day: Jeremy is more dimply, Jonty has *slightly* more angular cheekbones. I could be wrong, but I'll go with that.

'Arrest her!' adds Jonty.

'And she's stolen my shirt!'

Paisley steps in front of me as they reach us. 'Hello, Jeremy, Jonty. It's lovely to see you again.' They stop to air kiss.

'Do you know her?' Jeremy asks, again jabbing a finger in my direction.

'Alice is a new friend.'

Jonty is rather red in the face. 'Well, did you know your *new friend* locked us out of the barn house in the middle of the night? We had to sleep in a *tent* like commoners!'

I'm fairly certain Paisley is disguising a smile with her delicate cough. 'Well, gosh, that's awful. On a normal day, I'd have Alice escorted from the site at once. However, given that you drugged Alice, one can only assume with an eye to sexually molesting her while she was unconscious, one can hardly blame her. Wouldn't you say?'

Oh, wow.

Both twins freeze for a second. 'It was him!' they say at the exact same moment, pointing at each other.

'So you don't deny it?' Paisley asks coolly. 'It's interesting. Weren't you at my opening ceremony yesterday afternoon? I thought I made my high regard for consent plain. Didn't you?'

The twins squirm.

'What did you give her?'

Neither twin says anything.

All in a flash, Paisley raises her mallet and smashes it down on Jonty's left foot. He's wearing docksiders, and howls in pain. He hops away, swear words echoing off the mansion behind us.

'Don't make me ask again,' Paisley says to Jeremy.

'Just a tiny bit of GHB,' he mutters. 'It was nothing, she'd have been fine. It was to help her relax, that's all, she was freaking out.'

Paisley swings again and now Jeremy screams.

'*That's all?* Did Alice expressly consent to taking GHB? Did she?' Neither twin answers – too busy cradling their left feet – so she rounds on me. 'Did you?'

'No. No, I had no idea.' I've never taken GHB. I know from Olivier it's the drug of choice for a certain type of gathering in Vauxhall but I've only heard of it as 'the date-rape drug' which doesn't exactly fill me with confidence. I recall Violet whispering something in Paisley's ear … is that how she knows what happened? I can't imagine either of the twins would be forthcoming, so that means Cat must have somehow informed Violet … or at least started the rumour mill turning.

'Admittedly I'm in no rush to invite the police to my party, but I think it's important justice is served, don't you, Alice?' Paisley rests her mallet on her shoulder.

'I … I … well, yes, I suppose so.'

'Paisley,' Maxim speaks up. 'Just call the cops when we get back to London. Let them deal with it.'

Paisley gives Maxim a look which conveys exactly what she thinks of that suggestion. 'Who's going first? Jeremy or Jonty?' she asks.

Both twins look suitably scared. I'd feel bad for them if only I didn't. 'Paisley! We weren't going to do anything!' they cry in unison.

'But you did. Do I have to repeat myself again?'

'Jonty!' Jeremy announces. 'It was Jonty's idea!'

'You shit!' Jonty pushes his brother.

Paisley gives her security guard a nod and he seizes Jonty, shoving him before her. 'Lie down.'

'What?'

'Is there a problem with my volume? Lie down, or I post what you did to Caterpillr.'

'You wouldn't?'

'Try me,' she says with a smile.

Jonty glowers at her, but does as he's told. He lies flat on his back, staring up at the sun.

'Alice,' Paisley says. 'It's your turn.'

'No … it's Maxim I think …'

Paisley shakes her head and picks up the remaining blue ball. She carefully places it on Jonty's crotch. 'Take your shot, Alice.'

'No way!' Jonty protests.

'Hold him down.' A pair of security guards pin Jonty down by his hands and feet. 'Alice?'

'But …' I can't. As angry as I am, and as fitting as the punishment seems, I can't swing a mallet at Jonty Tweedle's crown jewels. I'm not, and have never been the violent sort. Well, my indiscretion with Genie Nugent aside.

'Alice. Take your shot. Don't hold up the game.'

I look to Maxim and Olivier, but they avoid my gaze. Paisley smiles. The Flower Girls giggle amongst themselves.

I don't suppose I have to hit it particularly hard. I'm not going to apologise to the young man who most likely had designs on raping me. I step up to the side of his body.

'Be sure to hit it good and hard, Alice,' Paisley says.

I take the shot and, although Jonty squeals and flinches, it's actually a fairly square hit. The mallet makes contact with the ball and it flies off. It rolls over the lawn and comes to a rest against the first hoop. Not bad.

Maxim claps. 'Good shot!'

I look back and smile at Maxim but I see his face fall. I almost miss Paisley lunge forward and swing her mallet directly into his groin. Jonty howls in pain and curls up into a ball. It's a horrible, sickening noise, like a dog being kicked.

'Oh my …' I stumble back against Maxim's broad chest.

'If you want a job doing …' Paisley mutters.

'Fuck, Paisley!' Jeremy rushes to his brother's side.

'Choose your next sentence very carefully,' she says, jabbing him in the shoulder with the mallet.

I'm about to say something but Maxim takes hold of my wrist and pulls me back. This doesn't feel right. People often confuse being psychotic – or having psychosis – with being a psychopath. They are different things. *Psychosis* is seeing or hearing things that aren't really happening. A *psychopath* is someone with a personality disorder who struggles with empathy and lacks inhibitions. I do question if we're in the presence of one now.

'I'm sorry! I'm sorry,' Jeremy says, literally begging on his knees.

'You will be,' Paisley says. She sighs and lets the mallet fall to the lawn. 'Lily, Violet, Rose, let's see how quickly we can get the Tweedles cancelled online, shall we?' Her inner circle must be allowed phones, and they get to work.

'Paisley! Please!' Jeremy's face turns a sickly puce shade. For an influencer, it would have been kinder to slit his throat there and then.

'Willie?'

Willie Zong steps forward from the sidelines. He takes out his phone, from where I dread to think, and taps away for about five seconds. 'It's done.'

A Caterpillr just toppled an empire.

The twins look at each other, the awful truth sinking in: they are *cancelled*.

Paisley claps gaily. 'Wonderful. Let's get back to the game, shall we? What time is it?'

'One,' Lily says.

Instinctively, I look back and check the sundial. Sure enough, the shadow falls across one. Although, in this case, it isn't a one. For some reason, or possibly no reason at all, the clock has twenty-four hour numerals. The shadow lies on XIII. Thirteen o'clock.

When the clock strikes thirteen, it'll be off with her head.

My stomach drops like I'm plummeting from a very great height and for a second I feel weightless. Somehow, and I don't know how, I sense what's about to happen.

Now is the time.

Off with her head.

I wipe sweat from my top lip. I feel sick. I scan the garden: groups of lizard girls sunbathe, basking on the grassy slopes, sipping iced coffees or mimosas. Some people are still waking up, milling in and out of Gryphon Hall lazily after the heavy night. The funfair is operational down on the riverbank.

And yet I know she's here somewhere.

I look back to the hall. Even in the bright sunshine it looks mottled and grey, a tombstone against the sky.

And there she is.

On the first-floor terrace over the back door, I see Bunny's plume of hair almost glowing. She's wearing big black sunglasses and a grave expression on her face. With precision, she raises a long black shape. A hunting rifle. She rests it on the balustrade.

170

She leans in and looks into the scope. Oh my …

'Paisley!' I scream. The name almost catches in my glottis, but I spit it out. It's a horrid noise and everyone looks my way. 'Get down!'

Paisley's flawless face crinkles for the first time, genuinely confused. 'What?'

I throw myself into her as a snap cracks through the air. My chest crashes into her arms and I get an elbow in my stomach.

We fall to the lawn in a messy heap at the same moment a chunk of turf about a metre away is torn up. Maxim seems to realise what's happening and covers us both, his big arms enveloping us.

It's on the second shot – another miss – that people start screaming and running for cover.

'She's got a gun!' Willie yelps, clinging to Violet.

'Fuckeeng hell!' Olivier dives down and crawls behind a privet hedge. Maxim, Paisley and I scramble to join him, although I'm not entirely sure what a bush is going to do to save us from bullets.

I dare to look over the top of the hedge parapet. I stare directly up at Bunny. She pulls the shades down her nose, and looks in my direction. Her expression changes to one of surprise. I wonder if she's shocked to see me here. I wonder if she'll shoot at me. I wonder if she's lost the fucking plot. I knew she was a little kooky but … *cripes.*

I only see her for a second. She retracts the rifle and ducks back into Gryphon Hall.

'She's gone,' I say, collapsing against the bush. My heart feels to be beating in my throat. The thought that's she's stopped shooting because I'm here feels bubblegum-pink in my chest. Although that's probably not what I should be focussing on. I'm lucky to be alive.

The Flower Girls scurry over. 'Paisley? Are you all right?' Lily comes to her aid.

Paisley stands and dusts herself down. 'I'm fine.' She barks at her security team. 'Well? What are you doing? Get in there and find her for crying out loud!'

'Should I call the police now?' Rose asks.

'Did syphilis rot your brain?' Paisley glowers at her. 'If I see anyone touch a phone, I'll break the phone and then their fingers in that order. Is that clear?'

I help Maxim up – not an easy ask for a six-foot-four lump on crutches.

'Pais, come on … she's got a fucking bolt action rifle!' he says.

I finally realise the reality, or rather unreality, of the situation. This is not the real world. This is Wonderland. And Bunny – beyond all reason – has a fucking *gun*. We're not in Kansas any more, Toto. Or maybe we *are*, the USA has highly questionable gun laws.

Paisley ignores Maxim. 'Lily, Rose, Violet: spread the word the range is now open for clay pigeon shooting. People can head down all afternoon. Apologise for any alarm.'

The Flower Girls look uneasily to each other.

'Is the syphilis contagious?' she says, sneering. 'NOW!'

The three of them skulk off. My poor, befuddled brain tries to make sense of what's unravelling, but Paisley seems unfazed. She sidles up to me and plucks a privet leaf from my hair.

'Alice, darling. That act of selfless heroism has earned you a seat at my dinner table tonight.'

I'd rather sit next to a plague rat. 'I … I …'

'I insist. In fact, why don't you join me at six in the master bedroom and we'll beautify together and have a glass of champagne. I often think getting ready is better than going out, don't you?'

'I …'

'Good, then it's settled! Don't be late!'

'Paisley …' Maxim starts.

'Oh, Max, stop fussing, you're like an old woman. Far scarier people than Bunny Liddell have tried to kill me. It's really par for the course.' She gestures to the croquet lawn. 'Now! Whose turn was it?'

XXI

ALL TEA, ALL THE TIME

'Boats sail on the rivers,
And ships sail on the seas,
But the clouds that sail across the sky;
Are prettier far than these.'

'Is that yours?'

'Christina Rossetti,' I tell him, not bothering to look up. I lie in the bottom of the boat, looking up at the blue, blue sky.

'Is she from St Agnes?'

'No!' I chuckle to myself. Bless him.

Paisley and Olivier thoroughly thrashed us at croquet. Well, of course they did. With the exception of Paisley, everyone's nerves were shredded. We feared for our lives, and going through the motions was a ridiculous charade. I could hardly stop my hands from shaking. Paisley must be a cyborg, seemingly unbothered by the attempted assassination.

Again, I might need a minute for that to sink in. I just survived a live shooter situation. In leafy Berkshire of all places. That's where we are according to Maxim.

As for the shooter herself, well she has enough people looking for her now, she doesn't need me sticking my oar in. When Maxim asked me to afternoon tea at the boathouse on the other side of the island, I accepted the invitation without hesitation. It's not like I can get back to London; I need to collect my things from his yurt anyway, and it kills the time until my inevitable date with Paisley before dinner. Maxim assures me the waterway is both the fastest *and* most scenic route.

The river is picture-postcard beautiful. *For they were young, and the Thames was old, and this is the tale that River told.* Willows dangle over the riverbank and blossoms twirl through the air like confetti.

'Are you sure you're able to row?' I ask my boatman.

'There's nothing wrong with my arms,' Maxim says, and I can only agree, staring as his biceps strain against his shirt. He lowers his voice. 'And strictly between you and me, there's nothing wrong with my leg either.'

I get up and sit on the little bench of the rowboat. 'I beg your pardon?'

'Can you keep a secret?'

'I keep so many, I'm forgetting most of them.'

He shakes his head slightly and I sense he thinks I'm exasperating. 'My leg has been fine for a while now. Keeping the boot on just gives me a reason to hide away from the world.'

'Or at least rugby?' I say, pretending to peer through an imaginary magnifying glass.

'Bingo.'

'I get it,' I tell him. 'No one expects very much from me. My parents are delighted that I bother to turn up at school frankly. I can only imagine what it'd be like to be St Barnabas's star player.'

'It seems I didn't have much to offer beyond my rugby prowess. I feel invisible all of a sudden. I quite like it.'

I smile. 'The young ladies of St Agnes would beg to differ.'

'Yeah?'

'You are far from invisible, let me assure you.'

He winces a little. 'They think I'm a player?'

'Let's just say it's a good job you're not a girl, you'd be called much worse things than that,' I tell him. 'You know, it's a curious thing. It doesn't matter how many hearts you trample on, there's always a steady stream of girls lining up to be the next.' I twist a lock of hair around my finger, thinking about all those men on the apps who want to pin me down in anonymous Premier Inns. 'I sometimes wonder if we're all masochists and, deep down, curious to know what a shoeprint on a heart feels like. Pain has an allure. Some girls take scissors and razorblades to their skin and others simply choose terrible men.'

He makes an *oof* noise. 'Ouch. But fair. I deserve it.'

'I don't know about that,' I say. 'Do you promise these girls anything?'

'No, never. And I don't lie.'

'Then there are worse.'

His eyes dip, bashful.

While he steers us into dock, I look back at Gryphon Hall. Only the turrets are even partially visible through the treetops. The last I heard, following a very thorough sweep of the house, Bunny was nowhere to be seen. The house is enormous and Bunny is very tiny. There are a million nooks and crannies she could be hiding in.

I mean really, though. I knew Bunny was highly strung, but

this all seems a tad extreme. Anyone who met Paisley would want to fire a rifle at her, but that's neither here nor there. Whatever beef exists between them must be … considerably beefy.

As strangely affable as Maxim is, he's also my best shot at finding out what's going on. I can't help myself, I've always been nosy. I came here because of Bunny, but I'm starting to think I might be best off out of it. I guess I know she's at least alive now. She's armed … but alive. Our night in the hotel, my misty memories, feel trivial compared to whatever else it is she has going on. It feels like I've stumbled into the third act of someone else's melodrama. She's got bigger fish to fry. And there isn't a frying pan on earth that'll fit Paisley.

I want to go home now.

I do not belong here.

I'm discordant, as incongruous as a plastic bottle on the seabed.

Let's put my gender to one side and say I'd started St Agnes with any sort of desire to fit in, I'd have still been tainted by my 'made money' status. I'm a decade shy of poor. *Nouveau riche; a parvenu; a social climber.*

I am not of the same fortified blood as these people: Paisley and Royce; Maxim; Bunny; they're all cut from the same platinum cloth. They, and their fathers, and their fathers' fathers, ad infinitum, were born into vast wealth. Money beyond numbers, money beyond actual money. This fantasia is all they have ever known. To them, the extraordinary is ordinary.

Contrary to tabloid belief, I don't think my transition makes me very interesting. I'm neither unicorn nor mermaid. Just an unlucky girl whose mother got lucky. I, and others like me, are day tourists. We have a temporary queue-jump just so long as the money lasts. And on the day it runs out, our surnames don't provide a safety net, and we, like that poor woman in Shoreditch, kiss the pavement.

The river widens out, forming a lagoon. The boathouse and terrace are Mary Poppins quaint, a jetty running around the lip to dock rowboats. Swans, geese and ducks hover at the edges, hoping for scraps and crumbs.

Maxim rows us in and then a helper hooks us with a crook, and tethers the boat.

'Let me help you, sir.' The boy in the boiler suit, not much older than us, offers Maxim a hand, and I give the malingering scrum-half a glare. He at least has the decency to blush as he clambers onto the walkway.

Maxim, in turn, helps me out of the boat. Shameful for a feminist to admit but accepting his paw-hand does affirm my femininity.

'Thank you,' I coo, and hate myself at once.

'You're welcome. Now, would you care to join me for afternoon tea?'

'I'd be delighted.'

Taking my arm, he leads me to the tearoom in the boathouse. I recognise some current St Agnes girls and notable alumni: Genie Nugent, Nevada Charles. The *real* Sailor Birling is having lunch with Arabella Campbell-True. Heads turn to get a good gander at the latest girl on Maxim Hattersley's arm. I feel oddly proud. A guilty pride, but pride nonetheless. Is this what it feels like to win at Being A Girl?

Each dainty al-fresco table is shaded by a pink and eggshell-blue parasol and it all feels very Regency. Timeless and elegant. I like it, but I feel very underdressed in the stolen Tweedle ensemble. Less Mary Poppins, more Eliza Doolittle.

We find a vacant table and a young waitress takes our order. We're about the same age and I bet she attends a local school or college. I scan her face, hoping to send some sort of psychic message: *I'm a pleb too, I'm still human.* I search for a glimmer of recognition from her, but she won't meet my gaze. To her, I must look like one of those awful East London art school types, designer-slumming it, with an enormous trust fund. And aren't I? Maxim orders tea for two and she rushes off.

A couple of tables away, I see a very tall, very thin, very beautiful black girl, her face partially occluded by some comically large Dior sunglasses.

'Don't make it obvious,' I tell Maxim, 'but I think that's Clara Keys.'

'Really?' He pretends to yawn and looks over his shoulder. 'Yep, that's her.'

I try to listen in to her conversation. The supermodel is having afternoon tea with a flamboyant (a lazy euphemism for gay, but I don't like to make assumptions) Irish man.

This is the maddest thing. I cut a picture of this woman out of *Vogue* and stuck it into my Art sketchbook, and she's *on the next table*! I could reach out and poke her! She's flesh and blood! I lean in, trying to play it cool. 'But why is *she* here?'

'It's Wonderland,' Maxim says, as if it were obvious. 'Who isn't here?'

'She's iconic! Can I tell her I'm a fan?'

'Not if you don't want me to run and hide. Be cool.'

'Maxim. I have bad news. I'm *really* not cool.'

He beams a little. 'Ah, I dunno. I think you're pretty cool.'

I feel my cheeks burn. As we wait for our food to arrive, we talk idly about our very different lives at St Barnabas and St Agnes.

'What *did* happen to your leg?' I ask. 'Really? I've heard about twelve versions.'

'Such as?'

'Drunk driving? You pissed off the wrong boyfriend or brother? Paisley took a croquet mallet to it? OK, I made that last one up myself.'

He shakes his head. 'Nothing so dramatic. I fell in a ditch outside the pub when I was staggering home in Esher, sozzled.'

'Oh.'

'But you see I was on my last warning – both at school and at Harlequins. I've been dropped.' If he's aiming to be insouciant, he just missed. The last word is overstuffed with failure. 'Harlequins let me go.'

'But …' It doesn't need saying. If *I* knew that was supposed to be his future, so did he.

'I'm a liability!' he says jovially, painting over the hurt in the same pastel hues as the parasol.

'I'm sure you're not … there must be …'

The waitress arrives with a three-tier tray of afternoon delights. The top tier holds powder-pink macarons and petits fours; the second scones, jam and clotted cream; and the third has genteel finger sandwiches filled with a choice of ham, salmon or egg.

'You're not a liability,' I tell Maxim once the waitress has gone.

I help myself to an egg sandwich and I don't even care if it pongs.

'Aren't I?' He laughs. 'I had some orange juice last week and I thought it had gone off because it tasted so strange. Turns out, it just didn't have any vodka in it.' He reaches into his blazer pocket and produces a hip flask. He pours some whiskey into his tea. 'Let's make it Irish. It's after midday, after all.'

'Somewhere in the world, it's always after midday,' I say.

'I like your thinking.'

I tilt my head. 'Do you need an intervention? Shall we pull a Lexi Volkov on you?'

He laughs again. This time louder.

'What?'

'Well, that's how all of this started.'

I stir a spoonful of pink sugar crystals into my china cup. The spoon tinkles against the sides. Terrible etiquette. 'I don't understand.'

'Bunny.'

I swear to goodness, my heart stops, just for a second, before clunking onward. 'What about her?'

Maxim rams an entire ham sandwich into his mouth. 'Do you remember Antonella Hemmings?'

'Of course.' The poor girl was practically canonised after her death. We've all sat on that memorial bench at some point. It has pride of place at the centre of the Green under the sycamore tree.

'Well,' Maxim says. 'We killed her.'

XXII

SOMEONE ELSE'S FLASHBACK

'Antonella was the girl I pictured when I first ever masturbated. I'd have been eleven or twelve, and she was two years above. I remember seeing her for the first time, leading prayers in chapel, and I thought she was the most gorgeous girl I'd ever seen. That long black hair; olive skin; her lips; her eyes. I always did have a thing for that one from *High School Musical*, I guess. Antonella stood in front of the stained-glass window with her prayer book, and it was a religious experience. She was a goddess. She was Aphrodite. I was in love.

I plucked up the courage to ask her out when I was thirteen. It was the week before Xenia Blenheim's deb ball and I asked if she'd be my date one afternoon on the Green. She was sitting with Lexi. You know those two, they were pretty much inseparable. At first she laughed, but her smile dropped when she saw I was serious.

"Oh, I'm sorry! I thought you were … like, doing a dare or something."

"So, will you?"

"God, no!" Lexi chimed in on her behalf. "Dream on, Pooh!"

I didn't look like this then. Puberty hadn't fully kicked in and I was just a tubby ginger kid with freckles. And Lexi was right, I looked like Winnie-the-Pooh. Antonella slapped Lexi's hand.

"Maxim. You are so sweet. But I can't go out with a Lower

Three. It'd be like paedophilia or something."

"Of course," Lexi said with a laugh, "it's totally fine when *we* date older guys."

"That's different!" Antonella hit her again. "I'm sorry, Maxim. But you're very cute for asking. I won't tell anyone."

"I will," Lexi said.

And she did.

A year or so later and I looked very different indeed. My stock was on the rise. It was Florentine Hervey-Lenk's Sweet Sixteen at some bar on Clapham High Street. It was sick, totally off the chain. I don't know how, but we got hold of a load of champagne and stuff. I think that was the first time I did coke, actually. And there were girls, mostly girls in fact.

Antonella was there, and she was crying outside in the doorway of a closed charity shop. I was trying to look hard by having a cigarette when I saw her. Clapham High Street is pretty feral at night, I didn't think she should be alone.

"Antonella?"

She looked up at me and wiped her eyes with her palms. "Oh, hello, Maxim."

"What's wrong?"

"Nothing. Nothing, I'm fine."

I pointed back at the bar. It was vibrating with bass and lust, everything tacky from Jägerbomb fingers. "Do you want me to go find Lexi?"

She shook her head. "She already left." She was wearing one of those tiny *Love Island* dresses that's barely there. I could see her nipples through the sheer fabric. It was awesome. "Take a seat, Max."

I squished up next to her on the step. "Sure you're OK?"

"I will be. Maxim, I'm going to give you some advice: *never* date an actor! Their grip on reality is tenuous at best."

I laughed. "Got it! Which one?"

"Does it matter?"

"Want me to beat him up?"

"A kind offer, but I'll pass. I don't doubt you could though." She gave my bicep a squeeze. "I can't believe I'm about to say this but: have you been working out?"

I could feel my cheeks going beetroot-red. "Just a bit. Every day. Twice a day sometimes."

"Well, I can tell. You look *mad buff, bra.*" She smiled and I felt it right in my middles.

There was a moment of silence. I sensed, and I was right, that this was my chance. If I let it slip away, there might not be another one. "He must be a total dickhead to treat you like this."

She rolled her eyes. "And why's that?"

"Because you're the most beautiful girl at St Agnes. The most beautiful girl at any school."

She groaned a little but looked up into my eyes. "Is that your play, Maxim? Swoop in when I'm feeling dumped and vulnerable?"

"No. I don't have any 'play'."

She smiled kindly. "You have more than you think." She cupped my cheek in her hand and kissed me on the lips. I was in shock for a second. I'd spent so much time thinking about kissing Antonella Hemmings, but never actually about what I'd do if it happened. It was like kissing any other girl, but not daring to breathe in case I blew it away. It almost hurt in my chest. Not to mention the fact my erection was about to rip my trousers at the seams. "You're a good kisser," she said. "But don't tell anyone we did that."

"I won't."

"Maxim Hattersley?" she asked.

"What?"

"You wanna get some fried chicken?"

And so we did. We went down to the KFC next to the gay club, and had Zinger Tower Burgers and Diet Cokes.

After that? She kept me in a holding pattern for the next year. The rules were never formally set out, but we didn't talk at school and I only saw her when it suited her. Her father was an envoy or ambassador or something, and they had this astonishing house near Regent's Park, not far from the zoo. When her parents were out or away, she'd have me over. I board at school, so it was just easier that way, I suppose.

For me, it was a big deal, but I mostly think I was there to stop her being lonely. Lexi had started seeing that douchebag Kurt Blakeney and I think she felt a bit cast aside. Girls are weird. I'd go over and she'd be in a big, saggy T-shirt or sweatpants. Her hair would always be up in a topknot; no make-up on. I thought it was nice she felt so relaxed around me. Of course, I see *now* that she just didn't feel the need to make an effort. I wasn't worth it.

"Are you fucking anyone else?" she once asked after we'd had sex in her parents' bed. She wanted to try anal to see if it hurt. I only got it like halfway in and she said we needed ... what? Why, isn't it relevant? OK, I guess you're right.

Anyway. Afterwards, she sat up, naked, to smoke a fat blunt

she'd just rolled. Her parents were never there, they'd never know. The pot smell would be long gone by the time they returned.

So she asked if I was seeing anyone else and I said I wasn't.

"You should," she replied. "I am."

"What?"

"Max. You're fifteen. I'm sixteen. I hardly think we're going to get married, do you? It freaks me out when people our age play at Mr and Mrs. It's like watching toddlers stomp around in heels and pearls."

"But ..."

"But nothing!" She held the joint to my lips and I sucked on it obligingly. "Max, you're a massive ride. Go out there and sow your wild oats or whatever. Don't wait for me. It might never happen."

I sometimes wonder if she knew. Like, she was going to be one of those 'Candle in the Wind', 27-Club types. Burn bright and fizzle fast, like that joint.

Anyway. As ever, I did as I was told and started putting it about in the hope she'd get jealous and change her mind. Around the same time, Royce, Paisley and Bunny came up with this business idea: to start a club night to end all club nights. It makes sense, right? Clubs and bars and parties in Mayfair or Chelsea were literally paying us to go to their piece-of-shit nights and post about them on socials anyway. Why not cut out the middleman?

I joined the venture; I quite liked the idea of being an entrepreneur. We were too young to run a venue, but we could plan the parties and guarantee a solid gold guest list which meant the bottom feeders would pay whatever we wanted. It was genius. And it worked: Wonderland I was just at Annabel's, obviously. Wonderland II was more ambitious and we took over a disused part of the London Underground. Wonderland III was at an abandoned mosque in Catford. We got Apollo to guest DJ.

It was the biggest party yet. It wasn't our best – it was a little out of control and we couldn't keep gatecrashers out like we wanted to.

You know the rest.

I saw her that night, yeah. She was already pilling off her tits when we ran into each other. She was covered in sweat and glitter. Her pupils were like fucking golf holes. She put her hands around the back of my neck and kissed me, hard and tonguey.

"Aren't you worried someone will see?"

"No," she said. "I love you."

"That's the pill talking."

"No, I do." She put her index finger to my mouth. "I just don't tell anyone. But I do. One day, one day it'll be our time, Max. After the adventures … after all the adventures we'll find each other again and that's when it'll be time. You're Endgame." She kissed me again. She smiled sleepily over her shoulder and vanished into the crowd, like she was sinking into human quicksand.

I lost her and then … well, I heard the sirens and saw blue lights, but just thought it was the police breaking up the party. It was …'

XXIII

AND THAT'S THE TEA

'It was the ambulance. The police only came later.'

We've scarcely touched the mountain of cakes in front of us. My stomach is a tight figure eight.

'Oh, Maxim. I'm so sorry. I had no idea.'

'No one did. No one does.'

'But ... you didn't ... you didn't *kill* her.'

'We made Wonderland.'

'You knew Antonella a lot better than I did. Did she seem like the type of girl who did things she didn't want to do?'

He shakes his head slowly. 'No.'

'You know sometimes girls have to pretend to be a lot sweeter and more innocent than we really are. The world wants cupcakes.'

He feigns a smile, but he's run aground in memories now. A shout-out to all those lovers and mistresses invisibly mourning the loss of their clandestine paramours.

'What's the etiquette when one loses a secret girlfriend?'

'She wasn't my ...'

'Maxim ...' I say gently.

He shrugs. 'I thought it advisable to get thoroughly cunted, and I'm not sure I ever really sobered up to be honest with you, Alice. When I'm not drunk ... I just remember she's gone.' For the first time a tear runs down his broken nose. 'Oh god. I'm a hot mess.'

'It's OK.'

'She's gone. She's fuckin' dead. And the last thing she sent me was a picture of her tits. How? How can that be all I have of her? I'm waiting for her next message and it never comes. I can't … I can't get her out of my head. I feel like I'm losing my fucking mind. Is that what it is? Have I gone mad?'

I take his mighty hand over the table in both of mine. 'I'm afraid so. You're entirely bonkers. But I'll tell you a secret … all the best people are.'

He laughs and some snot shoots out of his right nostril. He catches it with a napkin. 'Jesus, I'm fucked. You know my father is threatening to send me to Sandhurst?'

'The *army*?'

'He thinks it'll straighten me out.'

Maybe it will, or maybe it'll finish him off.

'I know I was kidding before, but Maxim, your family has limitless money. What about a stint at the Clarity Centre? Worked for Lexi, or so they say.'

He shakes his head. 'No. I can't. There's a lot going on in London at the mo.'

I pour us a fresh cup of tea. 'Is it something to do with Bunny?'

This time he nods. 'Someone told the police that Paisley supplied Antonella with the drugs that killed her.'

'Did she?'

'Fuck knows! Alice, there must have been about fifty people dealing that night. It was a huge party. It was all covered up, naturally, and Paisley was sent to Switzerland while it died down. But *someone* told the police, and Paisley thinks it was Bunny.'

'Why would Bunny do that?'

'Fuck knows that either! Why would Bunny do anything Bunny does?'

And finally it all makes sense. I see the sequence in my head: Bunny getting the invite to Wonderland IV in her pigeonhole, and knowing it could only mean one thing: Paisley was back in London and back in business. Paisley must have then summoned her on the night of the funfair. I intercepted her outside the ghost train and she decided to hide in the hotel with me instead of facing her nemesis. I guess, at some point in the night, Bunny must have decided the best course of action was to actually kill Paisley dead.

'Eat or be eaten.' I pluck a mermaid-green macaron off the top tier, and take a bite.

'What?'

'I really think Bunny thought Paisley was going to kill her so she's going to try to beat her to the punch. *Did* Bunny report her?'

Maxim shrugs. 'Paisley seems to think so. It wasn't me, and it wasn't Royce, that's for sure, I doubt he'd know to dial 999 to be honest.' His forehead wrinkles. 'But, wait, how do you know what Bunny was thinking?'

My mouth hangs open. 'Um ... Bunny ...'

His eyes light up. 'Oooooh, I see! Did you fuck with her?' I must flinch. 'Don't worry. We know all about her *slumber parties.*'

Now I feel my eyes sting. 'I saw her the night she disappeared. She was so scared.'

He shakes his head. 'No, no, no! Don't be taken in by Bunny Liddell. You said it yourself: she's not nearly as sweet and innocent as she looks ... or did you miss her using us as target practice earlier?'

I say nothing.

'It's an act, Alice. Bunny's been batting her eyelashes and getting her own way for eighteen years. She's manipulative. She makes people think she's some helpless little waif and turns them into weapons. I've seen it happen time and time again.'

Why is he taking a flamethrower to that night? He's shitting on my perfect white night of perfectness.

'No. That's not what it was.'

'Wasn't it? You're here, aren't you? Because of her.'

'She couldn't know I'd find her invitation. No way.' Anger starts to bubble up in my stomach. He doesn't know what the night in the hotel was like. You can't fake what I felt and Bunny isn't that good an actress. 'I came because I wanted to help.'

'Why? You hardly know her.'

I don't have a reason. 'What you said last night ... about science and magic.' I sigh and throw my hands up. 'It's not sensible, or logical. It felt like ... the right thing to do.'

Maxim considers me. 'You're too good for all this. Sorry you fell headfirst into our slurry pit.'

'Well. I'm here now.'

Maxim pours me the last of the tea from the pot. 'That's why I saved your ass at brunch. I felt bad. Bunny slid into my DMs and told me she was coming. I promised I wouldn't tell Paisley, and told her to meet us in the yurt last night. I thought I might be able to smooth things over.'

'So I *did* fucking see her?'

'You did. And you freaked the fuck out and ran for the hills before I could explain. My guess is Bunny heard a girl's voice in the yurt and thought you were Paisley.'

'Jesus, Maxim, I thought I was having … I thought I was seeing things.'

'I'm sorry. I did try to stop you … but I was too fucked.'

Inquisitive little birds – blue tits and sparrows – hop around by our feet, pecking up crumbs and then retreating to the safety of the trees.

'So … what now?'

Maxim downs his tea. In his mammoth hand, the cup looks like something from a child's tea set. '*We* do nothing. I'm officially out. We leave Paisley and Bunny to their feud and get absolutely mashed at the closing party tonight.'

I frown. 'What? Even if that means them killing one another?'

'Lexi, Antonella, Paisley, Bunny. If I've learned one thing about London, it's that there's no shortage of beautiful psychopaths ready to knife each other in the back at a moment's notice. It's the circle of life.'

XXIV

I JUST HAD SEX WITH
MAXIM HATTERSLEY

And very nice it was too.

I might need a minute to compose myself.

I'm flat on my back, with Maxim's head nestled on my shoulder. His breathing is deep and rhythmic, and I assume he's fallen asleep.

The luxury tent smells of me and him and cum, which – on reflection – smells a bit like hair dye. Rain pitter-patters like pins on the canopy overhead and I'm very grateful to be inside, and under the duvet. Our clothes and his boot thing are scattered over the floor, stepping stones to the bed. I'm dying for a glass of water but I don't have the heart to move him.

OK. I'm ready.

Let's wind it all back.

XXV

SEX ITSELF

'I think it's going to rain,' Maxim says as we stroll back towards the house through the forest. There's a woodland path to follow and, by day, it's much less baffling than it was last night. It's rather beautiful, in fact; all the greens, all twinkling.

In the distance, I can hear the bass coming from the main stage at the fairground. According to Maxim, The Eaglets are headlining this afternoon's entertainment. I'm not a fan of faux-folk-festival anthems, but I know enough to know they performed at Glastonbury last year. I have no idea how much Paisley must have paid them to do the secret gig at Wonderland.

I look up to the sky. Burly bruisers, wide-boy clouds are rolling in fast across the blue. It's so warm though. Muggy enough for some thunder and lightning. I do so love a storm … when I'm not caught in it.

'What will you do now?' I ask.

He's still hobbling on his crutches, keeping up the ruse. I suppose he'll have to phase them out gradually or else it'll look like some Tiny Tim miracle has befallen him overnight.

'I think the old hangover's kicking in. I might need to have a little disco nap before … well, the disco tonight.'

'Oh yes, I forgot the disco. What are you wearing?'

'I have velvet flares.'

'Are you serious?'

'As serious as velvet flares can ever be, yes.'

'I hope Paisley has something I can borrow.'

'Are you heading to the house now?'

It's only a little after four. 'Not unless I have to. I'll come to your yurt and collect my things if that's OK?'

'Oh sure. I'm probably just going to sleep to be fair, but you can stay and chill.'

'As in *Netflix and Chill*?' It's laced with suggestion. I mean it too, although I'm mostly bluffing. I'm stone-cold sober but that night with Bunny ... I think it's flipped a switch. It's been over a week, and although I've thought about it and touched myself rotten, I want to feel the feelings again. I keep in mind Bunny's reaction to my ... self. She didn't seem to care. Was it a fluke? A one-off? Is that partly why I'm so keen to find her? What if everyone else is repulsed by me? Is she my one shot at love? And what about the Tweedles last night? Was that the MDMA talking? God, so many questions, I honestly tire of myself.

I remember again what Paisley said yesterday: *Submit to your wildest fantasies. Test your limits. Enjoy the flesh, give in to carnal desires.* And then I hear another voice, weirdly, that of my mother: *Alice! Get out there! Live a little! Try new things!* What could be more novel than a fuck with Maxim Hattersley? Before yesterday, I'd have been scared to even talk to him, and now here we are like old friends, ambling through the sun-dappled woods.

I am hungry. And it's not a hunger I can eat my way out of.

I slam on the brakes. He's Maxim Hattersley, prime sirloin, and I'm Alice: offal.

'Well, I don't suppose we *have* to sleep …?' he says, his tone curving at the tail into a question.

I stop dead in my tracks. He wasn't supposed to call my bluff. 'What?'

'What could be more companionable than a nap?'

Neither Olivier nor Dormouse are in the yurt. I imagine they're at the concert. We arrive as the first thick droplets of rain spatter against the ceiling.

'Just in time,' Maxim says. 'It's, um, this way.'

There are two 'bedrooms' as it were: little antechambers off the main tent, isolated by a curtain which is presently pinned to one side. Inside, I'm surprised to find a low, Japanese-style bed with a crisp white duvet and a lamp on the bedside table.

'Well, I'm not sure this has any right to call itself camping really,' I say. 'I've been in worse chain hotels.'

'You sure you wanna do this?' Maxim asks. 'After what the twins did?'

I hover at the threshold like a bad smell. 'Um, yeah. It's … it's just …'

He plonks his behind on the bed, and manspreads. Wish I didn't find the overtly masculine display arousing, but there's a kick inside. *Horny*, the lesser-known eighth dwarf.

'It's just what?'

'I … there's something … I …'

'Is this the whole trans thing?'

My mouth hangs open. 'Oh.' I gather my wits. 'So *everyone* knows, then?'

He grins lopsidedly. 'Sorry. Was it meant to be a big plot twist?'

'No,' I mutter. 'I just didn't want people … to think I was a freak. I just wanted to be a normal girl.'

He shrugs. 'What makes *normal girls* normal?'

'Well, their plumbing for one.'

'Are you saying girls are just walking vaginas with arms and legs?'

'No!' I yell a lot more loudly than I intend to. 'That's not what I'm saying at all.' I'm getting fired up now. I didn't realise my own head was such a minefield. 'You know, girls like me get killed for who we are.' But then I think that *all* girls get killed for who we are and another mine blows off another leg.

'I'm not going to hurt you,' he says. 'But I gotta say, I think about trans girls sometimes. I've seen videos and …'

I stifle a laugh. 'If you're expecting a pornstar, you're going to be sorely disappointed.'

He holds his hands up. 'I'm not. Alice … do you see yourself? You're beautiful and so …'

I groan. 'Please don't say *exotic*.'

'I was going to say *interesting*, but I thought it sounded like baloney. You're not the *average* St Agnes girl, mind you. They're normally a lot more prim, much keener to impress.'

'I don't know about that.' I shake my head, aware I'm probably talking my way out of some perfectly good sex. 'I'm sure that we all think *we're not like the other girls*, but there's nothing wrong with being a girl, and there are infinite ways to be one.' He looks a little hurt. 'But I'll take beautiful,' I concede. 'Beautiful on my terms, I think.'

He holds out a hand and pulls me gently towards the bed. I think he's about to kiss me, he leans in. I wait for it. I feel his warm breath on my mouth.

'What about Bunny?' he whispers.

'What about Antonella?'

'I think she's less likely to mind, given that she died a year ago.'

'I don't know.' I reach up and run my hands into his gingery hair. Even that feels taboo. 'I just ... I'm just curious. I wonder what it'll be like.'

This time he does kiss me. His jaw is rough, stubbly. It's an entirely different sport to kissing Bunny, or anyone I've kissed before.

'There are worse reasons, I suppose,' he says with a smile.

I like, and know best, the world of words and ideas, but I'm becoming increasingly fond of the sensual world. Any child can tell you about sight, sound, touch, taste and smell, less perhaps how to harness those five senses. It's funny, I think, how Bunny and Maxim are so different and yet with both of them those five things have unlocked a sixth sense: want, a specific want: desire. A magnet that lives in my middle. The one that pulls me this way and that.

I watch Maxim undress. He pulls his rugby jersey over his head. His body is muscular, strong, covered in a smattering of freckles. He's rough and hard in all the ways that Bunny was soft and curvy. He's block capitals, she's cursive script.

My fingers trembling, I unbutton the stolen shirt.

'Let me help you,' he says. He runs a hand over my breasts.

'They're so little ...' I say.

'I like them.' He traces my nipples with his thumbs.

There was a time when I'd have rather died than be naked in front of another, but the night with Bunny made me believe my body might not be a total horror show. I see his eyes linger on my breasts. It seems my visuals are working for him too.

I know what boys like *and* I know what girls like. What canny skills to possess! I'm strangely proud of myself as I reach out and rub him through his boxer shorts. Crikey, his ample size goes some way to explaining how he became the stuff of legend.

He goes to undo my shorts.

'Wait,' I say.

'Alice, I don't care.'

Well, I fucking do.

And I think that's probably a lie. He'll either be disgusted or aroused, but I find indifferent hard to buy. In Mother's room there's an antique chaise longue she refuses to sell despite the fact it clashes with the rest of the much more modern furniture. There's nothing *wrong* with the chaise, it simply doesn't *match*. That's pretty much how I feel about my body.

Well, if it's to happen I'd rather do it myself. I let the shorts and briefs drop to my ankles. I stand before him, offering up my cursed body like some sort of curio. Oh god, I want to run away. I want to cut myself. I can't look at him.

'Still just seeing "girl" to be honest,' he says. 'I don't know what I was expecting. I … I thought it'd be … more different.'

'Thank you.' What else can I say?

'Now are you gonna come here or not?'

I sit beside him and he takes hold of my face to kiss me

again. I need to get out of my head and occupy my body. I was not 'born in the wrong body'. I was – for better or mostly worse – born in *this* body. And it's alive.

He rolls onto me, dwarfing me. How strange that that should arouse me. Right now, I have what I guess I need; I want to feel small and feminine. The contrast between our bodies excites me. I want him to fuck me, to be inside me.

Why do I want that? It's so animal. I suppose we are. Pure savages and carnivores. Mammalian.

We kiss and he lowers his weight down on me. I lie back on clouds of cool white linen. I like it. I like how he feels on me. A good squash. It's like I'm sinking, sinking into the bed.

I loop my hands around the back of his thick neck and pull him as close as we can possibly get.

The whole world seems to tip.

And it does.

It feels like falling.

XXVI

DADDY ISSUES

I doze off a while and when I wake up, I feel refreshed, recharged. Maxim is still sleeping, splayed out greedily across the bed, pushing me to the very edge. I roll over. He is adorable. I am also a little sore, despite stealing some Liquid Silk from Olivier's luggage. That was very quick thinking on Maxim's part.

His profile looks like some Roman statue, carved in marble. Goddammit. Could I please just enjoy sex with someone without instantly falling in love?

While I know it's the oxytocin hangover, a peptide hormone flooding my poor brain, that knowledge doesn't render it any less potent. Love *is* a drug, and right now I'm very, very high on it. Already I want to do it again with him. He's so handsome as he sleeps, so male. I fight the urge to lick his exposed armpit.

Images take shape in my mind. Hope is a drug too, a dangerous one. It's compelled a great many to do some outrageously stupid things, doomed to failure. Could I become the sort of girl Maxim would court? I see myself with hair like my sister's, sans nose ring and eyeliner. I'm wearing a Burberry trench coat and scarf, walking through Hyde Park with Maxim. We're hand in hand. Would he take me to Henley Regatta to meet his parents? Would I use the correct fork? I'm no Antonella Hemmings, even if her public and private faces were very different. Would he proudly tell his parents he has a transgender girlfriend?

Well, that's the holy fucking grail, isn't it? Oh, I follow every last transgender celebrity on social media, brushing at the crumbs of their lives like an archaeologist, digging for clues they have *normal* relationships with *normal* people. Partners who'll pose for pictures, not just send decapitated dick pics. Any trace of evidence that there's a place for me in the future.

And now *our* future – mine and Maxim's – keeps unspooling at a hundred miles an hour: pop off to Durham or Edinburgh for three years; get The Op …?

(Side note: Maybe I don't *need* to … neither Bunny nor Maxim seemed to care. Factor in Henry, and I'm three-for-three on sexual bedfellows who liked my body just the way it is. So it really is whether or not I *want* to.)

Let's say I do, then get a nice job on a charity board, or an internship at a publishing house, until it's time to pop out the next generation of Hattersleys, and package them for St Barney's or St Agnes. OK, I can't give him genetic babies, but a little clan of ginger adopted ones could be so cute! But would I want to?

No. No, I don't want that. That's not who I am.

I didn't wait so long, and work so hard to be Alice, only to throw it all away on becoming Mrs Maxim Hattersley.

As if he'd want you.

Oh, not now, head. Can't I have one fucking hour to myself?

That life isn't for you.

You don't deserve it.

She's probably right.

I know, the sweet turning sour rapidly, that he's gonna end up with some honey-blonde pony-woman called Hermione or Persephone. Someone who won't cause any trouble. Someone his mum approves of; someone who'll provide heirs to carry on the Hattersley name in accordance with his dad's wishes; someone who doesn't rely on two pills a day to keep her from going under a train.

I look at him and my heart aches. Other Alice is right. Normal love is for normal people.

I'm crying. A tear rolls down my cheek because the fantasy is lovely and I can't have it. I'm stuck outside on the rainy kerb, window-shopping.

I gasp. My father, my biological father, is standing at the end of the bed, watching us. I look at Maxim, and he's still zonked out cold. I turn back and he's still there, exactly as he was on the one day I met him.

I know this isn't real.

But I shiver.

I screw my eyes shut. Felicity time again. Count to ten; breathe in for seven seconds and then out for nine; feel my pulse.

I open my eyes and he's still there.

It's not real.

He looks real. I could reach out and touch the rough, blue-grey jaw, the bulbous red nose and greasy, thinning hair. I can almost smell the BO, the dirty grandad shirt and denim jacket. Again, senses can be a tricksy thing. Not entirely trustworthy.

I'm sweating. Maxim can't see me like this. I have to go at once.

I slip out from under the covers, taking care not to disturb him. I step over a discarded condom, and tiptoe around my father, so statue-still. I locate my shorts and shirt at the foot of the bed. I cannot wait to be rid of these clothes.

I dress as quietly as I can. Before I leave the bedroom, I stand in front of my father. It's like the memory is being projected out of my head and into the room. Why now? What is it about what I've just done that's conjured such a frightful vision?

Daddy's girl.

I've got to get out of here. Tipping my head upside-down, I read Maxim's Rolex: it's ten past five. Near enough time for my date with Paisley. I listen and the rain seems to have stopped. The storm is over for now.

I step out of the yurt to be greeted by *that* life-affirming soil-after-rain odour. The wild garlic is truly wild, it hits me like a wave. Drips run from the leaves onto my head, but I like it, makes me feel like I'm *here*. I don't always. Sometimes I feel I'm in my own dimension, wading through time, lagging a second behind the normal people.

I get away from the tent, from the apparition of my father, as fast as I can. It seems fitting I'm disgusted at my own flesh and blood, and yet. It's true. Thinking about that day turns my stomach and it feels like ants burrowing under my skin.

I was twelve. It was the summer before I started St Agnes. Mummy had just given that fateful interview to the property and home supplement in the paper. She should have been more careful, a mention of the local pub pretty much gave away our exact location in Notting Hill, and that's how he found us.

It was after school and I was eating Nutella on crumpets in the kitchen when the doorbell went.

'Alice!' Mother called down. 'Can you get that? It's a delivery for Felix!'

I didn't even think to check the entryphone camera. I just trotted upstairs and flung open the front door, crumpet still in hand. The man waiting on the threshold didn't look much like a delivery man. For one thing, there was a crusty stain all the way down his front.

'Hello, Lorina. Can I come in?' He had a tooth missing from the top row.

'What?' I said dumbly. 'Who are ... Mummy!' I called back up the stairs.

'Do you not recognise me? It's me! Your old dad, Lori.' His gravel voice rattled like a bag of nails.

'I am not Lori.' My hair was longer then, almost down to my waist after years of refusing haircuts.

He looked very confused for a second and then something spread across his face. Something a lot like repulsion, and it was a mirror of the expression I could tell I wore. 'Charles? Charlie?'

No. 'Mother!'

I heard her footsteps thudding down the stairs behind me. 'Oh, for crying out loud, Alice, what is it?' And then she froze in the hallway. Her skin went zombie-grey. 'Jonny ... what ... *how*? How did you get this address?'

'Can I come in?' he asked. Mum always knows what to say, and I'd never seen her speechless before. 'Well?'

'Um ... yes,' she said, negotiating with ghosts. I vividly remember the claret shade she'd just dyed her pixie cut. It was cute. 'Come on through. Do … do you want a cup of tea or something?'

'Yeah. Yeah, a coffee would be good.' As he came into the hallway and slid past me, I got a strong whiff of booze. Stale, like he was sweating yesterday's whisky out through his pores.

'Is that my dad?' I asked, my voice budgerigar-shrill.

He looked to Mum.

'Yes,' she said. 'Alice, this is Jonny Radcliffe, your father.'

He eyed me up. 'Alice, is it?'

'Yes, it is,' Mother said firmly. I chose the name because it's what she'd have called me if I'd been born … correctly.

'You left us,' I stated. The hall was dark, the afternoon already turning to a drizzly dusk. The tiles were icy cold on my bare feet.

'I did. I'm very sorry about the way things ended,' he said sheepishly. Or, the performance of sheepishness, the way a schoolboy apologises to avoid detention.

'I don't remember you.' It was like my filter was broken, every stray thought was popping out uninhibited.

He looked at me and I looked right back, searching for a sign of genuine remorse … or joy at finally meeting the real me … or *anything* really. Again, I only saw somewhat rehearsed puppy-dog eyes.

'Come down to the kitchen,' Mum repeated.

I hovered while Mum made him a coffee. He sat at the dining table, playing with his hands. It was brighter in there and I could see he didn't look very well.

'Why are you here?' I asked him after he'd told us *how* he'd found the house.

'That's something I really need to discuss with your mum, poppet.'

'I'm not your poppet.'

'You are, that's what I used to call you.'

'That's what you used to call *Lori*,' Mother said with a sigh, bringing him his coffee. 'Alice, can you let us talk, please?'

'But …'

'Just do as you're told!' she clapped back.

Stung, I skulked off, but not very far. I listened, quiet as a mouse, on the stairs. Who wouldn't? Was this him trying to build bridges? We had nothing to go on – no foundations, no scaffolding. He was nothing to me. It would be starting a relationship with a perfect stranger.

'I see you're doing good, Lou,' I heard him say.

'Yes, it's going well, thanks,' she replied curtly.

'I'm happy for you and … what's your fella called?'

'Felix.'

'I am, I'm really happy for you.'

'What is it you want, Jonny? You could have just emailed my agent. Her details are on my website.'

'I wanted to see you and the kids, though. It's been so long and I saw how well you were doing in that magazine and …'

'What do you *want*?' she said more firmly. 'You couldn't get away from us fast enough seven years ago.'

And I, of course, wondered how much that had to do with me. *Act right in your head; talk like a boy; don't sit down to pee; man up*. Instead, he took a long, deep breath.

'I'm in trouble, Lou.'

'Ah, there we have it.'

'It's not like that …'

'Isn't it? I haven't seen you in the best part of a decade. Have you ever tried explaining to a five-year-old how her father *might* be dead?'

'And I'm sorry about that. I was in a really bad place, Lou. My head wasn't good, you know that. I had to get away, I thought I was going mad.'

'So you can see,' she went on, ignoring him, 'why I'd be somewhat suspicious that you show your face again now I've made a bit of money.'

'More than a bit,' he said.

'I've worked bloody hard. You left us with less than nothing.'

'Lou, I'm just asking for some help. I'm in a bit of trouble …' he said again.

'Nothing ever changes, does it?' I could so easily picture Mum's weary facial expression without needing to be in the room, I've seen that look a million times.

'I'm getting help, I am, I swear.'

'I can smell drink on you, Jonny.'

'I know, I know. I just need some help to get back on my feet.'

There was a slight pause. 'Did you have any intention of coming here to see Lori and Alice, or was it just the money you're after? Do you have any idea how much we've been through? Do you think it was easy? Everything with Alice?'

I felt a stab of pain between my ribs. I have made life hard. Me being me hurts people.

Another pause. 'No, no I would like to get to know them. I can't believe that's little Charlie …'

'*Alice.*'

'You know I've got another little boy now too? I'm not with his mum any more but I see him sometimes and …' I have a half-brother? The news was dizzying. I'd always thought of myself as the baby, but it turned out I was someone's big sister. I wondered what his name was, and if Mother would ask.

'How much do you need?' She cut him off.

'What?'

'You heard. I want you gone. I don't want you anywhere near my girls.' From the stairs, my eyes widened. I'd never heard her voice so cold. 'You are toxic, Jonny, and you poisoned me for years. I won't have you dragging my daughters down with you. I used to worry, you know, about nature and nurture. That some part of you was inside them. This was all for them. Every word I write is for those girls, to give them all this, and to stop them from becoming *you*.'

'Fucking hell, Louise. Bit hard, don't you think?'

'Not even slightly. What *was* hard was realising my girls were better off without a father than having you as one. But I'm going to give you the money, whatever you want, because without you I wouldn't have the two most precious things in my life. I suppose I owe you that. So: how much do you need to go away and never come back?'

The punchline? It wasn't even that much money.

I skulked silently up the stairs before my cover was blown.

Later that night, unable to shake a chill nausea, I sat in a hot bath. It didn't do much to defrost me. I watched Mum's fifty-pound Diptyque candle glimmer, and couldn't help but think she burned through money. The aroma – oud – was woody and strong, and my eyelids felt heavy.

There was a tap at the door. 'Alice? Can I come in?'

I covered my feminine mystique with a facecloth. 'It's open.'

'Are you OK?' Mum asked.

I pulled my knees up to my chin. 'I'm fine.'

She put the toilet seat down and sat on it, crossing her legs. 'Can we talk about what happened this afternoon?'

'What? Dad?'

'He isn't your dad. He's just a man I once knew. Father is a verb not a noun.'

I let that sink in. Felix is the only dad I've ever known and I love him. Mother chose wisely. Before that day, I half-thought *all* dads were auditioned, invited to join families, not a genetic birthright.

'What's wrong with him?' I asked.

'What do you mean?'

I hunched over my knees. 'He was … weird.'

She sighed deeply. 'He's not well. He has a lot of problems. But so do many people and it doesn't make them assholes. Sorry, I shouldn't swear.'

I wasn't a child – or at least I thought I wasn't – but I knew enough to know he was my father and fifty per cent of my DNA came from him. I'd always wondered about him, trying to Pritt Stick the few memories I had to the even fewer photos that Mum kept. I knew he was a poet and musician, and wondered if that's why I loved music more than Mum and Lori did, so always pictured him as a skinny-jean clad hipster with flowing hair. I didn't imagine him to be a shivering drunk with missing teeth.

I chastised myself for picking on his appearance, especially when Mother had just said he was ill. But I also knew that illnesses can be inherited.

'What does he have?' I asked.

'Addiction problems. Manic depression, although we call it bipolar these days.'

'Can I get it?'

'Alice, baby, no!' She rubbed my back with a soapy sponge. 'It doesn't work like that!'

Only, of course, it does.

XXVII

GIRLTALK

There's a security guard manning the main entrance to Gryphon Hall, bald with no neck like a human potato.

'Miss, the grand hall opens for the gala dinner at seven.'

'I'm here to see Paisley. She told me to come at six.'

He presses his earpiece. 'Come in, Bill. I have a girl here for Ms Hart. What's your name, love?'

'Alice Dodgson.'

'Alice Dodgson. Right. Thanks. Over.' He stands aside and waves me through. 'Ms Hart is in the master bedroom. Upstairs, third door on the left.'

I stifle a gasp as I step inside. Time hasn't been kind to the sleeping beauty house, but it's still breathtaking. *Too posh for me*, Grandma Dodgson would say, but then she says that about brown bread too. Cracked chessboard tiles stretch out before me, leading to an imposing staircase. Amber afternoon sunlight pours in through the windows on one side and, on the other, my progress is watched by a procession of marble busts all wearing cobweb wigs. Stone columns hold up an intricately painted ceiling. The mural is very, very faded but I can more or less make out what I think is Lucifer being cast out of the heavens. A naked winged figure falls into swirling smoke and fire.

I'm alone, although I can hear distant kitchen noises: plates and pots and pans as the staff get ready for dinner. Who lives like this? It's more like a museum piece than a home, a relic of an Olde Merrie England we don't quite seem to want to let go of. I can't say I blame the Dormans for choosing to live in the city, but it's a shame they're letting such a handsome estate crumble to dust. Install a dinky gift shop and sign it over to the National Trust, I say.

I make my way up the grand staircase, feeling very *Beauty and the Beast*, and tap politely on the third door on the landing.

'Come in!' I hear Paisley's voice. I enter to find her having her hair styled by a whippet-like man, while a woman kneels at her feet giving her a manicure. The Flower Girls lounge around an impressive master bedroom, sipping champagne. The décor is fussy, frilly, old fashioned, and reeks of Mr Sheen and mildew. I could quite easily picture Henry VIII tying one of his kinkier wives to the oppressive four-poster bed. Tapestries hang over the oak-panelled walls.

'Ah, Alice, you made it.' Paisley has her back to me, but she catches my eye in the mirror. She's wearing a silk dressing gown in deep burgundy. 'Champagne? Cocaine?'

On the bed, Rose snorts a fat line off a hand mirror and offers it to me. 'I'll just take the champagne, thanks,' I say. 'I'm irritating off coke, I hate to think what I'd be like on it.'

'Suit yourself.' Paisley accepts the mirror and inhales a pre-chopped line with a silver straw. 'God, I can't imagine trying to get through this weekend without coke. I know it's terribly common – coke is for brickies and Mummy's Night Off these days – but it serves a purpose.'

Lily hands me a glass of Bollinger.

'Thank you,' I say.

'Are we about done?' Paisley asks the hairdresser. Her hair has been curled tightly – almost, dare I say it, into a Diana Ross 'fro. Bit cultural appropriationy. Still, she looks very disco I suppose, which is no doubt her intention. The hairdresser finishes off by emptying a can of hairspray into the atmosphere, and he and the manicurist leave.

'Lily, Violet, Rose; you can go too,' says Paisley.

'What? Why?' Violet whines.

'Because I'm bored of you. Please leave.'

Three sulky girls file out of the bedroom, leaving us alone. I don't like it. I think I'd prefer witnesses to whatever is about to happen. Even Piglette is nowhere to be seen.

'Sit, sit, sit,' Paisley says, gesturing at the bed. Sitting on someone's bed feels oddly intimate but I do as I'm told. 'OK. We must get you out of those clothes. You look like you survived something.'

'I suppose I did,' I say quietly.

She strides over to a handsome armoire. On the pillow I see there's some sort of journal or scrapbook. It lies open, with numerous leaves of paper and documents poking out of the sides. I wouldn't pay it much mind, every girl's entitled to her diary and nothing in that diary – no pre-menstrual rant or tear-soaked declaration of love – should be held against her as evidence. But in this instance, I see a photo of my mother's face staring out at me.

'Blue's your colour, isn't it?' Paisley says, rifling through a rail of clothes. 'I always bring various back-up options, you're in luck. You're taller than me, but would you say we're about the same size?'

I force my gaze away from the notebook. 'Yes! More or less.' Definitely *more*, but we'll make it work.

'Let's see ...' Paisley returns to the wardrobe, her back to me. I lean over to get a better look at the journal. It *is* my mum. It's the interview she did with the *Observer Magazine* when her last novel came out. They sent a photographer to our house and they shot a portrait in the yard. You can just about make out the yellow lemons on the tree behind her.

But why would Paisley Hart, of all people, cut out and keep an interview with my—

'It's OK,' she says suddenly and I recoil, caught bastard-handed. 'You can look.'

'I'm sorry, I ... I just saw my mother sticking out and—'

Paisley crosses the room, brandishing a metallic peacock-blue dress. 'Here, see if this fits. Why, it almost matches your hair.'

The dress is fine, but the articles ...'Why?'

She joins me on the bed and scoops up the scrapbook. 'Why do I have clippings about your mother? Well, it's an interesting story actually, Alice. You see, I didn't put two and two together for a long time – what with her using a pen name and you being born Charles.'

From her collection, she presents my Year Four school photo. From it I grin, front tooth missing. I could be a little girl or a little boy to be honest, my hair was always as long as Mother let me have it, but now all I see in that picture is a child nigh on exhausted from expending all her energy on a wish.

Oh, that's a fucking kick in the teeth. My jaw feels actually dislocated. 'How did you get that? How do you ...?'

215

She pulls me off the bed to check if the fucking dress is long enough. 'How do I know you're transgender? Your sister is in the Oxford debating society with my cousin Rupert, and she said she had a transgender sister. It really wasn't difficult to track you down online and do a little digging. I wasn't aware it supposed to be a secret.'

Fucking Lorina, honestly. 'If it wasn't supposed to be a secret, I would have told people myself.' I try very hard to keep the annoyance out of my voice.

'Come now, Alice. It's hardly interesting, is it? It's not even the most interesting thing about *you*.'

That could mean any number of things. I'm experiencing a strange rising dread, a necrosis setting in at my feet and spreading north. 'I don't understand.'

Paisley points to her diary. 'In that piece your mother writes about witnessing a woman fall from a building in Shoreditch, and how it inspired her first novel.'

'Yes, that's right.'

She turns the page and it's a mish-mash of dog-eared, sepia birth certificates, newspaper clippings and family trees from the looks of things. 'Well, you see, Alice –' Paisley's eyes cut deep into mine – 'the woman that fell was *my* mother.'

Oh. I'm stunned, winded. My mother shielded Lori and me from the gory details. I never knew her name. I have only known her as "the woman who fell".

'I … I had no idea.'

Paisley sits and leafs through her journal, stopping on a slim newspaper column. '"Daughter of Earl Dead in Horror Fall". I can see how you wouldn't know. She was only referred to as her father's daughter or husband's wife, and the family paid to keep the details out of the press. It's interesting, you know. My father only made any money because my grandfather set him up. All the money trickles down from my mother's side of the family but, in the end, she's only really notable for her enormously histrionic death.'

'I'm sure that's not true,' I say, gingerly perching back on the bed.

'What was it like?' Paisley says, hardly blinking. 'What did it look like? You were there, weren't you?'

'Paisley … I don't think …'

Her eyes, the cold blue, as sharp as a dagger. 'You don't think what? That'll it remedy the trauma of my mother throwing herself from a hotel balcony when I was five? Probably not, but I scarcely see how it can make things worse, do you? So: what was it like? Seeing her fall?'

My mouth gapes uselessly like a goldfish. 'I … it was very fast.'

'Was it terribly horrific?'

'My … my mother pulled me away so I couldn't really see anything.' I relive it in my head. That moment of perfect silence as our minds processed what we'd just seen. A shape, a shape falling faster than our eyes could make sense of. It was only after, only when she was splayed on the pavement in a growing lake of blood, that we understood.

'But you saw *something*?'

'Yes.'

'We're all on tenterhooks, Alice. Enlighten me.'

'I just saw something move. We were walking through

217

Shoreditch. Everyone stopped. All of a sudden there was just a woman on the pavement. People started to scream. I didn't even really see her fall.'

'Did she bleed, Alice?'

'Yes.' A tear runs down my cheek.

'Why are *you* crying? It wasn't your mother.'

I wipe it away. 'I know. But I'm sorry. I don't know why I'm crying. I've thought about her a lot. What it must have been like, to fall. Whether she was scared, or if she felt … a sort of freedom.' I thought about her that day at the train station too. Another tear finds its way out. 'I … thought, once I was a bit older, that she must have been very unhappy … or sick … and that she might have … felt a sort of relief …'

Paisley takes both my hands in hers. Her eyes are still glacial. 'Do you know, I have often thought the same. Only, of course, I wonder if she thought about us, her children, at all. Have you ever wondered what it'd be like to be dead, Alice?'

'Yes,' I tell her.

'Me too. I think about it often. Oh, I know we all hanker for a cloud in heaven, but the realist in me thinks my mother craved the abyss. That absolute nothingness. Sometimes I wish she'd taken us with her. Some mothers do that, you know, kill their children, and then themselves. I'd like to know what nothing feels like. But, of course, it wouldn't feel like anything at all because that's what nothing is. I can see why Mother found the notion seductive. Death is life's best mystery by far.'

I wish I could blink myself a hundred miles from here. All the air has gone from the room and I can't breathe. 'Paisley, I'm truly sorry …'

Her jaw clenches and I swear, for an instant, that she's going to hit me. Pure rage seeps from her in crimson waves. Instead, she drops my hands. 'It's fine. I suppose she must have had a lot on her mind. Now, let's try this dress on. It's almost time for dinner.'

'Are you sure you want to do this?'

'Do what? Eat dinner? Of course.'

'But ...'

'But nothing. Try it on.' She holds up the dress expectantly. I sense she's waiting for me to strip. 'Come along, it's *just us girls.*' There's just a hint of mockery in her tone.

Reluctantly, and already feeling exposed, I unbutton the shirt. We're standing about a metre apart.

'You have a beautiful body,' Paisley says. 'It's nothing to be ashamed of.'

'I'm not.'

Her gaze falls on my breasts. 'Good. And the rest.'

'Paisley ...'

'What?'

Is she really going to make me do this? I undo the shorts and let them fall to the floor. I'm still wearing the Tweedle briefs but I feel thoroughly exposed.

'There. That wasn't so hard, was it?' She hands me the dress and I step into it. It's backless, tying at the neck, which means my hideous shoulders won't be an issue. Paisley slips her hands around my neck to help me secure it. Her skin is warm against mine.

She turns my body around to face the mirror. It is a *little* snug across my rear, but not unattractive. Womanly, dare I say it.

'It fits like a glove,' Paisley says, admiring me. She smooths it down my back, her hands brushing against my bottom. I don't know what to say. 'Which leaves only two questions.' She strides back to the wardrobe. 'One – what shall *I* wear? And two, who is hiding in my closet?'

I frown. Paisley thrusts both hands into a rail-full of clothing and drags someone out into the room. With a cry, Cat tumbles onto the rug, looking every bit as startled as I'm sure I do. Her hoodie falls over her eyes. One can only assume she's been in there the whole time.

'What the fuck?' I gasp.

Paisley looks unimpressed, standing with her hands on her hips. 'The closet? How droll. Are you trying to be ironic?' she asks Cat, before turning to me. 'Alice, I believe you've already met my sister?'

XXVIII

NEVE

'Your sister?'

Cat says nothing, so Paisley answers for her. 'Alice, meet Neve.'

'Were you listening to us?' I ask, knowing the answer full well.

Cat, or Neve, pulls back her hood and kneels up. 'I was keeping an eye on you and … actually I was mostly just spying on you. Saved your ass last night though, didn't it?'

I can't deny that. I wrap my arms around my body protectively.

'What are you doing here, Neve?' Paisleys asks with a bored sigh, selecting a scarlet garment from the wardrobe.

I have, of course, heard of Neve Hart, the eldest of the Hart children, although she was expelled from St Agnes long before I started. The last I heard she was at some Catholic reform school in Ireland. I guess it didn't take. She seems wholly unreformed.

'You know me, I love a party.'

'That isn't even slightly true.' Paisley drops her robe to reveal cherry-red lingerie, and steps into what turns out to be a flared jumpsuit.

'You're right. It's not.'

'Then why are you here? Or is it just to piss on my bonfire?'

Neve stands and shrugs. 'Curious, I guess. Time to check out the family business.'

'Wonderland is nothing to do with you, and it never will be. You're a gatecrasher, plain and simple.'

Neve grins. 'Party pooper.'

Paisley casts an unimpressed eye over her big sister. 'Well, you're here now, I suppose. You will attend dinner. Dress appropriately, you're an embarrassment. This isn't one of your dreary Camden metal nights for goths and bed-wetters.' She addresses me. 'Alice, take whatever clothes and make-up you need. You can both join me on the head table as guests of honour.'

'Can't wait,' Neve says with plentiful sarcasm.

Paisley finishes strapping some gold platforms to her feet and straightens up. 'I need to check on dinner,' she says, sidling towards the door. She pauses at my side. 'I think you two have much in common. But be sure to ask my sister why she wears the gloves.'

Neve smiles but gives her little sister a double-finger salute. 'What a fucking cunt, honestly,' she says, once the door has closed behind Paisley.

I can't argue with that. 'Why are you following me around?' I ask instead. 'I'm grateful for your assistance last night, but if you were a boy your persistence would be more than a little creepy.'

'I *am* more than a little creepy.' Neve picks herself up and plonks her behind on the dressing table, sending Paisley's cosmetics rolling to the carpet. 'OK. I admit it. I'm interested in you for the same reason Paisley is. It caused quite a stir – the piece your mum wrote. Dredged up the Hart family secret. Royce told me Lulu Carroll had a daughter at St Agnes … and it was you. You, Alice Dodgson, are hard to stalk. No social

222

media, no societies or sports at school. I found *one* picture of you on your friend Dinah's Instagram and I recognised you at the Mock Turtle. Your disguise was, let's be honest, shit. I was intrigued. You saw our mum face-dive the pavement. If you lost a parent as a kid, you'll know that's literally a lifetime therapist's bill.'

She's not wrong there. My dad may as well have been dead. It'd have been easier, perhaps, if he had been. 'I was five, Neve.'

'I'm guessing you remember that shit.'

I watch her from the mirror. I let my hair down and think about make-up. I feel naked without a lot of black eyeliner. 'I'm not going to repeat myself if you heard it all from in there. I told Paisley everything I remember.'

'Fair.' Neve looks at her feet. 'I guess … I guess I've always wondered about her face. Y'know, if there was a sign of that freedom you talked about. I hope it fixed —'

'No!' I say more loudly than I intend. 'Suicide is a permanent—'

'Fix to a temporary problem, I know.'

'Do you?' I say, still angry. 'Did you also know that last year I almost threw myself in front of the 11.37 to Portsmouth?'

She looks surprised for the first time. 'What?'

How much to tell her? I suppose I've opened Pandora's box now and she can see all the monsters inside.

'Things were bad,' I tell her.

'Bad how? How bad?'

'You really want to hear the whole saga? It's not some inspirational TED Talk moment,' I snarl. 'You won't grow or learn from it.'

'I don't care. Tell me.'

I do tell her. I was born on a Wednesday and you know what they say about Wednesday's child. Woe is me. The nice doctors at the gender clinic – once they were done trying to 'talk me out of it' – warned me about pinning all my hopes and dreams on finally getting my little mitts on oestrogen. *I'll be fine once I'm a girl*, I would tell myself every single night as I fell asleep and then again when I woke up. It was the agonising delay in treatment that was driving me to self-harm, not *me*.

Some days I couldn't get out of bed, veins all full of cement and tar. So low, I was pressed into the mattress like a waffle. But it would all be fine once they JUST FUCKING GAVE ME THAT PRESCRIPTION.

And then they did and … nothing changed. Oh, the first couple of days were joyous. Finally, I'd proved to the clinic something that was abundantly obvious to anyone who had ever met me, and they gave me the pills I thought I needed. But then a week passed, and then a month and … nothing. My body changed very slowly, but my head … my head didn't change at all.

What a fucking idiot I was. What did I think was happening inside the head of a common-or-garden girl? Pink kittens? Ballerinas and nail varnish? Popcorn and pot pourri?

No, there was still just me. And still *her*. Other Alice.

Because I had *always* been a girl.

A very poorly girl.

Oh so slowly my *body* went on the journey it was always supposed to take. And the baggage came with it.

I'd been through so much to still feel so rotten. The prettier the outside got, the more I felt the mould and maggots inside; the louder Other Alice became, until I *only* heard her. I couldn't tell the difference any more. And so I started to plan. The train station; what the note would say; the way out. Thinking about dying was all that got me through the day.

Even thinking about it now reminds me of the allure.

It was a symptom, it was a symptom, it was a symptom. I cling to that mantra. And I believe it. I do.

And I really should have brought my medication with me.

'In a weird way, I'm glad it all happened,' I tell Neve, 'because I finally got the help I needed. I'm sorry, but I don't accept there was anything in your mother's life so dire it couldn't be remedied. A year ago I *really* wanted to be dead, and now I'm really, *really* glad I'm not. What if I'd done it?'

If I'd gone under that train, there'd have been no Bunny, no Maxim, no nose-ring. No milkshakes with Dinah. I'd have never read *The Bell Jar* or *Bonjour Tristesse*. I'd have never seen *Rosemary's Baby*, or *Hamilton*, or Sister Sonika live at Brixton Academy.

'Sorry you went through that,' she says. I sense she's about to dispense a similar misery memoir but the cat's got her tongue. 'And what about us?' she says quietly, after a moment. 'Me and Paisley and Royce. Weren't we reason enough to stick around?' She goes over to the bed and plucks a faded, dog-eared photograph out of Paisley's scrapbook. I see a smiling family portrait of Mr and Mrs Hart and three small children. My gaze lingers on Mrs Hart: a stunning brunette with a striking resemblance to Paisley.

'Why didn't you just tell me who you were?' I ask gently.

She nods in the direction Paisley just went. 'I didn't want her to know I was here, she'd send me packing. Paisley knows *everything*, though, I should have known.' She grins. 'Also, I liked being Cat. It's nice to be someone else sometimes.'

I turn and walk to the dresser, looking amongst the cosmetic debris. 'Do you have any black eyeliner?'

'What do you think?' She smiles again. 'Miss Dodgson, would you accompany me to dinner?'

XXIX

THE BATHROOM QUESTION

I find the Flower Girls in the bathroom, getting ready and hoovering lines of gak off the toilet cistern.

'So you're transgender?'

'So you were, like, born a boy?'

'How old were you?'

'Did you just know?'

'How did you know?'

'Do you think children really know when they're that little?'

'What if you change your mind?'

'Are you a girl now?'

'Like a real girl?'

'Were you born in the wrong body?'

'What was your name?'

'Did you have a sex change?'

'Did you have a penis?'

'Do you have a penis?'

'Did you have The Op?'

'Will you have The Op?'

'When will you have The Op?'

'Is it like a real vagina?'

'Can you have periods?'

'Can you have babies?'

'Are you sad you can't have babies?'

'Will you adopt babies?'

'Which toilet do you use?'

'Do you sit down when you pee?'

'Do you think trans people should have a special toilet?'

'Do you think rapists might pretend to be trans to rape people in toilets?'

'Do you think trans rapists should be in women's prisons?'

'What about the Olympics though?'

I add one question of my own: 'Um … can I just use the toilet, please?'

XXX

WHAT'S THE TIME, MR WOLF?

Arm in arm we descend the great stairs. I don't know where Neve found a tuxedo that fits her, but somehow she has. She looks incredible – both beautiful and handsome at the same time, a gorgeous equilibrium of masculine and feminine. She's swapped the leather gloves for some pristine white ones.

I'm wearing my Docs with the satin gown because I can't even pretend to walk in heels, and I don't exactly relish being even taller than I am. As other guests arrive via the main doors, I see them scowl up at us and I feel a curious swell of pride in my otherness. I am glad I am not like them.

'This is going to be awful, isn't it?' I say.

'Oh, totally,' Neve replies. 'But I get the company of a beautiful girl for the night.'

I wonder what magic Wonderland has, how upside down it is, that here I seem to be significantly more desirable than I am in the real world. It occurs to me that a couple of hours ago, I had Maxim inside me.

I rather like Neve's attention.

And Bunny's.

Even Paisley's.

I am in bloom, so it seems, attracting bees.

'I'm your date?' I ask.

'I don't see how you're not. Although I understand I have mad competition.'

'We're all mad here,' I mutter to myself as we join the steady procession heading into the banqueting hall. I look up and see portions of the ceiling are missing entirely. I can see the pink twilight sky, a faint crescent moon slinking in.

Neve whispers in my ear. 'There's nothing sexier than watching a girl turn.'

I tut. 'I'm not *turning* in any one direction, thank you kindly,' I tell her sharply. 'What about you?'

'Lesbian.'

I smirk at her. 'Old money.'

'Exactly. When did *lesbian* become a dirty word?' She leans in again. Her lips brush against my ear. 'I love it. I am a girl who only fucks girls – cis or otherwise, I'm no fucking TERF. I am, therefore, a lesbian. I like it, I like that I'm part of a lineage of proud lesbians: Roxanne Gay, Audre Lorde, Anne Lister … all the way back to Sappho herself. It's a powerful sisterhood and I wouldn't ever let a man absorb any of that sexual energy.'

I'll take that sugary validation where I can get it. That's both straight men *and* gay girls today, so I must be doing something right. Do I think Maxim stole my Girl Power through the tip of his willy? No. I think it's simply a different energy and I'm partial to both. Sweet and salty popcorn. 'I'll be sure to remember.'

I see Maxim is already seated at the head table and put some space between Neve and me. I'm not aware of a solitary sexual encounter equating to a betrothal, but I do feel a twinge of guilt about leaving without telling him.

Like any well-bred gentlemen, Maxim and Willie Zong stand to greet us as we arrive.

'Neve,' Maxim says, surprised to see her apparently. 'I thought you were ...'

'In prison?' Neve asks as she takes her place. 'Not right now.'

'You were in prison?' I find my name card sandwiched between Maxim and Neve's and I can't help but think Paisley planned this for maximum awkwardness. Like Neve says, I'm starting to think that Paisley could well be omniscient.

I wonder if there are no electrics in the ballroom. Cables with bare Edison bulbs criss-cross overhead, lighting the hall. It's enchanting, halfway between inside and out. I think of *A Midsummer Night's Dream*, only this is a queendom with a Titania but no Oberon. A quick scan of the name cards confirms only Paisley and her idiot brother will be joining us. There is also, I note, a place setting for Bunny Liddell next to Paisley. I'm not sure *I'd* leave a place at the table for someone who tried to shoot me, but different strokes for different folks.

'I was,' Neve says enigmatically. 'Well, a young offenders' institution.'

'Why?' I blurt out. Is it terribly uncouth to ask?

'There was an accident,' she says.

'That was no accident,' Willie chimes in. 'Your father may have taken out a super injunction, but the court records made for very interesting reading.'

Neve smiles broadly. 'God, it must be boring knowing everything, Willie.'

'On the contrary. There are always new things to learn. Isn't that right, Alice?'

231

'I don't know what you mean.' I pick at a bread roll. I'm not sure I like this feeling of being a tourist in my own life. I'm far from home, everyone's speaking a foreign language and I definitely don't have the currency.

'I don't mean anything other than that you look lovely, my dear,' continues Willie. 'Why, you're on the verge of fitting in. Have you worked out who it is you are yet?'

I ignore him.

'You do,' Maxim leans in closer. 'Look lovely.'

'Thank you,' I say.

'Why'd you take off like that?' he says quietly.

'I …'

Neve reaches over me to grab some bread. 'So do you want to know what it is I did?'

Maxim sighs.

'I …'

'I tried to burn down my school in Dublin,' she announces in the same manner you'd explain you burned the toast.

OK, she has my attention. 'What? Why?'

She shrugs. 'I thought it'd be pretty.'

'Jesus, Neve, I'd forgotten how full of shit you are,' Maxim says.

'What?' she says innocently.

'And was it?' I ask. 'Pretty?'

'Sensational. It went up really fast.' She takes off her gloves to reveal badly burned hands. The skin is shiny, silver and taut. She waves her fingers over the candle and I hold my breath. 'Nothing beats the rush of seeing something catch fire, it's addictive. Watching a tiny little flame baby gobble and gobble everything in its path until it becomes a big, fat, roaring monster. There's a point when the see-saw tips; it burns out of control, when it becomes bigger than you, with an almighty WOOF. It's ... scary, sure, but you can't stop watching. Where's it gonna go next? What's it gonna do? It's alive, you know: this baby you made.'

'Ignore her,' Maxim tells me. 'She's plain nuts.'

Neve looks at her hands. 'Guess I stayed and watched a minute too long, huh?'

Looking around the table, I can't help but think I'm trapped in a basket of vipers, all slithering over one another, each as dangerous and deadly as the next. I'm starting to think I was far better off hiding in my bedroom.

But then Neve smiles warmly and I remember that she sat at my side all last night to protect me from Jeremy and Jonty. And Maxim. He's arrogant, yes, but he got me out of a pickle earlier – and I believe Paisley could and would pickle me given half the chance. These people aren't necessarily *loathsome* as I'd always assumed. Instead, it transpires all the money in the world isn't some sort of brain condom protecting you from mental health problems. It would be only too easy to hate them, yet I do not. I suppose the difference is Maxim and Neve have their issues *despite* their class, not *because* of it. I love how I place myself in a different circle on the Venn diagram, like Mummy's wealth hasn't bought me shortcuts and bonuses. It comes back to what Felicity says about insight. If you *know* you're privileged you're probably not the worst of the worst.

'Well, here we all are.' Paisley and Royce arrive at the head table and join us.

'Neve!' Royce seems genuinely pleased to see his sister and

the two embrace. 'Pais said you were here! When the fuck did you get out?'

'A while back.' Neve doesn't elaborate further and sits back down. 'Are you OK, baby brother?'

'You know me,' Royce says, and I note that doesn't actually answer her question.

'I hope you're ready for a feast,' Paisley says. 'Willie, Maxim. How is Wonderland treating you?'

'My dear, you've outdone yourself,' Willie says. 'It's a flight of imagination.'

'Best yet,' Maxim says simply.

'Thank you, Max. It's a shame you're still out of action, isn't it?' And in that moment I know Paisley knows Maxim is feigning his injury. It's all in her sly delivery. Unlike her sister, I'm happy to sign off Paisley as both mad *and* loathsome.

'Tuck in,' Paisleys says, pouring for her guests. 'Who wants the red? I selected it myself. Full-bodied, fruity, delicious.'

'Is there white?' I ask, scanning the table. I don't especially like any wine, I think grown-ups only drink it to look sophisticated, but I will tolerate a glass of white wine to be polite.

'I don't care for white,' Paisley says. 'Have some red.'

I reluctantly hold out my glass. Ghastly. It smells of something I'd drizzle over a salad.

The first course is delicious little cheese and tomato tartlets followed by a zingy lime sorbet palette cleanser. Royce does the majority of the talking, trying to enthuse Maxim about the looming rugby tour to South Africa. Healed or not, Maxim is tagging along, but I can see from his eyes that his heart's not in it.

'I mean, bruv, it's going to GO OFF. Dooley's defo confirmed, as are Brent and Hammo. Winky has to get his grades up, but that's fine, and Greggle is trying to get out of a family holiday. I mean it's going to be *sick*.'

I have no idea. He's a giddy simpleton child trapped in a man's body.

'Are you OK?' Neve asks as her brother brays on.

'I'm fine,' I say. I keep thinking of Felix and whatever chaos I've created back in London. 'I think it's time to go home.'

'Depends on your home.'

'Enough. I'm tired of riddles, Neve.' She says nothing. 'I'm sorry, that wasn't called for.'

'It probably was. Talking nonsense is so much safer than saying what you mean. It usually gets me in trouble. For example, I could just say *I like you*, but that's scary because I don't know what you'd say back.'

'You barely know me,' I say kindly. 'According to Willie, I don't know myself. I'm not sure what there is to like.'

'Now who's talking in riddles?'

We share a smile.

'Oh, look,' says Paisley, clapping her dainty hands. 'Here comes the main course. We have a special treat.'

A waiter strides up to the table and, with great flare, places before us a roasted piglet, a red apple in its charred mouth.

'Oh my god!' I cry. 'Is that …?'

'Jesus, that's fucked up, Paisley!' Maxim barks.

'What?' Paisley's glare cuts him down. 'How is it any different from the bacon you had at brunch? Now: who's going to carve?'

'She replaces them when they stop being cute,' Neve says,

turning decidedly pale. 'And she calls them all Piglette.'

I can't hold back a second longer. 'That's …'

'That's what, Alice?' Paisley says. Is this what she wants? A fight? A reaction? My horror? I'm a puppet on her strings dancing to her fucked-up concertina tune. 'Don't be shy. It's what?'

'That's disgusting.'

'Is it now?'

'I'm vegetarian.' I've never been more convinced, in fact.

'Very well. There was no need for the outburst.' She instructs the waitress to fetch me the vegan option. 'The rest of us shall enjoy the pork. Royce? Do us the honours.'

I'm served a pea-and-pumpkin risotto, a true sign the chef holds vegetarians in low regard. Risotto is one step up from scraping the meat off the plate and serving what's left. It's passable. I don't care for the red wine, the taste almost muddy. Instead, I stick to my water and wait for a server to bring white.

'So what *was* that about, earlier?' Maxim asks, when Royce is distracted for a second. 'You should see the bruise on my ego.'

'I … didn't want to rouse you. You looked very content.'

A faintly smutty smile crosses his lips. 'I was. Until I woke up alone.'

'Keep your voice down!'

His face falls. 'Why? Ashamed?'

'No. Why would *I* be ashamed?' And I can't really give him a reason beyond that. I'm absolutely not going to tell him I had a psychotic episode and hallucinated my father, but perhaps he's a little bit right too. I've cultivated a reputation as a rogue agent, a free radical who exists above and beyond the St Agnes social strata. What could be more crushingly predictable than schtupping Maxim Hattersley? It's very off-brand. 'I don't know.'

'You don't know if you're embarrassed?'

'Maxim, I am categorically not embarrassed. Maybe ... I ... I didn't think you'd be up for spooning and cuddles.'

Now he smirks a little and I feel a twitch from below. He lowers his voice 'Alice, I thought it was fucking hot.'

I sigh. 'Yes, it was.' And I'd do it again.

I honestly can't decide which of Dante's circles of hell this dinner most resembles. It feels like I'm being punished in different ways from all sides.

And that's when I see *her*.

I stop.

I blink.

I look again because I can't always trust my eyes.

Oh, it's Bunny, all right.

It's a *good* wig, but I can *always* spot a wig or a toupee. A strange gift to possess, but it never fails me. She weaves her way through the tables like a pinball. She's dressed in a server's uniform: crisp white blouse with a red bow tie. Her trademark hair is hidden under an unremarkable black bob.

With Herculean courage, she approaches the top table. The balls on this one, honestly. Maxim is still wittering on, *I don't say this to all the girls, but I had a really great time this afternoon*, but I don't hear him. She's brave or insane. She stands right behind Paisley's right shoulder. I mean, it's genius: hiding in plain sight. There's nothing more invisible to people like Paisley than the cleaners and waiters, especially those with Bunny's skin tone.

'White wine, love?' she asks in a thick mockney accent. She sounds like Dick Van Dyke.

'Please,' Paisley says.

Bunny pours her a fresh glass. I watch intently as she flips open a ring on her index finger and a white powder tips into the drink. I gasp. I don't think anyone else sees. But Bunny sees that I've seen. She comes to me next.

'White, madam?'

'Yes, thank you.' She leans over me to pour. 'What are you doing?' I hiss, almost inaudibly over the hubbub of the hall. She ignores my question. As she moves to the next table she looks over her shoulder and smiles sweetly.

I look at Paisley. She's polished off her serving of beloved pet and dabs her lips with a napkin. If she's finished eating, she's going to want a drink. She reaches for the wine.

And I hesitate.

I believe, without doubt, Bunny has just poisoned Paisley's wine. Would that be so bad?

I vividly picture Paisley staggering away from the table, clutching her throat, red-faced and mouth a-foaming. I imagine it'd all be over quite quickly. I expect people would cheer – internally if not aloud. Ding dong, the witch is dead. The Wicked Witch of West London to be precise.

Oh, for crying out loud. I've been in Wonderland too long. In the world, the real world, people our age don't just die. Poor Antonella Hemmings stayed in Wonderland too long and look what happened. As much as I think the world would benefit from an absence of Paisley Hart, that's not my – or Bunny's – decision to make.

I *also* know that everyone else around this table would happily throw Bunny under a Routemaster. While Bunny is adept at vanishing, I don't want her to spend a life on the run. What a waste of a life that would be.

Paisley picks up her glass.

'I just don't usually feel what I felt in that tent … there was a connection …' Maxim is still going.

I move quickly. I push my chair back, go to stand and deliberately plough into a male server who's clearing the table. As we collide, he drops a dirty plate in front of Paisley. She recoils, dropping her glass of wine onto the table. 'For crying out loud!' she snarls as it spills all over the crisp tablecloth.

'My fault!' I say loudly. 'I tripped.'

Paisley scowls at me, mopping up wine with her napkin.

'Alice?' Neve says. 'What's wrong?'

'Nothing!' I say a little too shrilly. 'I'm just going to the bathroom. IBS.'

I already see Bunny's bewigged head slipping out of the hall. I excuse myself and follow her, trying not to look too obvious as I weave past the other diners. I wait for a server to head into the kitchen and duck out behind them. I dare not even look to the head table in case one of them – *any* of them – saw me leave.

This is it.

It's finally time to catch up with Bunny Liddell.

XXXI
THE ROSE MAZE

The kitchen is all hustle and bustle, much too hot and garlic-sweaty. The caterers are lining up hundreds of red velvet fondant hearts, ready to be ferried out. I'm just in time to see Bunny vanish out of a fire escape.

'Toilets are the other way!' a stocky, lobster-faced chef barks, but I ignore him: chefs, in my experience, need less cocaine and more anger management. I cut past a kitchen porter to chase Bunny into the night.

The cool night air is pleasingly nibbly after the airless feast and I gulp in a cleansing lungful. The fire escape is to the side of Gryphon Hall. I hear footsteps crunching on gravel on my left. I dart around a covered-over sailboat festering on the drive and find the tennis courts, which also look like they've seen better days. Bunny's shadow swoops across the pocked AstroTurf and I give chase.

'Bunny! Wait!' I pick up the hem of my dress and hoist it up about my thighs.

I run across the tennis court and meet a wall of roses, taller than my head. I can't see if she went left or right, but I can hear girlish laughter from the other side of the hedgerow. I turn right and find her wig hanging off the bushes where they part to form an entrance. It's a maze. A very unkempt rose maze, and the roses are red.

I follow the path into the labyrinth and see crimson petals shed all over the well-trodden trail. She must have torn their heads off as she ran past. Like Hansel and Gretel, there's little I can do but follow her.

'Bunny!' I cry again, picking up speed.

The maze is so overgrown, it's hard to know which the dead-ends are. I suspect some valid routes are now almost grown-over, sealed up like old scars. I pick my way through, careful of thorns. Soon, I am lost. I couldn't go back to the beginning and start over even I wanted to. I feel panic climbing the rungs of my throat.

'Bunny! For fuck's sake!' The further in I go, the narrower the pathways become. The maze is starting to feel like a floral straitjacket. I walk straight into another dead-end. 'Fuck!' Bunny's bow tie dangles off the hedge. I feel suffocated, claustrophobic. I turn and head back.

Time to give up, Alice.

No, not her. Not now.

I see something move on the other side of the hedgerow and I recoil. Is it Bunny ... or her, Other Alice?

Someone is coming around the end of the maze corridor and she looks just like me. Only the eyes ... and the teeth ... the teeth are needle-sharp. Piranha teeth.

I run.

Round and round I go, dizzying myself. Twists and turns with no way out. I round a corner and come face to face with Bunny's bow tie again. I'm going around in circles.

A hand bursts through the tangled thorns and I cry out.

Aliiiiiiiceeeeee …

I pull away from the fingers and sprint in the opposite direction.

thisisnotrealthisisnotrealthisisnotrealthisisnotreal
You can't be crazy if you know you're crazy.

I pant. I can't breathe.

I'm about to scream for help when I see one channel open out into what I assume is a central atrium. I almost fall into it. There's suddenly so much more air to breathe and that feels like some sort of progress. At the centre of the opening is a moss-covered stone fountain, inoperative and dry. I think it's a long time since the goggle-eyed fish statue coughed out a spurt of water. I collapse onto the rim of the fountain and catch my breath. I wait for the maze to stop spiralling around me, or for me to stop spiralling in the maze. I'll take either.

What am I *doing*?

I mean that generally.

I should have stayed home and sent memes to Dinah all weekend. But no, I'm here, chasing girls, chasing boys, my mental health is worse than it's been all year, and there's not a single friend in sight. Really, this is all very, very sad. I should never have come here.

I let my head fall into my hands.

It's all too much and I cry. It's been bubbling up and now it all comes spilling out, sheer frustration finding its way to the surface. No tiny rhinestone Hollywood tears here, I feel my nose stream and I honk like a goose.

What did I think I could change?

I am an embarrassment.

I am an amusing novelty to these people, a toy. A cheap, disposable Happy Meal trinket. Next week, they'll get a new one.

'Alice, don't cry.'

I take my hands off my face and see Bunny kneeling at my feet. Her eyes are pools and she could well be a mirage.

'I didn't mean to make you cry. I thought the maze would be fun.' She tries a smile.

I look up at her through blurry tears. 'This is all a game to you, isn't it? Nothing ever matters.'

She looks hurt, big doll eyes impossibly wide. Her hair is plaited into cute pigtails. 'I'm sorry. That's not what I mean. I never thought you'd come here looking for me, Alice. It's the sweetest thing anyone has ever done for me, it really is.'

I wipe my eyes with my thumbs. 'I … I thought that night we had was special.'

And now she blinks, incredulous. 'It *was* special!'

'Then why did you leave?'

'Because I knew Paisley would eventually find me. I had to get out of London for a while. And I knew my Uncle Reggie had a gun I could borrow for a weekend. He's not my real uncle, of course, just a gentleman who likes it when I call him that.'

I'm leaving that titbit well alone. 'I … was so worried about you, Bunny.'

'Honey, I'm a cockroach. You can't get rid of me that easily.'

'But …'

She holds a finger to my lips. 'But nothing … all we have to do is get this weekend over and done with, and then life can go back to normal.'

Normal? Normal is highly relative. The next words linger on my tongue, but I have to know. I take the plunge. 'What about us?' And the thing is I already know the answer. It's like I'm looking down and see, for the first time, how thin the ice beneath my feet is. Perilous.

She blinks. 'What do you mean?'

'Do you think …? No, it doesn't matter.'

'Do I think we'll be the next It Couple at St Agnes?' she says with a smile. She leans in and we kiss. I'd love to enjoy it, but I'm frozen stiff. 'God, Alice, I can't say I've thought about anything other than the task at hand.'

And I've thought of nothing but her. Can I get those hours refunded, please? Be very careful who you let take your heart on a test-drive. I suppose that's that then. And, I knew, I think. I wonder if I crave pain as much as love. *Some girls take scissors and razorblades to their skin and others simply choose terrible …* well, *partners.* 'Bunny, you can't kill Paisley.'

'I'm afraid we might have to,' she says very sincerely. 'It's kill or be killed.'

'Eat or be eaten,' says a new voice. Neve ambles into the heart of the maze, not a care in the cosmos, hands shoved in her tux pockets.

'Did she see me?' Bunny asks her, suddenly business-like.

'No. I told her I was going to look for Alice.'

The penny drops, the light bulb comes on, the metaphor is stretched and I understand: Neve and Bunny are in it together. I look to the pair, aghast.

'You're *both* plotting to kill her? Are you out of your fucking minds?'

'I think we established that several chapters back.' Neve shrugs. 'Alice, I've spent literally all weekend trying to keep you out of the way. You weren't supposed to get mixed up in this. You don't understand.'

I actually laugh. I am very tired. There's salty, tearful phlegm in my mouth. 'I think I do. You're all fucking insane. Jesus, I thought I was bad.'

'Nah.' Neve shakes her head. 'I can see why you'd think that, and I'm not pretending I don't have my *issues*, but – in this case – we're just playing by the *old* rule book.'

'What are you talking about?' I shout. 'It's murder!'

'Please do yell that a bit louder,' Neve says. 'In your world, murder is punished. In ours, it's merely uncouth.'

'This isn't civilised society,' Bunny adds. 'It's *high* society.'

'Our families didn't get to where they are now by being good at business …'

Bunny inspects her fingernails. 'Or *good* at all.'

'They got there,' Neve finishes, 'through ruthless red blood and money. If the roots are rotten, Alice, you only get bad apples.'

'A journalist was going to write an exposé for the *New York Times* about my father,' Bunny says. 'So Daddy paid some kids in a gang to stab the guy in Central Park. The kids are in jail now, my father is … not.'

I think I do understand, if not accept. One set of rules for them, and another for us. When you have money, when it's in your blood, you can get away with anything. For every felled redwood, every Weinstein or Epstein or Blo, there are countless others getting away with it, often in plain sight. We shrug because that's how it's always been and we know our place. These people are so, so untouchable, this might as well be a game of chess. And, judging from their faces, one Neve and Bunny are quite bored of.

God, perhaps France had the right idea. Let's dust off the guillotines. Off with their heads.

I don't want to occupy a world where death doesn't matter. I think about Paisley's poor piglets, each replaceable, a new one bred for every one killed. I cannot imagine living like that, and nor do I want to. It's time for a reality booster jab.

'She's your sister,' I appeal to Neve in my calmest voice, the one the nurses in the unit used.

'She's a *monster*.'

'If she comes back to London, she'll make all our lives miserable. Yours too, Alice, you're on her radar now,' says Bunny. 'She could destroy you. Imagine the trouble she could cause at school: she could petition to have you barred from girls' toilets and changing rooms.'

'She can fucking try,' I say. I want to sound confident, but I know the rights I have at St Agnes were *gifted* to me by Grafton and they could just as easily be revoked.

'And your mother too,' Bunny goes on. 'A couple of phone calls here and there and no newspaper would review her books ever again. No festivals, no TV deals.'

'Balderdash,' I say, although that has also hit a nerve. 'Mum has an army of fans. What can one skinny seventeen-year-old girl do?'

'Exactly!' Bunny goes on, twirling around in the clearing. Crickets are chirruping away, and an owl sounds very depressed somewhere in the woods. 'Don't you see? That's how she gets away with it! To adults, Paisley is this adorable, charming, rich, well-bred young lady. They don't know her like we do. Worse still, they want to *be* her. She possesses youth and beauty and, even better, she's *cool*. Adults, whatever they say, crave youth the way vampires thirst for blood. They look to girls like us for guidance: what to wear, what to eat, what to listen to. All Paisley has to do is declare a club "old" and it's dead within days. Journalists, newspapers, magazines have their tongues so far up her ass, they're practically rimming her. Instagram, Twitter and Facebook have her over for tea, for fuck's sake. They all secretly wish they *were* Paisley. Through them, she can have people in Hull, Humberside and Harrogate dancing to a new tune every week if she so chooses. Do *not* underestimate her, Alice.'

'Life is better without her,' Neve says simply. 'It doesn't take long for people to realise what a cunt she is. She can only keep it up for so long before the mask slips. You think we're the first people to talk about … removing her.'

I spring up off the fountain, angry now. 'Still! You can't just *kill people*! It doesn't matter how rich and fucking famous your parents are!'

'Tell that to Antonella Hemmings.'

That curtails my flow. 'What?'

'No one else died that night, did they?' Bunny says, sharing a private glance with Neve.

I mull that one over for a second. 'Are you saying Paisley murdered her? Oh, come on.'

'They loathed each other,' Neve says. 'Antonella was the golden girl, toast of London.'

Bunny sighs. 'Antonella was the Princess fucking Diana of society girls. Can you remember the charity drives, and trips to orphanages, and washing the lepers' feet or whatever? It made the rest of us look bad.'

Now Neve slumps down on the fountain. 'Paisley had her sights set on Maxim too. Well, she did then. Now, not so much. He's a ...'

'Liability ...' I conclude.

'Two birds, one stone: she got a love rival out of the way *and* made her look like a fuck-up in the process,' Neve says sadly.

It sounds plausible, but even I can't envisage Paisley deliberately giving someone the wrong drugs. Antonella took a bunch of industrial-strength PMA thinking it was MDMA. An *accident*. The coroner ruled it death by misadventure, I remember it vividly. Thinking it through now though, there's a horrible likelihood to it. I do not think Paisley is stupid and I suppose the best murders are the ones that look like accidents.

'No,' I say in an attempt to convince myself as much as them. 'I do not claim to know what it's like to grow up in your twisted families but— Are you OK?'

Neve is resting her head in her hands and Bunny looks even more absent that usual. She staggers forward and I catch her.

'I've come over all queer,' Bunny says. 'How odd.'

I try to hold her up, but she goes floppy like she's been deboned. 'Bunny!'

'Gosh ... sorry, Alice ... I don't know what's ...' She's too heavy for me. I lower her to the ground.

'Neve!' I cry, then see that she too has slumped backwards into the dusty fountain. 'Fuck!'

The rose hedges rustle and I hear voices coming close. I worry for a second I'm hearing things again, but these are *male* voices. Bunny's eyes have rolled back into her skull and her mouth sags open. I rest her head on the dirt.

Felicity once taught me that anxiety is nothing more than fight-or-flight kicking in at all the wrong stimuli. Now it's very much real. I can stay and fight whoever approaches, or I can get the fuck away.

My feet really want to take Option B. I need time to think.

Standing, I assess my escape routes: there are four exits back into the maze, but I don't know from which direction the newcomers approach. I don't think I have time to work it out. I bound into the exit furthest away from the house.

I'm only just around the bend, when I hear *her* voice. I look through thorns and knotted branches and see a flash of red.

'Well, there are two of them,' Paisley says, flanked by her security team. 'Find Alice.'

I run.

XXXII

ALL ANGELS

I thought I imagined the first drop of rain on my head, but then I felt another, and another and soon it's tipper-tapping through the leaves and branches, and I'm soaked to the skin. It's that voluptuous summer rain, and the air does feel charged like a storm is about to crack through.

I crouch in the undergrowth, consider smearing myself in wet soil for camouflage. Between the rain and sheer terror, I'm wide awake now. Here, roots and vines create natural cubbyholes for me to hide in. I'm very thankful Paisley didn't equip her fleet with sniffer dogs, although, logically, I don't suppose a drug dealer would. I hide in my little den and watch the guards trudge past, griping about the turn of the weather.

Past the maze was the less expensive campsite where I was supposed to be staying. I dart from glamping tent to tent, hiding, until I reach the boundary of the estate and the forest. I hear a faint, bassy *thud, thud, thud* coming from the direction of the hall and I assume the closing disco is now in full swing.

I peek my head out and check the coast is clear. My mission now is now very evident. I need to head back to the house and find a telephone. There *must* be a landline or mobile in there somewhere. It's time, long past time in fact, to call the police.

Paisley, Bunny and Neve may well occupy some strange,

lawless dystopia where waiflike heiresses can murder with carefree abandon, but I do not. I live in the world where, all being equal, no one is above the law.

Kidding, obviously, even I am not that naïve. When our newspaper-appointed leaders are the most corrupt of them all, I have precious little faith in *fairness* any more, but I trust in the police sufficiently to (at least temporarily) derail whatever Paisley's current plans are. I can throw a spanner in the works and buy us all some time. Neve and Bunny *must* have been drugged. What else would explain their sudden illness? And Paisley seemed to be expecting it. The red wine – it must have been – she was so keen for us all to drink it, while switching to white herself. But Bunny wasn't with us … Oh, I don't know, Paisley has spies everywhere, and is always one step ahead. Paisley must have grown tired of toying with her mice.

My dress is black with mud and moss and grime, but it's less conspicuous than the bright blue. I stay off the paths, picking through hedgerows, taking care to avoid brambles and nettles with exhausting elephant strides. It's a starless night, and the forest is darker than blind, I have to scoop my way through it like it's tar.

I hear voices and drop to the ground, flat on my stomach. A sharp stab of pain flashes through my hand and I stifle a cry. I've cut it on something on the waterlogged ground. Biting my lip, I hold it up and pluck out a tiny shard of glass from my palm.

'Where the fuck is it?' A male voice crashes through the forest. I press myself as low as I can.

'Just follow the path!' someone, another man, shouts back.

I hear footsteps and dare to peek up. One of the security

team, Bill from earlier, tramps down the path, a body slumped over his shoulder. I can't be sure, but I think it's Willie – I recognise the hair. Where are they taking him? Bill vanishes into the trees up ahead before the second man follows him. This one is pushing some sort of cart. In it is Maxim, head lolling to the side.

I realise I'm not breathing.

What the fuck is going on?

The cart grinds past about five metres from where I'm hiding. I lay flat as a slow-worm. I wait until I can't hear the wheels any more and crawl forward through the undergrowth. The caked, sodden clothes drag me down. I rise to my feet, shivering all the way to my jangling bones. I check my hand and it's bleeding, but it's hard to tell how bad it is when I'm so covered in mud.

Crossroads. In one direction, the path leads back to the house, the other into the unknown. The guards are taking Maxim and Willie *away* from the hall. Why? I run the mathematics in my head. Once more I feel time galloping past me. If I go back to the house to find a phone, it'll be minutes, hours even, before the police get here – we're in the middle of nowhere. That's time that Maxim and Willie might not have. If they have any time left at all.

She *has* poisoned them, they might already be dead. It can only be the red wine and I had but the tiniest sip. For all I know Bill and his friend are taking them to be buried. Or burned. Fuck, this is Brontë-bleak.

Maybe I'm mad not to prioritise calling the police, but it's all fucking mad around here, so I find myself fitting in.

Apparently, at Wonderland, the normal rules are suspended

and chaos rules. This is life now. I can hardly remember a time when I wasn't scared.

'This it?' Bill calls back.

'Yep!'

I duck behind the nearest tree. I forget about my hand for a second and press it painfully to the bark. I peek out and see a church – a small chapel – no doubt belonging to the house. It's so dark I can only just make out the clock tower, but pale yellow candlelight hums behind the leaded windows. The guards take Maxim and Willie inside through the main doors and not into the graveyard, which offers some hope. I hang back for a second before gingerly making my approach.

A peeling sign on the edge of the graveyard reads ALL ANGELS CHAPEL, GRYPHON HALL. I hear the door creak open and I duck behind a headstone.

'That the last of them?' Bill asks his colleague.

'Aye. She wants us to keep looking for the tranny, though.'

I beg your pardon? I nudge the rage to one side. Now is *not* the time to leap out and lecture him on hate speech.

'Fuck that,' Bill says. 'Cuppa?'

'Now you're talking.'

The evil henchmen, who probably live entirely normal lives in the suburbs when they're not doing Paisley's dirty work, walk out of the church grounds in the direction of the hall. Satisfied they're gone, I slink out from my hiding place and edge towards the church. It's horribly quiet aside from the polite patter of the rain on leaves. I press myself into the alcove by the doors and try to sneak a look through the gap where Bill left it ajar. The candles give off a deceptively welcoming glow, like Santa's grotto. Every year, when I sat on that chubby pervert's lap, I always wished I'd be a girl come Christmas morning. You can imagine how disappointing a stocking full of boys' toys was.

I can see only the back row of some wooden pews. There doesn't seem to be anyone moving around inside.

Gritting my teeth, I dare to prise the door open a couple of inches and slip through. There's a draughty entrance vestibule with piles of mildewed Bibles and old collection bowls. An overbearing mustiness, and the scent of fox piss, catch in the back of my throat. Rank. All Angels church is in an even worse state than the main house. A tarpaulin flaps and billows off a gaping hole in the roof. I step into the main chapel cautiously, eyes peeled for Paisley. I think the coast is clear, but *someone* has lit dozens of candles around the perimeter. They flicker and dance as wind chases its tail around the hall. It'd be quite enchanting if I weren't so scared. I realise I've forgotten to breathe again.

A leg in a plastic brace juts out into the middle aisle down at the altar. Taking another sweep of the church I hurry forward and find it's where they've dumped Maxim. I drop to my knees alongside him.

'Maxim?' I tap his cheek, the way I've seen them do it a hundred times in movies. 'Max?'

I rest my face on his chest. He's out cold, but – thankfully – breathing.

Behind us, further up on the altar, are Neve and Bunny, similarly zonked out. I run over to them and give Neve's leg a shake, but nothing.

'Wake up!' I hiss at her. To my left, propped up against the bottom of the pulpit is Willie. Below him is Royce Hart.

'Excellent! You've saved me the trouble of finding you.' Her voice echoes around the church. Paisley stands on the threshold, now wearing a sleek maroon roll-neck and matching leather trousers. Her hair is tied back severely into a knot. She's dressed for no good. 'You look like shit.'

'It's a festival,' I say, voice flat.

'You just can't fucking help yourself, can you?' she replies, proceeding down the aisle, some lone bride. Red wedding.

I stand up, still sandwiched between Neve and Bunny. 'What is this, Paisley?'

'Do you have like a condition? A spectrum disorder or something? You just can't keep your nose out of other people's business, can you? Why are you even here, Alice?'

I go to answer, but find I still don't have an answer readily available.

Paisley continues down the aisle, candlelight glowing red in her eyes. It's like I'm seeing inside her soul, and it's an inferno. 'I'll ask again. Why did you come to Wonderland?'

'I don't know ...'

'You don't know?' She comes closer. 'You just followed Bunny blindly? Doubt it. You wanted to fuck with the cool kids? No, that doesn't ring true. There must be something more to you than *curiosity*. No one's that fucking curious.'

'It was the right thing to do!' I shout the words. I add more rationally, 'Bunny was missing and no one cared! I fucking stepped up.'

She stops dead in her tracks. 'Oh. *Morals*. You know, you did intrigue me briefly. A transgender girl would have been a great addition to the squad but I'm starting to think I was wrong.

There's nothing special about you, is there, Alice? So you cultivate these eccentricities to make yourself seem more interesting: the blue hair; the nose ring; the over-baked vocabulary. It's all a façade and there's nothing underneath. You're … just a girl.'

'Fuck you,' I mutter. She is, of course, spot on and I could weep. Maybe there isn't any filling to me. I'm a bauble. None of that matters now, I'll save it for therapy. Right now, I have to stop her from graduating from school bitch to spree killer.

She looks down at Maxim's prone body. 'It's a shame. I had no quarrel with you. You've wholly inserted yourself into someone else's mess. You were supposed to drink the wine, fall asleep and wake up safe and sound in the morning at the hall. But you've seen this now …' She tails off. 'It's a shame.'

I think I already know the answer, but I ask anyway. 'What are you going to do?'

'What? You think I'm going to do some big dénouement speech?'

'Probably, yes.'

She smiles. 'No, too cliché. Why don't *you* tell me what you think is going to happen?'

I quickly scan the chapel for a way out. There *must* be a second exit somewhere through a vestry or something, but I can only see the front doors. It's a small church, perhaps there is only one way in and out. 'You're going to … kill us?' The words feel ridiculous on my lips, but there we are. And now it's real.

'Yes,' Paisley says simply, stalking amongst her prey like a tigress. 'And now, tell me why?'

'Because all of us know what really happened to Antonella Hemmings.'

She nods, and I wonder if she's impressed I've worked it out. 'It's the only way, unfortunately. When the police started sniffing around, Daddy got me the hell out of London for a year, but have you ever been to a Swiss boarding school? It was like being in a PG 13 purgatory, and I thought about following in my mother's footsteps every single day. But then I thought, hold up, why do *I* have to lose *my* life? I didn't pour pills down Antonella's throat. She was the one knocking them back like they were Tic Tacs. I'm coming home, Alice, and I can't do that if there are rumours swirling.'

'Killing us won't fix that!' The words spill out of my mouth in a stampede. 'Olivier is the gossipiest bitch at either St Barney's or St Agnes ... half of London knows! You can't kill all of us! And anyway, you already got away with it! Everyone thinks what happened to Antonella was an accident.'

'The rumours aren't going away, though. But I'm banking on the suspicious death of my inner circle sending a fairly unambiguous message to anyone else who might choose to utter my name alongside hers. And who's going to miss these nuts and rejects? Each of them does nothing but drag a heritage family name through the manure. There's a reason they're all boarding school exiles. Look. It's the way it's always been done. Every mafia has its godfather.'

I shake my head. 'Paisley, listen to yourself. You can't kill six people.'

'Why not? There's nothing else to do, is there?'

'What?'

'What's the point in me? I'm so bored. I could kill a hundred people and it'll all get swept under the Persian rug. Nothing I do matters.'

My mouth hangs open. 'Am I meant to feel sorry for you?'

'No. You're meant to be terrified.'

Oh, I am. 'It's insane!'

She barks a harsh laugh. 'Oh, I know! I know that it isn't normal to have these serpents in my head whispering all through the night. It's certifiable. And you'd know all about that, wouldn't you?'

I feel a bit sick. Is this really happening? Just for a second, it's not Paisley Hart in front of me, but Other Alice. I close my eyes. I count to five and open them. It's Paisley again, waiting for my response. 'I don't know what …'

'You were sectioned last year. I got hold of your notes. Suicide attempt, right? Bipolar?' I don't really need to say anything. It's certainly not worth denying it. 'Was it awful?'

'Yes.' I take a step towards her. Lion tamer. 'Yes, it really was. But then I got better.'

'Yeah, you look *great*,' Paisley says sarcastically.

I try to pull some textbook therapist shit on her. 'What you're feeling is *guilt*. Antonella died on your watch and you feel bad. That's normal. I know what it's like to have a head that won't shut the fuck up, Paisley. It's not for ever though. I beat it, and if I can, you can.'

She looks at me with thinly veiled disgust. 'Are you suggesting I fuck off to the Clarity Centre or something and weave baskets like Lexi fucking Volkov? No thanks. I know I'm putrid at the core, but I've made my peace with it. Sadly, it's our legacy. Me and Royce and Neve.'

'What do you mean?'

She smiles again. 'Do you want to know a secret?'

XXXIII

BLACK/HART

She beckons me closer and, so help me god, I cannot resist.

'Can you remember how I told you my grandfather gave my father a job? It was a pay-off. You see, my father was his son.'

'What?' I blink. What is she saying? Also, did I just see Maxim move? I think I did – his head just turned slightly, like he's dreaming. Keep her talking. 'I don't get it.'

She rolls her eyes. 'OK, a potted history of my family. My grandfather, Earl Titus Black, married into Dutch royalty in the Swinging Sixties and had my mother, Selina. However, at the same time he had an affair with a society girl – a go-go dancer-turned-model called Panda Hart. Together they had my father, Regis. She threatened to go public and, terrified of a scandal, he vowed to provide for both her and her son.

'That would have been the end of it if my father hadn't been such a fucking failure at both St Barnabas and then Oxford. Although Panda had married and divorced one of the Rolling Stones by that point, she made Titus find a position for Regis at Black Plastics, his corporation. And that was how Regis came to meet my mother. My mother wrote in her suicide note that the shock of discovering his children were fucking was what killed old Titus back in 1990. His heart just stopped one afternoon and he slumped face-first into his crab linguine at The Ivy.

'Of course, my mother and father knew nothing of it until Panda confessed everything on her deathbed. It's a thing, apparently, Genetic Sexual Attraction, look it up. Relatives who meet as adults describe feeling a powerful sexual connection. By the time Panda died, my parents already had three inbred children.

'And that, my mother said, drove her to throw herself off a hotel balcony twelve years ago. My siblings and I are a repulsive natural disaster.'

The cogs in my brain clunk and grind, trying to make sense of the yarn she's unravelled. Cannot lie, I did not see the incest twist coming. 'Paisley, that's not your fault. Your parents didn't know ...'

'We're an *abomination*!' Paisley screams. Up this close, I can see a white crust in her doll-like nostrils. She's coked up, which explains a lot.

Did I see Maxim stir again? I will him to wake up.

Paisley goes on. She looks down at her brother and sister with pure loathing. 'Neve is fucking unhinged, Royce is profoundly stupid and as for me ... well ... I don't have a heart.'

'Paisley ...'

'It's true, Alice. I don't feel things. I don't feel *anything*.'

There. I hear it. A bum-note of sadness in her voice. I think she *does* feel it. And if there is a heart there, I can change her mind.

'Paisley ... listen. Sometimes we don't let ourselves feel things. It's ... safer that way. I've done it all year, but I think if you block out the bad, you block out the good too. Sometimes you have to ... let go.'

'I can't. If I stop now … it'll all come undone.'

'You mean *you'll* come undone? Everything you told me is royally fucked up, but none of us are slaves to our lineage. For years I thought I was going to turn out like my father: some fucking howling lunatic. He's a drunk. He ran away. He left me.'

Suddenly, I understand. It breaks like dawn.

'And that's why I came to Wonderland. I wouldn't, couldn't leave someone like he left me. I am *not* my father. We are not our parents and we don't have to repeat their mistakes. If you do this … it's like you're giving in to fate.'

And with that, I have nothing left to try. My lips are cracked and dry.

Paisley's slight shoulders sag. 'Maybe I'm not as strong as you. Do you know what? I'm *holding back*. The urges I feel … the violence of them. It'd shock you, Alice, it shocks me.'

In real life, there are no mad queens, no wicked stepmothers, sea witches or bad fairies. It's never that black and white. There are people doing terrible things, but they usually have a reason. But what about here? I have to believe that a part of Paisley, some starved root, is still connected to reality.

'I … I spend a lot of time asking if I'm mad,' I say. 'We all do. We are all hanging on by a thread and we all need help. Please let me help you, Paisley. My mum once told me that just because you're ill doesn't mean you have to be an asshole. You don't have to do this.'

She seems almost bored now. 'No, I think I do. All I have is my work. I'm good at it. I could run London one day. The queen bee. And these miscreants pose a threat to everything I've built.'

'No!' I shout, and try another tactic. I sense compassion is a dead end. 'Paisley. If you're already on the police radar after what happened last year, won't this look really, *really* bad for you?'

She shakes her head like I'm missing the obvious. 'That's why I made sure Neve was coming … by forbidding her from coming. Catnip. It's convenient to have a pyromaniac in the family.' Paisley picks up two bottles of vodka and tips them over Maxim, then Royce and Willie. 'Accident waiting to happen really, and Neve will insist on playing with matches. The church will burn, and I'll survive to tell the tale. Then my life begins. The only heir to the Black/Hart fortune. Sure, I'll still be an inbred wretch, but I'll be a very rich one.'

'You'll fit right in with all the other inbred wretches,' I say coldly.

She shakes her head. 'You're not one of us, Alice. You never will be.'

'And may I say thank fuck for that.'

Her face hardens. She insouciantly pushes a candelabra over onto the wooden pews, also covered in liquor. With a mighty woof it bursts into flames. I feel the heat on my face.

No time to waste. I run.

I sprint to the left of the altar and down the side of the chapel. Paisley races down the right-hand side to cut me off at the pass. I reach the entrance about two seconds before she does and throw myself at the double doors. I yank on the handles but they don't budge.

I feel her hands on my hair and she pulls me back into the chapel.

'You'd need the key.'

'Ow!'

I swivel around and push her off me. I shove her hard and she tumbles back into the aisle, flat on her bottom. I fall over her, but spring back to my feet first and step over her. She tries to grab my leg, but I kick her off and lurch back into the entrance hall. The main doors are locked, but where else is there? In the vestibule, there's an inconspicuous side door. I grab the handle and it swings open. I hurl myself through the gap and slam it shut. Paisley barrels into the other side and I throw all my weight against the door to close it. With a cry, I manage to slide a rusted bolt into place. I fall to the floor exhausted. Paisley continues to pound on the door.

Only now do I look around to see where I am. It's a stairwell, wooden stairs zigzagging up and up. It sinks in. I'm in the bell tower. The only way is up. Fuck.

There's a sudden crash behind me and an axe head splinters through the door. You have got to be kidding. Where the fuck did she get an axe?

I turn and flee up the stairs, taking two at a time. If nothing else, this gets me further away from the fire. Perhaps I can call for help or something. Whatever, I have precious few choices.

Round and round I go until the air changes. I feel cool, fresh wind cutting across the top of the tower. But I also smell smoke. It's oddly homely: log fires and barbecues. I remind myself who is on the grill.

The stairs open out onto a viewing platform. A big old bell

covered in verdigris is at the centre of the shaft. There are no windows at the top of the tower, only archways in the masonry which look out over the surrounding woods. I race around the full perimeter, looking for any partygoers who might have come into the forest.

'Help!' I scream, the smoke already scouring the back of my throat. It's a black column surging out of the hole in the chapel. In the dark of night, the smoke is blacker still, a velvety absence. 'Can anybody hear me? Help us!'

I bang both fists on the side of the bell and it gives only the most pitiful, half-hearted bong. Then I hear nothing except the crackle of the flames. I see the first few tongues licking at the hole in the roof. For a second, I picture the others down there, burning alive or choking to death …

'Help us!'

'No one's coming, Alice,' Paisley says, her voice steady, as she reaches the top of the stairs. I back away from her. 'You'll only die slower up here. The stairs are wooden.'

'I'll jump!' I shout. I look over the shallow ledge. From below, the church didn't look very tall. From up here …

'Either way, you'll be dead so … go ahead.'

'You won't get away with this.'

She looks genuinely confused. 'Of course I will.'

And she's right, she will. I look down again. The church grounds are overgrown, knotted with weeds and creepers. You never know, they might break my fall after I break both legs.

I've come so far since that day on platform six. I don't want to die. Gosh, the powerfulness of that certainty actually startles me.

I really don't want to die.

Being alive is fucking bonkers, but it's certainly an experience, isn't it?

I'm not done trying the flavours.

You know what you have to do.

Other Alice is standing right behind Paisley, a slight smile on my, on her, lips.

I do.

Kill or be killed.

I know.

So do it.

A thought occurs to me.

A mad thought.

Truly, truly mad.

I go.

I charge for her.

I am bigger than Paisley Hart.

My feet stamp across the platform.

Smoke swirls all around us.

Other Alice laughs.

Or is it me?

Paisley's eyes widen as she realises what's about to happen.

She's too late to swing the axe.

I shove her.

She grabs me.

There's no stopping either of us.

Over we go.

Sometimes
I
dream
that
I'm
falling.

I fall and fall
light as a lullaby
my fingernails clawing at thin air.
Blue sky
above and below
down and down
down
and down.

And it's funny because
in real life
when I fell

the ground comes up at you really fucking fast.

XXXIV

I WOULD ADVISE AGAINST 'AND IT WAS ALL A DREAM'

I'm late.

I have places to be, I'm sure I do.

I try to move but there's nothing to move.

If this is death, it isn't the nebulous nothingness Paisley craved. I am aware, although I am bigger now than my edges. I have no sense of a homunculus, no sense of self at all. I feel untethered from the physical. I'm only aware of colours: salmon-pinks and duck-egg blues, watercolours. And I am warm, perhaps too warm.

And then the warm becomes more localised. Something is pressing down on me, so there must be something to press down on.

And my mouth feels dry which suggests there is a tongue.

There's a daffodil yellow glow behind my eyelids – I have eyelids and I know just where they are! – Sunday morning sunshine.

'She's coming to,' a voice says.

It is my mother's voice.

But then I drift away again, coming loose from my doll parts once more.

'Alice …?'

This time I do not recognise the voice. Female, bubble-bath tones.

'Alice, dear, it's time to wake up. That's right, good girl.'

My eyes feel crusty, but I open them. The room is white and bright, clean. Morning light. 'Wh …?'

'Don't try to talk, love. You're in hospital, Alice. You had a nasty fall.'

And all the queen's horses and all the queen's men couldn't put Alice together again.

'Is she awake? Can she hear us?' I hear my mother again. I look up and see her and Felix hovering nervously at the foot of my bed.

'Mum …?'

'Oh, thank god!' Mother rushes forward and lunges over the bed to hug me. 'Oh, my god, Alice.'

The doctor, a kindly Asian woman with a white mallen streak in her hair, takes a step back. 'Be careful, she's delicate,' she warns Mother.

'You had us really worried, Alice,' Felix says. They both look shattered.

'What time is it?' I croak. If it's light outside, did I sleep through the night?

'It's Tuesday morning,' Mum says.

'Tuesday!'

The doctor steps forward again. 'We put you in a coma, Alice, to reduce the pressure on your brain. You sustained a pretty serious head injury. And a very thoroughly broken wrist.'

Oh, hello, yes, there is indeed a plaster cast on my left arm.

Mother covers my cheeks in kisses. 'My baby. Oh, my love, I

was so scared. I thought I'd lost my baby girl.'

'How … how are you here?'

Felix sounds exasperated. 'Alice! You vanished off the face of the earth! When you didn't come home on Saturday night, I called the police and your mum caught the first flight back from the States.'

Little chunklets start to come back to me. I think back to the fall. It did *not* feel liberating. I did not feel free as a bird. It was physical, wholly, in no way spiritual. I *fell*. Fast. All I felt was an ugly, gut-wrenching Alton Towers drop, my stomach in my chest, and the gruesome anticipation of the pain. And for a second, boy did it hurt. I don't know what happened to Paisley. I think I hit the ground first. Hard to tell, I had my eyes shut if I'm honest.

'Where am I?'

'King Edward VII hospital,' Felix says. 'Near Windsor.'

I want to go home. I want Heinz tomato soup and *Steven Universe*. 'Where's Paisley? The fire …?'

A man clears his throat. We all look around and *that's* when I notice the uniformed police officer sitting discreetly in the corner.

'This is Inspector Knight,' Mother says with distaste. 'He needs to speak to you about what happened. But only when you feel up to it.' She glares at him. 'I told him you need to rest first.'

Knight gets to his feet. He's a youngish, handsomeish mixed-race guy. 'Hello, Alice.'

'Hi.'

'Are you well enough to talk?'

'I don't know.'

He nods. 'Sorry to bother you when you're feeling rough, but I'm obliged to tell you that anything you say could be used as evidence and …'

'What happened to the others? The fire? Are they OK?'

'I think I'm supposed to ask you the questions … but no one else sustained serious injuries.'

How? 'But Paisley …'

'Paisley Hart?' That piques his interest. 'What about her?'

I stop. Even drugged out of my head, I need to be very careful. I shouldn't say anything at all. If she's alive she's very, very dangerous. A wasp is more dangerous when you try to trap it. I'm sure Inspector Knight is very nice and terribly good at his job, but he's as much use to me as a toy soldier. They haven't even sent a detective, which means they think Paisley – all of us – are dumb kids, out of control trust-fund brats. No. He cannot protect me from the likes of Paisley Hart. Perhaps there really *is* a safety net for people like her. The police are for real people, and, if I've learned one thing this weekend, it's that Paisley and the others don't live in the same world as the rest of us.

I play dumb. 'I don't understand. Is she OK? She fell with me.'

'Miss Hart was discharged on Sunday with minor injuries. She said you both jumped to escape the fire? Is that accurate?'

I don't want to commit myself until I know the full story so say nothing.

'Her friends were treated for smoke inhalation. Nothing serious.'

Good. That is good. But how? I saw it burn.

'What were you all doing in that church, Alice?'

All of them look to me expectantly. 'I ... I ... we were partying. It got out of hand.'

'I'll say. Are you saying the fire was an accident?'

I think of Neve. I wonder if, somewhere, she's being held responsible. I won't let her go down for Paisley. 'I don't remember.' I am biding my time. 'Sorry. It's all a blur.'

Knight frowns. Maybe he's sharper than he looks. 'We'll talk again later.'

'Sure,' I say. 'Sorry.'

In chess, the queen is the most powerful piece on the board: she can move any number of squares in any direction. That's not to say she's invulnerable. A well-placed pawn can take a queen.

Mother stays with me that night. She lies next to me in the hospital bed. She's soundly asleep, wind whistling through her nostrils. I've slept for three days so it shouldn't be surprising that I'm wide awake at one a.m.

I do so hate hospitals. Perhaps not surprising given I was once locked inside one. It doesn't matter how superficially nice they look, they're still places of pain and suffering. Alarms keep going off, people wailing for help.

I cuddle up against Mother and feel very loved.

I *am* loved.

There is love in my life. It pays to remind yourself once in a while.

Love isn't abstract, I can feel it in my chest. I have a gooey caramel centre like one of those sponge puddings that come in a little glass ramekin.

I wonder if that's the difference between them and me. Those unloved wretches, out of sight and out of mind, abandoned at boarding schools or institutions. I'm not sure precisely what's wrong with them, but they should try a bit of love.

They are very rich, but also very poor.

I snuggle closer to Mother and close my eyes.

XXXV

SLAY QUEEN

They could so easily be a fashion campaign. They're a ready-made billboard. They recline across three levels of the amphitheatre on the Green, the lawns that sit between St Barnabas and St Agnes. It's summer solstice, the hottest day of the year thus far, and there are only two weeks left of school. I observe them discreetly from the other side of the lawns, a hundred other students buzzing in and out of the hive between us.

Regis Hart must have pulled all his strings because Paisley is back at St Agnes. She sits on the highest tier, her uniform pristine, her hair tied back in a high ponytail with a red ribbon. Bunny, Maxim and Royce are on the next tier down. Maxim is out of the leg brace and back in the St Barney's rugby kit, doing exactly what's expected of him. Bunny, her face inscrutable, wears plastic heart-shaped sunglasses, and strokes Maxim's hair idly.

Apparently *that's* a thing now.

The jury's still out as to whether Bunny Liddell is a needy chick or a Venus flytrap. Fuck it, they deserve each other and it's so much easier to be codependent as a pair.

Ouch. That's bitterness talking, and you mustn't store envy in your heart as it soon sours, but I thought my night with her was special. Scratch that, it was special to *me* at least. I'm glad I had a night like that in my life. I hope there will be others, with people who deserve me more. I wonder if a thirst of suitors will spend a lifetime chasing after Bunny, trying to pin her down, only to discover there's nothing terribly tangible to affix to. She's perfume.

Alice, release the toxins. It's much too hot to be angry; London slumps like a melting sundae.

I'm not sure what I want, but I want something *real*.

On the bottom tier, appropriately, are bottom feeders Olivier and the Flower Girls.

It seems you can miss a lot if you take a fortnight off school to recuperate. My head feels fine, the cast will be on my arm until the end of term. Thankfully, the St Agnes gingham summer dress is short-sleeved, so I don't feel too hot and bothered.

I can't believe I was so determined to stay in the closet all these years. I didn't even get a *Vanity Fair* coming-out cover, posing in my knickers. If they didn't know before, everyone knows now and precisely nothing has changed. St Agnes girls *still* hold me in very low regard. It's pleasingly consistent.

'Alice!' It's Dinah, galumphing across the Green with her cello. She struggles over to the bench where I'm sitting in the safety of the shade, reading Virginia Woolf. Perhaps fittingly, the protection from the brutal midday sun is provided by Antonella Hemmings's commemorative tree. Dinah parks the cello and wraps her arms around me, squeezing like she's testing an avocado for ripeness.

'Careful! My wrist!' I squeal.

'How are you feeling?'

'Much better, thank you.'

277

'Look at you! Alice, I scarcely recognised you!'

I reach up and touch my hair. During my convalescence, I went to see my mother's hairdresser and had it dyed a golden-blonde shade, a slight variation on my natural colour. It's presently pushed off my face with a … well, a blue Alice band. I guess I'm finally ready for people to see my face first, hair second.

'Do you like it?'

'Yes! Very much so! Thank god you're back! Where have you been all morning?'

'I had to go see Ms Grafton.'

'What for?'

'You'll see. In time.'

She frowns. 'Alice, what happened at Wonderland? It's all anyone is talking about.'

I smile. 'Really? What are they saying?'

Dinah looks warily over her shoulder like she's worried people might be eavesdropping. 'Some people are saying the bipolar trans girl tried to kill Paisley Hart!' I'd expect nothing less. 'Others are saying there was some sort of suicide pact, or that Wonderland is secretly a sex cult, or that Neve Hart tried to burn everyone alive …'

I laugh gaily. 'Sex cult? Amazing! It's more fun, I think, if I let people tell their stories, don't you?'

'But you'll tell me what really happened?' Her eyes widen.

'Dinah, when *I* know what happened, you'll be the first to know!'

'Good!' She smiles sweetly. 'Crap! I have to get to my cello lesson, but I'll see you after school, right? Milkshakes?'

278

'Sure! Milkshakes would be perfection! And doughnuts too. Glazed ones.' I hug her tight. 'I missed you, Dinah.'

'It's only been two weeks!' she says.

'No, it was longer than that.' This is the first time I've been fully here in quite some time. I thought I was back, and my body was, but there was still a lot of fog in my head I couldn't quite see through. Sometimes it's only when you're well you realise you weren't. It won't last for ever, of course it won't, but right now – I'm doing OK. OK is OK. I'll keep working towards good and great.

I spot Willie Zong at the edge of the Green, loitering under a lace parasol. 'I'll meet you here after sixth period,' I tell Dinah and kiss her farewell.

I watch her heave her cello across the gardens, past where the A-list are sunbathing. They're laughing at something their queen is saying. It's perplexing. They *know* she tried to kill them! Do they care? Or are they scared?

Maxim catches my eye for a moment. I stare back and tilt my head a fraction. *Well?* He has the good grace to flinch and look away. Maxim and I belong in that parallel world. Oh, we could try to make something happen, but I suppose it's safer, *easier*, for him to play happy families with a girl like Bunny. And who can blame him? If the wheel of fortune had made me a phenomenally rich, white, straight cisgender boy, I'd be sorely tempted to kick back on cruise control too. Above all else, I think, Maxim Hattersley is lazy. Pussy.

And speaking of which, I can't stop thinking about the time we had mind-blowing sex. And that is fucking infuriating.

'I know you're there,' I say loudly.

'How?' Neve replies.

I crane over the back of the bench and see she's leaning against the back of Antonella's tree, throwing cashew nuts into the air and catching them in her mouth.

'I don't know,' I tell her. 'Some sixth sense. Or maybe it's your fragrance.'

'I'm not wearing any.'

'Then it must be the former.' She looks back at me and smiles. She's wearing a slouchy Metallica vest and denim shorts with stompy black boots and fingerless leather gloves. 'Are you following me, Neve?'

'Do you want me to be?'

'Are we still answering questions with questions, because I can go all day?'

She laughs. 'Just wanted to make sure you were safe, I guess. My sister is ...'

'A psychopath? Oh, I know. I'm not sure you're any better.'

'She let us out of the church, you know?'

Interesting. 'Change of heart? Or was it that she knew she wouldn't get away with it?'

Neve shrugs. 'Little of box A, little of box B? Maxim woke up first and got everyone out of harm's way. Then me. I was already out of one of the windows and I saw you both fall. Paisley was hurt, not badly like you, but she couldn't run. I'd have fucking throttled her and she knew it. I made her open the doors for the others. It's a funny thing: fires aren't as fun if you haven't started them yourself.'

'Who knew?' I say. 'And who called the police?'

She shrugs. 'I don't know. Someone saw the church burning

from the house and called them.'

I nod, grateful to my mystery saviour. I wonder … if Neve hadn't already escaped, would Paisley have snapped my neck and left me at the foot of the bell tower? Probably.

'She'll try again,' Neve says gravely.

I watch Paisley, laughing and joking with a group of people she recently tried to murder. 'I don't doubt it. Does she know it was you?'

Neve frowns. 'Know what was me?'

'That grassed her up to the police? About Antonella?'

She grins again. 'Ah well, that's still a mystery. Someone gave the police her name. It wasn't me and it wasn't Bunny. So that leaves only two …'

'It wasn't Maxim. At least he said it wasn't and I don't see why he'd lie. So …' That leaves only Royce. I look over to the amphitheatre. The lughead is currently competing – against himself – to see how many Chicken McNuggets he can fit in his mouth at once. '*Royce?* No way!'

Neve seems to consider her brother sympathetically. 'I wouldn't be so sure. He's the male heir to a family empire that Paisley has her eye on, and she's Daddy's favourite. Do you *really* think he's going to let his baby sister usurp him? I've learned there's a certain power in playing the fool. No one expects anything until it's too late. If Paisley is stupid enough to underestimate him …'

'She isn't,' I say quickly. The Hart children are a Shakespearean tragedy waiting to happen. *King Lear* on ket.

'I gotta get gone,' Neve says, pushing herself up. 'I shouldn't be here. Got people to see, sisters to bring down.'

'Where will you go?' As contradictory as it sounds, given she's a serial arsonist, and an accessory to attempted murder, I feel safer with Neve around. Meh, she's never tried to kill me. It doesn't hurt that she's gorgeous, I suppose.

'Here and there.'

'But ... will I see you again?'

She smiles broadly and I can't help but grin back. She's curiously contagious. 'You will if you want to?'

I just give her a coy smile. At least I hope it's coy.

'In that case, I'll ... be around.' And just like that, she's gone, vaulting over the iron railings onto the street. She turns back and gives me a salute. She calls back, 'Give 'em hell, Alice.'

Oh, I will. The application forms are folded neatly in my teddy bear backpack and ready to give back to Grafton. I gather the remains of my jalapeno mac and cheese to put in the trash, and follow the path back towards St Agnes.

'It's good to have you back, Alice,' Willie says softly as we pass on the thoroughfare. I almost don't hear him.

'Isn't it?' I rubberneck to face him.

He looks out from under his parasol. The lace casts intricate shadows across his face. 'A little dicky bird tells me you're planning to run for head girl.'

'Gosh, news does travel fast.'

A faint smile crosses his lips. 'A certain someone won't like that.'

'Yeah,' I say, wearily. 'I can't just let her win. It wouldn't be right. I'll be better than her. I *am* better than her. I'll beat her.'

'And how do you plan to do that?'

'Dust off the guillotine? I honestly don't yet know. But I will.'

He takes out some tiny brass opera binoculars and looks towards the amphitheatre. 'I can't wait to see how it all turns out.'

'I remembered who I am, by the way,' I tell him. He nods and doesn't enquire further. I bid him farewell. I feel more like myself, more Alice, than I have done in some considerable time. A couple of years ago, I got lost in myself. I feel a little bit closer, now, to finding my way out. I forget that, when I was a very small child, I did something incredibly strong, and then somehow managed to convinced myself I was weak. Well, no more.

With the summer sun on my back, I walk towards the redbrick cloisters of St Agnes. I've got an awful lot of work to do.

ACKNOWLEDGEMENTS

No wise fish would go anywhere without a porpoise and I am so very lucky to have a wonderful team steering me right:

The White Rabbit – Sallyanne Sweeney
The White Queen – Sarah Lambert
The Marc Hare – Marc Simonsson
The Caterpillar – Ivan Mulcahy
The Cheshire Cat – Nicola Bailey-James
The Duchess – Emma Draude
The Dormouse – Emily Thomas
The Mad Hatters at Hachette who keep letting me write books like this one
The King of Hearts – Max Gallant
And all the Alices – my readers, new and old

SUPPORT

WONDERLAND is a work of fiction. Alice is fictional, but many young people struggle with issues including mental health, self-harm, sexual assault and drug use. Help is out there. For more information on where to find support, you could consider the following sources:

CHILDLINE:
A private and confidential service for young people up to age 19. Contact a Childline counsellor about anything – no problem is too big or small. Available 24 hours.
Call free on 0800 1111 or talk online at childline.org.uk

MIND:
Offers advice and confidential support to anyone experiencing a mental health problem. Helplines are open 9am–6pm on weekdays except for bank holidays.
Call on 0300 123 3393 or find them at mind.org.uk

THE MIX:
Offers advice and confidential support for under 25s, including a crisis messenger. Helplines are open 4–11pm every day and web chat is available 24/7.
Call on 0808 808 4994, text THEMIX to 85258, or find them at themix.org.uk

SAMARITANS:

Confidential and emotional support for people who are experiencing feelings of distress, despair or suicidal thoughts. Lines open 24/7 and 365 days a year.

If you need a response immediately, it's best to call on the phone.

Call free on 116 123 or find them at samaritans.org

FRANK:

Offers facts, support and advice on the use of drugs and alcohol. Lines are open 24/7.

Call on 0300 123 6600, text 82111 or find them at talktofrank.com

Don't miss Juno Dawson's award-winning CLEAN

Addiction, redemption, love and despair –
CLEAN will have you hooked from the first page.

Read on for a sneak peek...

Face-down on leather. New car smell. Pine Fresh.

I can't move.

I'm being kidnapped.

But I can't move.

My arms and legs feel like they've been deboned, dangling like jellied eels. Sick or dribble is crusted on my chin and cheek. With great effort, I peel my face off the seat.

My lips and tongue are chalky dry. I open my eyes, and blistering daylight burns them right out of the sockets. It hurts. I screw them shut but snatch a glimpse of Nikolai. From this angle, I only see the back of his head; his high fade haircut, and his hands on the steering wheel. I recognise his Rolex.

I don't understand what's happening.

Where am I?

Where *was* I?

Rewind the night. The last thing I remember, I was at the hotel. Yeah, that's it. We were in a penthouse. I got a key from reception. Me, Kurt and Baggy and that girl. The Fashion Week party . . . the bar . . . we left the bar to get high.

Oh yeah. The blue chaise longue. A needle.

Shit.

Is this what an overdose feels like?

I can't remember anything after I came up. I run a trembling hand over my body and I'm still in the gunmetal Miu Miu dress I was wearing last night. I'm covered in a scratchy plaid blanket. My feet are bare.

'Nik?' I croak. My throat feels like it has barbed wire stuffed down it.

'It's OK, Lexi. I'm getting you help.'

What now?

Oh fuck me hard, it's an intervention.

I start to argue, but my eyes catch fire again. I squeeze them tight and let darkness wrap around me like a sushi roll.

Also by Juno Dawson

A timely exposé of the dark underbelly of the fashion industry in an era of #TimesUp and #MeToo – this might just be Juno Dawson's most important book yet.